EndEarthers

By

Charles Mitchell Turner

EndEarthers

Charles Turner

Published by Charles Turner, 2024.

This is a work of fiction. Similarities to real people, places, or events are entirely coincidental.

ENDEARTHERS

First edition. July 31, 2024.

Copyright © 2024 Charles Turner.

ISBN: 979-8227384607

Written by Charles Turner.

QUIET BENEATH THE MOON
CHAPTER ONE

It is evening of a long, trying Sunday. Driven by insomnia, driven by my acute isolation, I spend hours walking on the beach after sunset. Once the unbearable sun has rolled away for the day, I'm toiling like a bug over the deep Long Beach sand. The scudding moon hangs over my shoulder, listening as I ramble on. It makes a good companion, the moon. For its sake I stick to the small talk, not wanting to make him depressed. This evening he's a white sliver. I call him "Toenail Clipping." He doesn't mind. I can call him anything. He sticks with dog-like loyalty. He just wants to hang. But, unlike a dog, he lacks the power to alert me if someone runs up behind me. Which is happening now.

I spin, alarmed, because I hear pounding footsteps over the wet sand at the water's edge. I freeze, weighing the situation for possible danger.

I see a gangling male start to flail his arms when he hits the dry sand. He gets in my face in the time it takes to slow and quit wind-milling those long arms. By then it's too late to throw up my hands to block him. He gets nose to nose and stands, panting. I discern big square teeth, a great mustache, a swarthy grin as he grabs my shoulders. "I'll be damned," I tell Toenail Clipping; "it's Doc Ramos."

Doc draws me into an embrace. "I missed you, Denny the Wizard," he says through his teeth, looking into my eyes with eyes as black and bottomless as the holes of time.

"Me too," I say stupidly.

We pause, each waiting to see where we go from here. Doc's panting is slowly easing. He looks at me in an odd little way that says he's heard of my doctor's prognosis, but he doesn't know whether to mention it. I catch my gaze on the great ship that's moored directly behind him. It's the Queen Mary, secured as close to the shore as practically possible. I see pensive, patient Toenail Clipping high over the Queen Mary,

waiting in vain for me to rejoin him. I slide my eyes into Doc's sad stare, feeling a bit sorry for him. "Don't worry, Doc; I'm holding stable. I've a few alternative programs to sample yet."

Doc shakes his head. "You're going to lick it."

"Yep; I am. Let's go to my place. I've got to piss."

"Hang it out here."

"We'll go to my place."

"You writing lately? I don't see a new book in nearly three years."

"I have pieces of books in boxes. Hell, I'm no good for work anymore. I'm living on Social Security and dribbling-in royalties. What brought you to Long Beach?"

"Looking for you, Denny the Wizard; looking for you."

"Until the first of February I lived in L.A. How did you know to come here?"

"I called your brother to find out if you're kicking. He told me how you've taken to always walking this beach."

"After fifty years, you just came to visit?"

"Well -" Doc stops in his tracks and jambs a cheroot between his square teeth. He chips a wooden match with a thumbnail until it ignites. My eyes ride the flame to the

cigar tip and along the shaft to Doc's teeth. I notice how stained those teeth are, and that there is a chunk out of one. When I last saw them they were still white and clean, in gums that held them as steady as posts in concrete. I note the creased face, the loosening jowl, and I realize, he has aged, same as me. We are old. Two old fucks with broken teeth. I clap his shoulder as he moves ahead again.

We scale a grade that peaks against the grey wall of a sidewalk. We gain that plateau with its high street-side curb and go left to cross Long Beach Boulevard at the intersection.

"So; how's Mexico?"

Doc chews the cheroot, meditatively. "Painful; desperate; beautiful; maddening; inspiring - It's very spiritual."

Doc flips his smoke into some palmettos growing in front of a stucco building. The

building's outside lights go on. Despite what Doc has said, I privately conclude that it's something more than a simple visit that brought him here.

Doc goes on about Mexico. "Me? I don't work. I am like an itinerant preacher. I roam the country, talking about the same things I did during the protest days, only adapted. At first it was hard. They thought I was a lazy hippy. They didn't trust me. But I was running with Anglos so much I forgot how to be with my own people. So I told them that. I humbled myself to the most menial existence until they felt pity and began to like me. Now when I come to a town the poorest of the poor offers to share everything they have with me. There is so much need there. Sometimes I have to leave there and that's the

hardest part. I got to recharge the batteries, Denny."

"Do the authorities bother you?"

"Oh, yeah. I spent two years in jail. But they could never find me guilty of nothing. So they let me out."

"You're the only one that hasn't changed, Doc."

"That is where you are wrong. That's a bunch of bull. You're still the same. You just got disconnected." Doc takes a turn in front of me and stops. "Do you have a car, Denny?"

"I have a Taurus wagon."

"You know, you don't look too good. How do you feel?"

"Aw, I'm all right. There's a certain strain to being alone in this. But I'm okay. I'm strong."

Doc digs in his shirt pocket, fishes out another cheroot and fiddles with it. It's nearly too frazzled to be smoked.

"Doc; why are you really here?"

"Seriously - I got in trouble with some drug people. I wasn't doing anything, but they think I did. So they want to kill me."

"What a dumb-ass move."

"It was a set-up. I didn't do nothing wrong."

"Tell it later, Doc, I can't think when I got to piss."

"Yeah; let's get on to your place. Now I got to piss too."

We approach from the driveway, coming upon the Taurus. It sits, dappled by a

mercury light that shines from above through a chinaberry tree growing too close to the

house. Heavy dust hides most of its sheen. It appears in the darkness to be black, but in fact it's indigo. It's so neglected looking because it *is*. Doc runs a hand across the hood, streaking the dirt. "I got here by bus," he says, wiping the hand on his pants.

My house is old, with falling gingerbread, peeling paint and crumbly shingles on the low pitched a-frame roof. Too much rain and humidity are ruining all that wonderful craftsmanship. The landlord seems not to care. Inside, the house meets one's expectations, if they are not high. The sheet vinyl floor shows wear where the sub floor is loose. Dirty beige walls, low ceiling, with a fan light that strains to exude a yellow glow. I've furnished with gaudy furniture and outlandish do-dads to counteract the depressing pall.

Doc quick strides ahead of me to get to the commode first, unzipping and pointing in a fluid motion so that an unrestrained stream begins to flow into the pot.

Crap! My bladder's sides strain like a water balloon. "Hurry, Doc; I can't wait any longer."

Wordlessly, Doc keeps pissing.

"Doc - Shit."

I power walk through the kitchen. The doorknob rattles when I give it a violent turn. I throw the door open; then, in the fenced-in enclosure, where a barbecue pit is nearly lost in an overgrowth of weeds, and the nasty little mosquitoes whet their vampire noses, I hang it out. At last, the piss flows, to a chorus of warbling angels.

After, utterly calm, I'm zipping my fly, floating into the house. Doc's rifling my 6

books; says he's looking for a road atlas. "I haven't been on a road trip in a long time," he

says.

Doc leaves the books disheveled. He throws himself into the divine softness of the recliner, looking at me with eyes that proclaim his tiredness. "Denny, we got to plan us a

new adventure. Something to say we still count for something in the world."

I move to the kitchen, stalling an answer. At this point I'm really hungry. "Do you want something, Doc? I'm making myself a concoction of veggie juices. But I can fix you a juicy porterhouse. I've been saving that for something, but you're welcome to it."

"No, nothing. I don't eat."

"Organic carrot, spinach, apple and barley juice. One glass, three times a day. Since I've gotten used to this stuff, I actually look forward to it."

There's no reply. I return to the room, sipping a bit, seeing his sprawling form asleep in the recliner. No wonder Doc's being so quiet. I pause in that naked moment to look upon my old friend, gratified that he's come. I marvel that his mustache and hair are mostly black, while my own hair has blown away with the tumbleweeds. I smile. "Rest it; I'll see you in the morning."

After drinking my juice up a bit too quickly I find myself cleaning in the kitchen. Juicers are a pain in the ass. As I put all the parts on the drainer and wipe up the counter, Doc begins to snore, becoming louder and louder. Amused, I stand in the doorway and watch him sleep. *I wish I could die like that.*

Then I spy the little packet of white powder, all but freed from his pocket. It should be no surprise, really, as I continue to look on, now with moistening eyes, cursing the way

life changes, where even the saints can't remain saints. Suddenly weary, I go to the

bedroom. Giving up seems the only option, as I lie on the bed with all my clothes on,

A few hours later, Doc comes in and shakes the bed, not seeing that my eyes are still wide open. "Hey, fucking *gringo*."

He shakes the bed again.

"Hey, Doc. You didn't rest very long."

"I got too excited thinking how we are going to be together again. What's wrong? You look like you're struggling with something emotional."

"I'm okay. You can nest here indefinitely if you want to, Doc. I'm too settled; not going anywhere."

"Okay." A restless hand moves over the content of Doc's shirt pocket. He darts his

eyes away, but they can't evade me.

I tell him, regretfully, "If you want to keep going I can take you out along the Grapevine, or I can put you on a bus. '

"Or you could lend me the car!"

"Out of the question," I reply firmly. "I'm driving to LA next week."

My shoes fall over the side, taking my feet to the floor. "Sorry, Doc. I don't do long trips anymore."

Doc speaks over my shoulder, following me all the way to the kitchen. "I have to keep moving, Denny. I can't be sure if they are able to track me. I can't be out on the road. I can't take any public transport."

I put on the light over the sink and begin cleaning up the teapot. "I want to be

supportive," I begin -

"But, you could give me the key if you want to support me. It's the only way."

"Or I could tell you to keep on traveling the same way you got here if I want to hard ass an old friend."

"Friend," Doc laments, his face clouding with what appears to be anger.

There's no warning, as he attacks, growling like a demented bear. The instant his oversized hands wrap around my wrist and upper arm I cave. "All right, damn it. I'll drive you."

To my surprise, the assault continues. He slips his arm about my throat. Our struggle brings us into the living room.

"Give me the key."

"A-augh - I can't breathe."

Doc turns my pocket inside out to wrangle away the key. After, he flings me off to the side. I crash over a table, smashing a vase full of plastic flowers. His heels vanish out the door as I wrestle the table away before I can move. "Doc," I plead, "don't take my car."

Getting myself up, lurching outside.

The car engine revs and the lights go on. The back-up and brake lights work in

unison as Doc positions the Taurus on the driveway. Once he rolls onto the street, I will have to consider reporting my car as stolen.

Inexplicably, he stops. The car shuts down.

I rush the passenger side and Doc obligingly unlocks the door. Scrambling in, as my ass hits the seat, I become aware there is a squad car parked near the driveway

entrance. The cop face in the window is focused in this direction. Doc huddles, looking the way he did the first time we got arrested protesting, in 1965. "Let me guess," I snarl venomously. "No license? A warrant? What are you guilty of?"

"Close your hole."

"No. No, Doc. You practically stole my car. I want to know."

"I'll tell you later. Shit. The cop's turning in."

In surreal slow motion, the squad car inches near. The cop gets out. A lanky figure, he approaches from the driver's side, darting a flashlight about the car interior.

"What's going on?" he says politely.

Doc feigns innocence, becoming wide-eyed in the hard glare of the light. "Come again, officer?"

The cop, jiggling his flashlight, bends to speak directly into Doc's face. "I saw the two of you running. Why did you come out of the house like that?"

"It's his house," Doc says to shift the focus onto myself.

"It is my house, officer. We were having a disagreement, so my friend here ran away from me. He wasn't going anywhere, though; just teasing."

The cop considers a moment, his intelligent brown eyes continually probing, registering, analyzing. *Should I call back-up? Any way they're telling the truth?*

We hear his radio garble a short burst in cop language. The cop appears to ignore it. His curiosity about us remains unsatisfied. "Anyone inside the house?"

"No, sir. I could show you around. I have a photo of myself on the bureau and lots

of personal papers at my desk."

The cop radio spews a long unintelligible message. The cop turns off the flashlight. "You boys be careful."

He strides to the cruiser and quickly backs it into the street. With flashing lights and blaring siren, he's gone, leaving us stunned. I look at Doc, inquiringly. "Crazy fucker. What are you going to do next?"

"Still driving out of here. Still giving you the same choices."

"Look. Doc -."

Doc explodes. "God damn it, I got to save my own self. At least you got a chance. If I don't go now, I don't got no chance."

"I'll never see my car again, will I, Doc?"

Doc restarts the engine. "I don't know. We'll see."

As I reach for the door handle, he acts on impulse, putting it in gear and gunning it. The tires spew gravel all the way to the street, squealing, fishtailing the car across the pavement. We race to the stop sign, where Doc taps the brake pedal, then continues around the corner, not affording me the chance to get out. The sun puts its first beam in our eyes as we begin the race toward Doc's vision, our doom or our destiny.

CHAPTER TWO

"This is the Ridge Route Highway," Doc maintains. "The Grapevine part of the Ridge Route comes when we pass Fort Tejon. At the end of it we get in the San Joaquin Valley."

After I don't reply for the hundredth time, Doc prowls through the glove compartment, picking out a short pencil. He chews meditatively on the eraser end, soon making a face over the rubber taste. Flipping the pencil out the window, he begins patting the steering wheel, singing up-tempo Spanish songs. Abruptly, he finds another topic to flip out at me. "What happened to all those great books you were going to write? Each time I saw your titles I said, 'Maybe this is it.' But they were always about insane Martians, space guys trying to get laid, monsters looking like flaccid dicks, slithering across beach sand. That's crap, Denny, and you know it. You always said you planned to write The Great American Novels, a whole series of them, putting in the stuff the hacks like Mark Twain and John Steinbeck had to leave out. I never understood what that meant, by the way. What? What did they leave out? What did you perceive that anyone else didn't?"

Doc's right, of course. When it came down to it, I didn't measure up. The novels I've produced sold pretty well, but the audience couldn't care less about literary standards. There are some fuck books that are better written. I look out over the Tehachapi Mountains as at some ghost terrain where the spirits of long gone writers blow about with the wind. I tip an imaginary glass of wine to their honor, as Doc rambles on.

Dozing, unwilling to ponder any more - until he breaks through with a touchy subject we both had been avoiding. "My sister lives with some nuns, thank you very much for asking about her. She spends all her time praying and reading little Bibles. Her last guy really fucked her up." Doc is quiet a few moments. "She always wanted you, you know. You didn't give her the chance. You should have married her, fucking wizard." Another pause. "Hey, I'm talking to you!"

I smile, involuntarily. "You know, Doc, I could have had this conversation with you this morning, before you went all Dutch Schulz on me. Now I'm just some object riding along in the car, like that air freshener dangling over the windshield. Wake me when we get to the next populated car stop. That's when I'm going to turn you in and get my car back to Long Beach."

"Fucking *gringo*. At least now you're talking."

"No, I'm not."

"Then, God damn it, I'm going to drive like a bat out of hell. If you're lucky, the cops will stop me. If not, well, who knows about the car?"

"Drive away. We have enough gas to get twenty miles. My credit cards and my money are still in my desk."

Doc chuckles. "Then we got Suicide Run. See you on the other side, *vato*."

But of course Doc would do it. So, I throw in the towel. "Look; If I promise to cooperate, will you be a good boy?"

"If it means you talk to me, yes."

"Give me back my car?"

"Shee - I was never going to keep it."

"Then pull over at the next diner. I'm starving."

"You got it. Damn I'm glad we're going to be friends again."

"Wrong, Doc. Friends level with each other."

"Fuck it, then."

That exchange leaves me grinning and Doc hunched darkly over the wheel.

I am wrapped into sarcastic thinking when Doc pulls into a place off the freeway, so I don't know where we are. I think at first it's a Stuckey's, but it's a private operation. I opt for a table until Doc becomes fixated on the woman at the counter. He slides in to sit before her and I of course follow suit. The woman has a cowboy face, long braids to the sides and a crooked smile. Very Kerouac. I note how the smile never really goes away. She's wearing a pink cafeteria style dress that says little about her figure, short-sleeved, so we see her arms have blotched skin. She pauses from wiping up something from

behind the counter. "Coffee?"

"Two," blurts the old Docster

"I'll have iced tea."

"That hair natural?" Doc inquires playfully.

"Coffee for you," she deftly slips the cup in. "What, honey?" She scoops ice in a tall glass and places it under the spigot.

"Your name Alice?"

"No, it isn't."

"I was wondering, because you look like Alice." Doc sugars the coffee, dumping in

two creams, singing barely audibly, "'You can get any thing you want....'"

Then he says, "I want a pack of them Mississippi Crooks to take with me. Two, I mean."

"And a chicken salad," I decide.

With her duties fulfilled, the woman busies herself at the far end of the counter, wrapping silverware, while Doc sips and I eat. I'm studying the rack of pies, trying to guess at the filling in each one, when Doc slips off his seat, saying, "See you in a minute," heading to the restroom.

"First give me the key, asshole. I'm driving if you're doing what I know you're doing."

To my surprise he transfers the key right away. Working on my salad, I continue to examine the pies, narrowing the scrutiny to what just could be blackberry. As I verge on ordering a piece, Doc breezes by and out the door. "Pay up," he says in passing.

Disappointed, yet relieved, I forgo the sugary mouth watering concoction. I shove the remnants of the salad back and approach the register.

"Can I have a water to go?" I say down the counter, bending to reach in my sock for a credit card.

"Sure can, honey." She hands the water, talking as she runs the card, her jaded green cowboy eyes scanning the Taurus. "Big boy like you, kid like that; something's not right here."

"I'm the designated straight guy."

"You be careful, you hear?"

"No promises; I'll try."

Her crooked little smile goes away for a moment. I go back and place a tip by my platter.

Doc is oddly silent as we hit cruising speed. It's me driving. He follows my actions at first, then settles to watch the traffic, his eyes inexorably beginning to shut. All the way into the San Joaquin Valley, he's still. I develop a tunnel vision, forgetting about him, barreling into a summer shower, the brief, heavy pelting kind. I ponder the cocoon-like state of today's auto passenger, the smooth ride, how we climb in, then get out a thousand miles away, almost as fresh as we began. Not like the old days, when travel was an adventure. Yes, sir. That was when we were each and every one of us Indiana Jones. All of a sudden, I find myself free-wheeling. Who should drop into the space between us but Salmon Rushdie! "Have you read my book?"

"Only a few pages."

"Did those pages create for you anti-Muslim sentiment or corrupt your perception of my religion?"

"No; I didn't get anything out of it. I was not mentally prepared to read such a book. I could not relate to the opening - found it boring."

"I see." Wise, impermeable pause. "Do you think you will read it in the future?"

"Look, I'm driving a treacherous road here. Do you think we could postpone this to a later date? I'm busy. You understand."

Wordlessly, Salmon continues his descent through the floor. He waves at me as he plunges out of sight.

Already, the rain is ending. Bright eye glare. I reach for sunglasses, noting Doc's face as I lean over him. The thought hits me: "He's dead; if not, dying." *Oh crap! Don't let him be dead. What am I going do? Get him out of the car! Walk him! Flag someone down!*

With the car wheels in the weeds, I fight like a wild animal to get him out on his

feet. I end up dragging his body over twenty yards, but his dangling legs don't move. We collapse on the gravelly shoulder. Weeping, I roll him on his back, repeatedly pressing on his chest. I won't give up until help arrives.

The brightness of a large hubcap, the stepping down of booted feet and Wrangler clad legs, a deep voice.

"Heart attack?"

"A bad dose of something illegal. I think he's dead."

"Let me have a go at him."

The trucker begins working Doc's limbs and slapping him from time to time.

"Do you know what you're doing?"

He rotates his big head, tilting to see beyond a cowboy brim.

"Nope. Did you?"

"No. I hope you called an ambulance?"

"I did do that."

We attempt to walk him between us, but Doc remains limp as a dead bullfrog. When the siren sound touches our ears we drop him, a bit hastily, grateful that the professionals can now make the call.

"Thank God," the sweating trucker grunts, pulling the plug from his mouth, spitting. His beer belly in a Harley Davidson tee shirt becomes the focus of my attention for the moment until they arrive.

It's like the beach at Normandy as the screaming vehicles swoop to the scene. Two rescue trucks, five cop cars, two or three VFDs. They swarm out, a highly trained battalion, each to their specific tasks. Paramedics go over the corpse. Right away, they strap it on a litter, then a lady cop asks me if the deceased belongs to me.

"No. I knew him from way back, but he just tapped me for a ride this morning."

"Next of kin? Where's his family?"

"Fresno. I forget the street."

"Put your name and address here. They may get in touch."

Surprised that I don't have to follow the ambulance, I say my thanks to the trucker.

We shake hands. Stumbling in the weeds, sweating profusely, I hike to my car. Luckily, we moved Doc's body far enough along the road to not block me in. I look down the highway as far as I can probe, in a momentary wistful glimpse of the past, almost able to see a young man in the heat waves trekking up the road, thumb out, heart on the hunt. He vanishes like a good little apparition.

Overlook this callous façade; Doc's absence is a hole in me. I intend to celebrate the man in my own quiet way. In the time of Denny the Wizard, we served together as ringleaders of the Waves of Love, loose-knit group of all-purpose-demonstrators and sometimes-runners-of-draft-dodgers-across-the-Canadian-border. That he was a Mexican so swarthy adds to the romance of the situation.

During the Chicago cop riot outside the Democrats' convention, near the spot where the Yippies nominated Phil Ochs' pig for president, he was the rescuer when I became the fallen comrade, with one planting his boot in my chest after swatting me to the ground with his club. Through teargas tears he took me beyond the maelstrom, then returned to do what he could for others.

After my parents both perished in a fiery freeway accident, I got really close to his family, to Mama Linda, and Nellie (Manuella). I still have the gas and indigestion from Linda's cooking, I think.

And Doc could sing. His rendition of America the Beautiful blows me away, over forty years later.

"Give concerts," Linda, and I often pleaded.

Unmoved by the requests, he preferred spontaneous renditions when one least suspected it. The proud peacock, he shunned the performer's spotlight. Go figure.

Somehow he found the time to read, for he knew the best sellers and would also quote the like of Yukio Mishima or John Steinbeck, at the drop of a hat. In endless discussions he goaded me to write, until I caught on fire, with my quickly failed magazine, The Moloch Eaters, being my first public effort.

As all of our friends took to proclaiming themselves ecologists, we knew then it was over. Nixon was having his way, despite all that the opposition could throw at him.

The only meaningful protests were being waged by the Veterans Against the War. Comrades in arms, Dale and Carl, had already drifted off and I had my writing to tend to. Doc's heritage called on him, urging the move to Mexico.

I am still unforgiving of the man who hijacked my car and claimed to be the same person. I don't bend easily. Perhaps in future days I may have a new slant on it.

A bit of history:

Conceived by me in the '60s, The Moloch Eaters magazine would be an antidote against the minions of Moloch, "eater of children." Figuratively, his beasts to be stripped naked and publicly flogged for their evil deeds. I'd be doing a small part in helping to break the power held over this land by predators of politics, engineers of war, leeches of commerce, purveyors of racism, oppressors of women. Everything making the people less secure. For, yes, these creatures from Moloch were and still are very real, to be fought with fury and conviction until a final struggle has been won.

My magazine became an early victim of miscarriage when my circumstances continually shifted and I was forced to abandon the project. At this time in history, sizeable portions of the populace were uprooted in the pursuit of justice as I was as we sought a different meaning to what we were being propagandized to follow. We could afford to do so, as the surging economy and the implementing of the New Deal made us feel the equal of the ruling class, so we pressed to be heard. My main focus was on war. That, and civil rights.

Ever since my grade school teacher brought us the breaking story of Emmett Till's torture and murder I had been aware of the black struggle to be regarded as fellow humans by the rest of society and was in to see it happen.

Regarding the war, my stint in the Navy almost turned me against my better nature.

I intended to re-up and go to 'Nam. It was during my break I investigated the why of the war and subsequently took a stand against the whole schmeer. I went marching, writing against it, and helping some resisters escape to Canada.

The Peace Movement coexisted with and fed each off of the other the Hippie culture, and although we gave our support our goals were not always the same. I think the tension with the law pushed us together. And of course Hippies often shared the philosophy of no more war. Our ranks were mostly filled with draft eligible males and women who supported them. And of course the older socialists.

I viewed our greatest victory as the day Lyndon Johnson not only vowed he would not stand for re-election, but he halted the bombing. Thereby clearing the way for the next president to negotiate the war's end. I don't think he anticipated a President Nixon.

Nixon pursued the war with a vengeance, expanding and drawing it out to the limit. Time was the grinder that wore down our movement. Time, yes, but also violence. Protestors were often attacked. The killings by troops at Kent State put the damper on it. By the time the war ended, just the Veterans Against the War were a viable force. "Now wait," one might argue; "What about the Students for a Democratic Society, their offshoot, the Weathermen?" It's a whole 'nother category for them. Although there were those such as me who felt only revolution could save us, virtually none, including myself, had reached the stage where guerilla tactics, such as the bombings they engaged. were at all helpful. As I said, the movement was over with. Observing the protestors turning away, as from a dream, as though our decade counted for nothing when the going got a lot tougher. It became apparent that the nation was moving into a more conservative era and

the Peace Movement, as well as the Hippies, were less noticeable. Our decade counted for nothing, in the end.

The world becomes increasingly hostile.

Moloch. Ruthless bastard.

As my friends drifted away, there was no place for me it seemed. I was there on the coast, now solitary as a spider. So there I stayed. All during our adventures I had kept writing in spiral note books, eventually producing near the end a first novel. You may recall, "The Lost Androids" nearly made the top ten best seller list. The follow-up books sell, but not as well. My social life starts then fizzles. Where fifty years has gone I dare not ponder. But that's where this story begins.

CHAPTER THREE

Then my doctor visit.

Doc Crowley wears a quizzical smile as his prune eyes probe my impassive brown ones.

"How do you feel? I mean, truly, on a day to day basis?"

I give him the patter of the old. "I've got these aches and stiffness in my joints, and I tire much too rapidly. Some days, all I want to do is take to my bed."

The doctor brushes me off. "Yes, yes. Advancing old age, not proper caring for yourself. I can prescribe you designer drugs, or you can beat most of it through natural supplements, good diet and exercise."

He shuffles some pamphlets but abandons them when I pose the big question. "What's the point, if I'm dying anyhow?"

He lifts his glasses so those prunes of his can meet my naked eyes. "That's just it. I don't find any more sign that the cancer is active. You're cured, but only for now. Once you've had cancer, you've got to protect yourself from recurrence the rest of your life. I have a few programs to recommend, some books for you to read - Aside from that, you're on your own."

A special milestone has been passed, making me feel like celebrating. As I'm walking through parking, I pay particular attention to the long suffering Taurus, which I realize deserves a part in the festivity. After cruising back into Long Beach, we pull off the street at Bubble and Wipe Car Wash for a thorough cleaning - get the dirt out of her

ears, so to speak. It's also a symbolic washing away of Doc's dying in her seat.

We sit in a line of fifteen cars, awaiting our turn, the faithful wagon and I, communing. Our thoughts and my thanks are with Doc Crowley, for giving me commonsense advice and treatment, and helping me work through my own program of cancer warfare, instead of insisting on chemo. As I appear to have come through it all with an immune system, I hope to live a long life without a relapse. Then Taurus is out of

my hands, getting vacuumed, scrubbed- - gussied up.

I watch her emerge from the storm of brushes, soap, and water from a safe distance, half expecting her to shake like a dog.

We drive away, new car proud.

Having completed the festivities, turning somber, I park under the tree, stirred yet to the core by the Doc Ramos saga, and now laden with soul shriveling thoughts that were deliberately sublimated before he appeared. Dark political thoughts, until now sublimated because it bespeaks a failed America and a failing humanity. It's common to blame Ronald Reagan for the collapsed fortunes of the poor and middle class, but for we old timers troubling signs were in evidence early on. For one thing, demonstrators have always been beaten under the rule of either party. Many union activists had to die before unions could take shape. These same unions, when strong, cornered Roosevelt to explain he was not just likely a one term president, but that a soviet style revolution could be looming if he did not come up with programs to help the people. The same forces that eventually led to a President Reagan worked tirelessly neutering and destroying the unions. In medicine we lost choices one by one. Roosevelt's plan for universal health care

was never considered, post FDR's death. When the stage was set Reagan merely provided the willing stooge. I admit to remaining silent even as I witnessed Bill Clinton bringing Reagan's voodoo economics to full fruition. My disappointed weariness toward my fellow lefties along with the perceived inevitability of democracy's groaning dysfunction had made me turn a deaf ear, for I was by now defeated. Doc's visit woke me enough to experience regret. Regret, but no action. By the time the sting of losing my friend eases, my apathy will have long been reinstated. In essence, my faith in humanity is nil. Make of it what you will.

I make my way in the gloom to my little writing room, which is furnished with a window air conditioner, a computer desk, row of file cabinets, and a chaos of papers - on the desk the PC that supplanted an ancient typewriter when the old machine couldn't cut it anymore. My intent is to begin a novel telling the story of a microscopic race that has occupied an Earthly niche for tens of thousands of years. They have been peaceful, but are

distressed because the race of humans has made life on the planet almost completely untenable. Solution: encapsulate a contagious deadly virus and sail with it into the entrails of an unlucky human.

First, I want to check my emails.

The old PC reluctantly begins to load for me. After a long pause the browser opens a page and I click on my email. Forty-one messages vie for attention. There is just one I want to pursue, the one from ddannyd. That's my brother Danny, who is a twin.

"Salutations. I got your message about Doc. I haven't responded because too heartbroken to know the words to say. I heard from Nellie today and she wants your addy.

What say you?"

And I reply, "Let her have it."

Now to my proposed book. The socialist race of microscopic beings . . . Working into mid afternoon until hunger intervenes. I make a sandwich of chopped sardines, red onions, garlic, and peppers, on mustard and mayo rye. Chased with cold black tea. Note to self: There are almost no groceries left. Get more.

On dressing myself, my stomach pushes uncomfortably against my trousers. I loosen the belt a notch and then sit to strap sandals on my feet, as I prepare to walk on the beach. The sun is still strong though hidden behind a thick blanket of clouds, I've got to be moving. Buttoning my shirt twice to correct wrong buttoning. Then, walking the blocks to the beach. It always disturbs me how few pedestrians I encounter. I haven't mentioned it, but my service in the Navy was spent here. In the early to mid Sixties the sidewalks carried its share of busy feet. Then the Navy base shut down. No more sailors equals a dead piece of Long Beach. Stores I once frequented are no longer within my range of notice. Even the Pike, a fun park, is no more.

An inviting little cove in the sand receives my body, where I can be comfortable while scribbling in my pocket notebook. Two minutes in, I pause to ponder what the gist of my new book ought to focus on. My personal opinions? Boring. The devastation sweeping the planet and driving the largest species, including humans, to extinction? Yes. Bingo.

Because we live in a world in which propaganda, intimidation, and distraction by way of games and memes chains us to our chairs. Then, the poison in our food and

environment weakens us further. So, we mostly don't even ask for justice and economic liberation.

My eyelids weighted as with lead, I slip the notebook and pen into my pockets, to lay back my head against the sand and doze. The sultry warmth doing a job on me.

From deep in the dark of my dozing a traveling light encroaches. It is a radiant globe, dragging its bottom, empty at first, until a shadowy figure materializes within, looking to be almost human, but with claws for hands and eyes like burning cinders. He regards me with malevolence for a time before speaking. "I am your life of sadness. I will kill you in the end."

He waves a hand and the Native American part of my grandfather's blood spreads a panorama of slaughtered native warriors, children, and young women over the centuries, the fruit of the Great Incursion, the scene folded over by fields of cotton, trees with the strange fruit of slavery hanging limp and rotting from the limbs.

All at once an animal with a body similar to that of a dog is lunging before me, with huge snapping jaws full of dagger-like teeth. I circle to the side. Its lean muscular body turns with me. Discerning its head to be perfectly positioned for me to bop it with my leather sandaled foot, I kick out, waking myself in the process. Almost immediately a strong feminine voice registers concern. "Are you alright?"

Not certain how embarrassed I ought to feel, I struggle to put her in my line of vision until I see freckles, frank blue eyes, and white streaks in a frame of dirt-blonde hair. Her beautiful lips enchant me. I struggle to my feet, with her reaching out to assist. "I'm fine," I tell her. "Just slept and had a bad dream."

"You look shaky. I'm staying with you until I'm sure you're going to be okay."

"I live within walking distance."

But my ankle is sore enough to cause me to limp just a little, when I step out and begin my journey home.

Her loose fitting bell bottom style slacks dance around some long legs as she paces

me and looks unwaveringly at my face. "I'm Karma. You don't have to tell me your name if you don't want to. I was just out on the beach to be alone after losing my job today. It hurts to be fucked over by some asshole who doesn't even know his job."

"I'm sorry," I say, wondering that "fuck" gets used so casually between strangers these days. "Do you have a line on anything?"

"I'm fine. Don't be concerned."

A cell phone makes its way into her hand and she's almost instantly connected and speaking to it. "Harold. I'm going to be late about a half hour. Go ahead and start without me. Okay. Thanks."

She hides the phone and gives a smile that's not really a smile. "Political meeting," she explains. "Helping Democrats who support the President."

I nod, stepping up the pace. Another coalition of Democrats sucking at the teat of a Republican administration. If she draws me out on the topic she is likely to grow angry. She is sensitive to the move, likely because of encountering it on a regular basis.

"We had to vote with Jay Smith to thwart Andrew Spud. Spud's a dangerous man. Who are you supporting?" she says, instantly prepared to do battle.

"Nobody at all," I reply. "Not a one of them."

"Then what are your politics?"

"Firstly, I'm a socialist. I once followed the likes of Chris Hedges, Richard Wolfe, and Shaun King, when I took the time to follow anything at all. Overriding even the socialism, I view humans as overstaying their welcome on the planet. Sad that we are taking the rest of terrestrial life and much aquatic life with us. I hope what evolves behind is kinder to Mother Earth."

Karma's ensuing silence could say lots of things, or else nothing at all. Then, a rueful look. "You to the far left are the reason conservatism has gained so much traction. Voting third party and even abstaining from the process ensures they win. That's why President Smith had to be elected -"

I halt right there, in the middle of the boulevard. "No. You President Smith supporters are saps. The ones taking away our tax money to fund endless wars and to

scam the citizens of what's left to further enrich the obscenely wealthy ensures conservatives win. That's on you. Voters are bottled into a no win situation. Neither Republicans nor Democrats serve the public good. Screw President Smith."

She would lose it if I made note of Democrats' unacknowledged admission that the party has lost their teeth, bark, and growl; hence the bolt to support a smooth talking Republican.

My ankle no longer hinders me. "You can go keep your appointment. I don't want any more help."

Again with the phone. "I want you to copy this ap and at least listen to a few of my pod casts," she says, holding it before me expectantly.

"Not interested."

"Come on, let me see your phone."

By this time we are moving again. "I don't carry it with me," I say at last. "It's anchored to the wall over the counter. It didn't go to ap school anyway."

Her astonishment is nearly comical. "Landline? Are you kidding me?"

Acid smile. "I live in the Twentieth Century. I don't like this one."

"You know," she says, "I almost believe you."

"Welcome to have a look," I say graciously.

By this time we've come on my street. A black streak near the stop sign reminds me of Doc each time I see it. He put it there with my car. We come in the yard, silent to one another, she likely trying to process the information I gave her, me wondering if I should offer her a drink. She waits calmly beside me as I work the locks and push open the door, then stand back to allow her to enter. She hesitates. "There aren't any animals in there, are there?"

"Not since Gretta there aren't. She was a small black spaniel, with wiry hair and a serious under-bite. I don't want another dog to miss like that."

Still she hesitates. "Don't let the flies out," I say, crossing the threshold.

She steps in and looks around, possibly surprised to find my house orderly, in a neglectful sort of way. She stalks across the living room to have a look at my phone and

finds it perched on the wall, pale yellow, with a heavy cord, marred with age. Turning, she approaches the television. "Ha," she says. "Flat screen."

"The old one died. So I upgraded from seventeen to twenty-four inches."

This time she goes all the way into the kitchen. After opening every single drawer and door, she says, "You don't have any food in here."

I storm indignantly behind her to expose the lie - kale, cabbage, peppers - and in the freezer a cube of butter and a pork chop. I look her in the eye triumphantly.

Her baleful response kills the instant.

Her police-eye spreads an all encompassing sweep of the house, the portion that I've revealed to her. "What do you do here all day?"

That's it. She's leaving. I get to save the two tea bags I had mentally pegged for in the event she accepted a civilized sit-and-drink. My dramatic move to open wide the door for her departure is marred by my ankle resuming the limp. Stumbling, I nevertheless get the knob under control.

Her gorgeous eyes no longer see me as she moves stiffly into the still sunny day and traverses the short distance to the sidewalk, with the legs of her pants languidly swirling with each long step. Then she's gone.

Resting a hand on the rail, watching to see she doesn't return. Quick movement, alerting that Lenny, the house gecko is about. He pauses near the corner post to regard me, with unblinking eyes set in a face mimicking the solemn features of Leonard Cohen. I tell him, "You guard the house. I'm going in."

Instead, he runs down the post and hides somewhere below the deck line. "Shirker."

CHAPTER FOUR

The deep dark night, when all souls should be sleeping, finds me treading barefoot in my underwear, fumbling to switch on the hall light. Next, bumbling through the living room, noting the round clock in the dimness how late - rather, how early - is the time. Three seventeen. The knocking at the door is pitiless. Damn it; if that's Karma - There is a chill and then a mild breeze as the door eases open.

"Your underwear," a husky feminine voice emotes as the woman moves forward, Tall black suitcase in hand.

I stand back, letting her in.

Dumping the suitcase in the middle of the room, she turns around to exclaim, "Danny's message got in the spam folder. I left out as soon as I discovered it. Too bad it's so late. But aren't you glad to see me?"

I gawk at Nellie. There's no other way to describe it. She looks a great seventy-five. My gaze sweeps a purple sheath dress, strong legs, black shiny slippers - and hangs up in her eyes. The deepest, blackest ports in the universe, blacker than were Doc's eyes. But momentarily out of place. For her face had been small, smooth as silk. The glow of young sexuality laser-beamed into my very protoplasm. Now there is a heaviness from gravity and longevity.

She returns the stare. Her black lipstick forms a tight grin. "Yes; I'm old, just like you."

"Would you like a cup of tea?"

"At three in the morning? I'm ready to crash in that easy chair."

I move to block the chair. "And wake up all stiff and unrested? Wouldn't think of it. There's plenty of room on my bed."

I guess she understands by my demeanor how harmless is the request, because she immediately slips off the purple dress and the slippers, then follows me in her underwear into the bedroom. "Pick a side," I urge, and she chooses my favorite nesting spot.

After slipping under the sheet, Nellie murmurs, "Sweet dreams," then closes her

eyes without waiting for me to cut the light and crawl in on the bed's bad side. Easing into the coolness, sheet thrown back, then just lying there, staring into the darkness, reviewing the past that never was and the reality resting beside me.

She had been in the old days a third wheel between the Doc and me rather than a romantic lover. If she wanted me the way Doc represented it, I never knew. I still can picture her grabbing up a tear gas canister, tossing it back, or spreading pamphlets, tireless for the cause. That we shared a few kisses due to spending so much time together was to me just innocent play.

Sleep eventually comes an hour or so before the accustomed trip to the bathroom. When I do wake up, Nellie is singing in the shower. Knowing she can't see me from there, I pee in the toilet, then get dressed for the day.

Yesterday's clothing makes the hamper the sole keeper of all the laundry, with that which is worn being discounted.

Sitting at the computer to make a few notes: Who is my race of microscopic beings? How close to human should they be? Are they men and women? The questions

get silly after that. Nellie comes out of the bathroom, dressed in fresh clothing. Black slacks, peach top - Where in hell did she get yellow lipstick? "Here I am," I call from my little space.

She poses in the doorway. "You look just like I imagined all these years, Denny." Moves forward. "Are you beginning something new?"

"Yes. Have you read my books?"

Blithely; "Not a one."

Undismayed; "Ah. Honesty. What writers do you read?"

"I haven't read any books since I left school in the tenth grade," she says. "I read the news, follow some video series online. I never liked fun reading."

Putting the computer to sleep, prepared to rise, I put my finger to her nose as I lean forward. "Are you hungry?"

"Sure. I want to treat you to breakfast, then sightsee Long Beach before I go home."

"Sightsee? Why?"

She's putting her phone inside her purse, already moving to go. "I like what I saw about it on my phone. I never knew Long Beach had so much to offer."

"Yeah, I don't care. I just live here. After breakfast you can sightsee on your own."

"My trip," she replies, "is just for you. If that doesn't suit you, we can just visit. If there is anything you want to do just let me know."

"Eat breakfast then return here," I say, adjusting my collar.

She adjusts the collar a bit more. Outside, we spar over whose car to take until Nellie climbs in her car and sits. We ride in bucket seats that remind me of the rides at

carnivals. The streets are less familiar to me where she takes us. The restaurant is bright and glitzy, but the menu has all of my breakfast favorites, but higher priced than I am used to. I'm all for leaving.

Nellie speaks as to a rebellious child. "You sit back down. I'm paying for this shit and you'd damn well better enjoy it."

Feeling properly chastised, I sit, head down, not even studying the menu.

At first she goes over her menu, then finally stares with unabashed bemusement. "You've changed," she says. "The Denny I recall was a brash, adventurous dude. You've shut down. It's not due to old age. What is it?"

Picking up my menu, I open to the section with eggs and pancakes. With eyes fixed on the beautiful stacks and whites with big yellow centers, I mull the answers one might toss off. And speak. "Imagine if you will a great air balloon sailing in the blue sky. Destination: equality, justice. Love, if you will. Mercilessly pelted from all sides, until the balloon damage sends it to a rough landing, not halfway there. Imagine the thrill of learning it's not possible. That humanity is beyond the point of expiration. Any form of life support just prolongs the agony." I pause to wipe my slightly runny nose. "I'm playing out the time I have left without antagonizing anyone. Let their fantasies sustain as long as possible."

"So you've given up. If I were a man I'd beat you right now. I'd slap your head until you got some sense into it."

"That yellow lipstick makes it impossible to take your kind of threat seriously," I

grin.

We study our menus, wondering where the waitress can be. Speaking over mine, I tell Nellie, "You're not at all like Doc described you. I expected this broken flower, this beaten down victim. Instead you have as much life spirit as ever."

"You could never believe fifty percent of what my brother told you, after he spent time in a Mexican jail, sick. He did almost the whole term in a fever that must have cooked his mind. They hooked him on drugs in there."

Our eyes lock. Tears spring to the surface. "Ah. That puts a new complexion on things," I say mournfully.

The waitress picks this moment to bounce up, brightly saying, "Hello. I'm Jasmine. I'll be taking care of your table. What would you like to drink?"

We both opt for coffee; hers with cream and sugar; mine black.

I pick up on the previous conversation. "They are ringing us in with weapons and poverty. A general strike could help, but they are masters at reneging. You'd best learn how to properly cluck, because to them we are no higher on the scale than caged chickens."

She looks sad. "Jesus, Denny. You make pessimists seem like Pollyanna."

The steaming cups are set before us. Nellie orders a waffle. I ask for the multigrain pancakes with eggs over medium and hash browns. No meat. We eat in silence.

On the road back, Nellie asks why I never married and if I am asexual? I explain that there were several women in my life, none of whom I could live out my life comfortably with. She then explains about her one marriage and the abuse that was inflicted on her. "He was nice the day we got married. I thought he was wonderful, so

solicitous of me in every way. He was the large inspiring type in appearance. He took me to shows, dances, the best eateries. I anticipated fairy tales and magic. Then one morning he hit me because I laid out his clothes for the day wrong. My reaction was to strike him back. He blocked my hand, then he smushed my face. For almost a week he berated and poked at me. Then one morning he awakened all beat up and I still held the bat, looking at him. He waved me off, in resignation. Took him maybe five minutes to clear out and

never returned for his clothes or anything."

"You always have been amazing," I reply as we turn in and pull up behind the Taurus.

We step out, but Nellie pauses. Her gaze is near ground level. "Is that what I think it is?"

Coming to her side, looking past her and detecting at once the object of interest, I assure her, "If you think it's a sheet metal screw stuck in the tire, you are correct."

Nellie pushes me to go in the house while she drives to the tire shop to have it taken care of. She's headstrong independent. I let her do it. Unlocking the door, hearing the phone ringing, I glance back as her sporty car makes a jaunty turn into the street and rolls away. Having her around makes me lighter. I should have stayed in touch with old friends like her. Inside, moving slowly toward the phone, reaching it at the same moment the ringing ceases. Knowing they will call back if it's important. I sit to turn on the midmorning news, mainly for the weather. The forecast looks chancy, a near perpetual state of the forecasts.

An authoritative knock resounds at the door.

Damn it. I told the Jehovah's Witnesses I wasn't interested. Taking extra time, strolling across the worn out linoleum, formulating a way to say, "Thanks, but fuck you" as pleasantly as possible. On the other side of the door is instead a man in a dumb looking brown suit with a blue and orange tie. A dumber looking brown hat with a crumpled brim and a dented crown. "Wexel's the name. Here for a welfare check."

Wexel comes forward with the authority of one who needs no stinking badges. Actually makes physical contact to brush by me.

"Look, dude -" I begin.

Already he is scoping out everything, going through cabinets, drawers, closets. Gawks at the bed. I realize for the first time that Nellie dragged half of the covering to the floor when getting up and simply left it. Then standing within a few yards of the entrance, filling out a form on his phone. Speaking, but barely distinguishable. I make out: "no food ... no clean clothes ... "

He turns treacherous eyes my way and says, pausing for an answer between each question, "Do you know what day it is? Who is the president? Do you know the name of the governor?" And other irrelevancies.

I humor him with correct answers.

He then stands silently, staring at the screen, and I conclude he wants to move me out of here. In the end he holds the phone before me and asks me to put my signature on there. Instead, I move to open the door, planning as civilly as possible to request he leave.

Another surprise, for Nellie walks in at this point. She pauses, possibly awaiting a signal to stay and listen or discreetly harbor outside. "Welfare check," I inform her. "I

think the dude's planning to railroad me into a public nursing home."

She turns on Wexel looking like she might pounce on him.

Wexel becomes all defensive when confronted by Nellie's hostile reaction. "Now, I didn't say that -"

"Of course not," she replies. "You sneaky sons of bitches make your moves on the sly. Mollify their fears until the trap goes off."

"The man's not taking care of himself," Wexel whines.

"He is perfectly capable of living on his own." She pauses a moment. Then, "But I am sent here to assist him. I will be here daily from now on, to cook, clean, grocery shop, wash his laundry, and anything else he may need."

Wexel finally lets himself out. Pausing on the porch, he advises that he's returning in two weeks for followup. Nellie pushes the door to, turns to sternly regard me. Her concern is devastating. "You are eighty, you know."

"So? What are you trying to tell me? That you're on Wexel's side?"

"I'm saying that I intend to move in with you," she says as if it's non negotiable.

"That's ridiculous. You can't abandon everything just to help me."

We have moved by incremental steps into the kitchen, where I produce my precious tea bags. The shiny tea kettle lives on the back stove element. Filling it with just enough water for two cups, then placing on the near element to heat.

After I adjust the switch to a high medium heat, I look her in the eye. "Go home,

Nellie. I don't need any help."

If a look could melt mortal flesh I would at this moment be settling over my shoes

with my clothing in a heap on top. "It never crosses your mind that you can be wrong about anything, does it?" she cracks.

Without another word being said between us she gathers her stuff into the suitcase and leaves the door wide open on her way out. I stand just out of sight listening to her door close and the car engine rev. In my imagination I see her back onto the street and go out of the neighborhood. In the scenario she may be fuming, but certainly not crying. Engine sound fades.

"I have my standards," I mutter weakly, closing the door, retreating then to finish making tea. Black English tea. Hearty robust black tea. I regret not having lemon or honey at hand. Sipping. Good anyway.

Already I miss Nellie's presence. Could it be the drive to hermit is loosening at the hub? No. I'm going to take to my chair and nap. You can carry on without me for now.

Dozing, with drone of TV to make me numb. I need this daily nap.

Goaded back to reluctant consciousness before sleep settles in by a tapping at the door. I don't want to answer it. But the door opens before I can decide. Rats. I need to start locking it always. Before I can stir enough to put my feet down, a tall black suitcase slides across the floor. A husky feminine laugh punctuates the arriving suitcase.

Black eyes and yellow lips.

"Damn, Nellie."

She gives me a Curly Howard wave. Stands with hands at hips. "Do you have laundry detergent? Dryer sheets? Never mind, I can see for myself."

The grogginess is slow to leave. My feet are on the floor but there is no will to

leave the chair. I remote the TV dead and listen for her sounds in the bath and laundry area. Disappointed to lose my nap, launching myself to toddle in her direction to holler, "This isn't settled yet." And, "You don't get to keep my side of the bed."

When she doesn't answer, I call again. "Would you like some tea?"

I come in on her sorting my underwear. "Do you want some tea?"

"I don't understand why you haven't done your laundry before now," she chides.

"I was taking a nap."

She feeds items into the washer before my watchful gaze. Then slips a pod into the receptacle. As she lets down the lid a trifle hard, I caution against slamming it down. "The lid switch breaks rather easily. I don't like paying the repairman to replace them."

Switch on, the washer begins filling with warm water. "The dryer is broke," I say nonchalantly.

"Why didn't we go to a coin laundry?" Nellie exclaims.

I blithely point to three plastic bins in the back. "That's for taking the clothes to dry."

She lets herself sigh at me, but I'm finding humor in the situation. "I'm going to make you some tea," I say, turning to go.

Seeing her reach for the broom in the corner, I warn her that she's accenting the fact I'm a slob and that's borderline insulting. "Go make that tea," she exclaims, waving the broom.

CHAPTER FIVE

The laundry building is decayed, with some of the brick façade crumbling, and the windows held in place by repeated caulking. But Rex the owner keeps the machines up and that is all one could ask for. Rex comes to the car to carry one of the baskets of wet laundry and even tosses it all into the dryers for us. Two loads. Nellie accompanies me to sit on an outside bench to feel the insidious warmth of the sun. It's hotter than we prefer. We just feel the need for sun to touch our skin.

I ask when she is returning to Fresno. "I'm not," she says adamantly. "I messaged Danny and he has agreed to go there and gather the items I need and come here with them. Nobody there is going to miss me."

The rays on my face are hot and I sometimes like it that way. Rex has ambled out and he takes a place beside Nellie on the bench. We sit in silence, each one urging the drying time to reach its end. Then Curtis comes to mind, colorful fixture of this particular neighborhood. "Where is Curtis?" I ask Rex. "He always comes when he sees my car."

Rex is two or three years older than me. He looks off with his bleached grey eyes in the direction the man in question always comes from and shakes his head. "Don't know," he replies. "I've had to throw out some sandwiches I brought for him. Ain't been around in about a week."

"Too bad he keeps his sleeping spot secret. We could check on him times like this."

Rex nods. "By the way; I'm closing this operation next month. Best get a new dryer."

He stands. "Wait as I check your laundry."

Waiting complacently. Nellie says, "So, you won't see Rex anymore. What about Curtis? Still driving here to see him?"

"Curtis is a good man," I answer. "No family, education or ambition, but lives for the moment in an improvised Zen. Pretty smart to be so ignorant. He will work for his food, as in cleaning up the place in exchange for Rex's sandwiches and the like."

By the time Rex comes out to let us know the clothes are dry I have extracted a five

dollar bill from my wallet, which I press into his hand. "For Curtis."

The laundry man stuffs the bill into his pocket. "Now I have something from him for you," he announces.

Producing two tens from another pocket, he shoves them at me. "It's from Curtis," he says. "He bought a scratch off with the last five from you and won back fifty dollars. He figures this twenty is fair, since he spent his own money for the ticket."

Waving it off, I advise him, "You keep it. You may need it once you've retired."

Unabashed, Rex stuffs it back in the pocket.

I'm all for tossing the laundry directly in the baskets and driving it home before sorting, folding or anything else. Nellie, intent on torturing the clothes further, insists on doing it all on the table right here. With a resigned shrug, I pitch in, only to be corrected as to methodology, until I am reduced to merely standing by, feeding a few pieces to her. Rex has gone to assist a new customer.

When finally we get the assaulted laundry in the house, I have to sit to recuperate, while Nellie dives directly into the distribution between hanging and drawer stuffing. It

ain't fun being old. I have the TV on to catch local news and weather. My eyes are heavy.

After the news slips blithely past, the weather forecast makes me sit up and pay attention. Some violent storms currently punishing the state will involve Long Beach tomorrow. That stuff has been deadly in a few places. It's a contest between climate change and the world war currently in progress to determine which will make us extinct.

Nellie has slipped by me probably to next take on the kitchen. I begin to wonder how I can get her to be slovenly like me. Turns out she is making a grocery list. I call out a few smoothie recipes.

Quietly aware of her activity, sitting very still, my nap finally shuts me down. Awakened later by the movement of a body transporting bags of groceries through and into the kitchen. On my feet, I call out, "Is there more? I can carry in the rest."

Assured there is, I end up making two trips.

Placing the bags to be easy to reach as she unloads them, I enquire how much it cost. She regards me with a sarcastic look and says, "Too damn much. Where do these

bastards get off charging so much for everything under the sun? I saw a package of hamburger meat for thirty dollars. Eggs. Unbelievable. Thirty-five dollar toilet paper. Thirty-five dollars to wipe your ass."

"I'm asking how much I have to give you for them," I say, interrupting. "I know how they rob us."

Nellie refuses to produce the receipt. "You've paid rent and utilities for this place. It's only right I share the burden."

She goes to my chair and drops down in it. "The wind is uncommonly strong out

there," she remarks. "Bad weather may be arriving a lot sooner than the forecast."

"Must have been between gusts when I went out there. There's nothing to do but hunker down until it's over. No walk today."

"Danny said you must have that sand worn out by now." Her black eyes are scrutinizing my features. "Okay if I sketch you this evening?"

"You're an artist?"

We set up at the table, as it's the only place to comfortably do this. She extracts a thick artist's pad and some pencils from the suitcase. I practice putting on my best face, watching her getting ready. When she begins flipping through some pages, I ask to see her work. She backs up to the most recent and names the subjects as she shows off three separate portraits. Her work uses bold strokes which she refines with more delicate shading in. I feel I could easily recognize the people depicted were they in this room.

She says, "I used to make drawings of the day's activities, in the protest days. There are lots of illustrations featuring you and Doc and even myself."

"I hope Danny's going to bring them. I would love to see it all."

She sets up the page and begins with vigorous strokes, dividing eye movements between the paper and my head. At one point her face is very close to the page. I can't see her features. Using a low sober tone she asks if I like her.

"Of course. I love you, Nellie."

"Not just as a person. Have you noticed at all that I'm a woman?"

"Nellie. The first moment you appeared at one of our demonstrations I saw a

dynamic woman whom a man would be lucky to hook up with."

She lifts her head, bores into my eyes with those blackest of peepers. "Then why didn't you try?"

Not feeling self defensive, really, but having never put it into words for myself even, I stutter at first. Then words begin to form. "I saw in you the woman I could pursue to the alter and then build a family with. Til death to part." My words falter. Then, "I grew up in the aftermath of the Great Depression. As the New Deal began to form and take hold, I already saw the elements of it falling apart. By the time we reached the Sixties I could see that the world is no place to build a family. I felt I could not ethically bring children into it.

With you, the need for procreation would have been inevitable. That is in fact why I never married anybody."

"We can't reproduce now," she answers.

"You married. Why no children?" I pry.

"Husband's boys shot only blanks," she answers. "But I learned to be happy he couldn't reproduce by me. Made a breakup easier, yet also made me not responsible for what he produces on the world."

She immerses herself in finishing up the portrait, speaking at the same time. "I would have gone with you, had you made a first move. I waited for it for over a year. Turned down some great prospects in that time."

"So," I mused, "it was you turning away Allen Cruz, not the other way around. Fascinating."

Nellie picks up the pad and turns it to display her work. She has given the image a somehow feral quality that is not observable inside my mirror. I nod approval. In fact I

tell her how much I love it. She beams in the light of adoration. She carefully puts the pad away. As she is standing over the now shut suitcase, I come from behind and embrace her. She turns in the circle of my arms for the full frontal effect. In the prolonged moments sharing the warmth, we listen to the escalating roar of nature.

The storm slams the house with unmitigated fury.

Five minutes later the power's out. A flashlight guides our movements in the

premature dusk before we take to cuddling in my chair with nothing else to do. I mentioned early in this narrative the crumbly shingles over the roof. Though it hasn't leaked in the past, a stream of water suddenly makes its way into the ceiling to cause a bulge threatening to bring it down. I fetch the stock pot from in the back of a lower cabinet before engaging a small stepladder to poke a hole in the drywall with a screwdriver. With the poke a swift gush runs down my arm, splashing on the floor. Nellie slides the pot under the hole. "This pot's too small," she says.

The plastic laundry bins are the answer. We replace the pot with the bigger bin, then empty the pot down the toilet. After that there's nothing to do, except return to the chair or lie in bed, although it will be necessary to return to bail out the bin.

"We'd better keep our clothes on, in case there's an emergency that we shouldn't tackle naked," Nellie says.

Wise words. But that doesn't stop us from violating each other's clothing. After a time, we fall asleep. Hours later, I arise to empty the bin. A spot from the flashlight shows it over the top. There's a great puddle on the floor. A shop vac would be just the thing to get it up. All I have is a mop and bucket. After bailing the water out of the bin I set to

picking up the other water with the mop and squeezing it into the bucket for transfer to the toilet.

Thirty minutes later, I'm leaning on the mop, listening to the disaster befalling the city. It's likely around three or three thirty, so back to bed. She feels me sliding under the sheet and moves nearer to share the warmth.

A major concern is an ancient oak tree that stretches high and wide in the neighbor's front yard. Oaks are notorious for falling during storms such as this. In my imagination I already see it falling against the house, crashing through my bedroom ceiling. I fight my imagination, commanding that it back off. Mercifully, a deep sleep prevails, lasting until morning.

The storm lashes Long Beach into the next day. On waking early, I gaze wistfully at the sheet-covered hump occupying what was my space in the bed. Can't help smiling. For some reason, Cyrano's Roxanne comes to mind - "One silken gown -" Later, when I

mention this to Nellie she retorts, "Except I'm not stupid like Roxanne. I could never be like that."

Hours later, after the rain has been stopped for a while, the electric power returns. Nellie busies herself cooking a pork roast that had thawed, while also giving the floor a thorough cleaning. Meanwhile I stand in the yard to survey the house and cars. The cars are fine, but for a few chinaberry branches on them. But a patch of decking shows on the roof where there once were shingles. It's about six square inches I would judge. Since there is a partial roll of aluminum flashing material behind the house, I see no cause to wait on the landlord to act. If I take a tin cutter and a few tacks with me, it should be easy

enough to work the right size metal under the shingles at the top, making it overlap at the bottom. A little plastic roof cement to cover the tack heads.

I'm leaning an aluminum ladder against the roof edge, when who should arrive at the scene but Karma, flanked by two friends. She's dressed in grey and her hair is bright even in no sunlight. They all three crowd before my ladder with their expressions of disapproval making them look like monkeys. "What?" I say, feigning innocence. "I'm setting it up for the repairman, whom I expect to pull up at any time."

Karma's reluctant to accept my explanation but lets it go. "We came here to see that you survived the storm," she says, "Apparently you're fine. I brought along Harold and Joseph in case the situation called for extra help."

"Just a simple roof leak and temporary loss of power," I say. "I do appreciate your concern, however."

"Well, okay," she replies. "I guess we'll leave. I want to invite you to our meeting tonight."

"I told you before, I'm no longer into politics," I begin. "I just -"

At this point, Joseph steps around Karma to make his pitch. His narrow face with eyeballs that look like blue aggies behind silver-rimmed glasses exudes maliciousness. "We are not going to argue," he states. "Do you mind if we just discuss it with you?"

Harold's head pokes out on the side. "Are you conservative or liberal?" He's trying to look pleasant with his heavy jowls and wavy black hair.

"If politically engaged still I would be socialist."

"But," exclaims Joseph, "socialist systems fail every time it's tried."

"If a big bully came at you every time you tried something you would fail too," I retort, wishing to remain calm.

They all three jabber at once, raucously alerting Nellie from inside the house. She steps down from the porch, pauses, observing for a moment. "Here," she says. "You're disturbing my patient."

They fall silent, turning to stare at the unexpected complication of a black clad figure with orange lipstick come to my rescue. "Who are you?" demands Karma, stepping forward.

Nellie stares her up and down, at her loose bellbottoms and tight-fitting shirt, at her beautifully sculpted head, before speaking. "Somebody that belongs here."

Karma stands her ground. "Well, we came because of the storm, to see that he's alright. We just happen to disagree politically and, since he's okay, we told him about it."

Nellie's orange lips curl in derision. "You brought a gang to beat him up. That's shameful. You're going to learn Denny doesn't take bullying and doesn't need my help. But of course he's getting it anyway. I've been with Denny ever since the Sixties. I know what's inside his head and I feel the angst and the anger just as much as him. You people playing at politics, wanting your side to score wins over the others, like a sports tournament. I hope Denny gives you the brush-off and doesn't talk to you anymore."

Karma's gorgeous lips purse, looking less gorgeous. Then she says, "I would like to hear it all from Denny."

"I'm going to sit in the sun to wait for the roofer," I reply. "Don't count on me for anything."

Harold dogs me to where I take a place on the porch steps, unable to let it go. "We need every hand, Denny. Why won't you give us that?"

Seated on the second lowest step, the sun streaming on my face, I regard him for a hard moment before I speak. "Read James Lovelock." Then I smile. "Do you like roast pork, Harold? Nellie has one on and it's a big one. Come back around dinner time and get fed."

"Seriously. I want an answer."

I search the porch to see if Lenny, the watch gecko is on the job. Sigh. You just can't find good help. Karma and Joseph move in close to hear my answer. I look them over, still smiling, only bitterly now. "Again; Lovelock. Although to me he's an optimist. His opinion that twenty percent of humanity will still be surviving in the year 2100 is a stretch. Read him anyway. Look; I'm in my eighties. I've spent most of the time watching you humans bring the planet to the precipice, preparing to throw it off. I opted out. I will go down with you, but I'm not one of you. We went beyond Brave New World and 1984 long ago, to face Imminent Extinction. I don't mind that you people are suicidal so much as mourn the fauna and flora innocently paying the same price." My voice chokes with emotion. "Fuck's wrong with you? You people get off of the property."

Nellie says, "I've got to mind my roast. You be gone by the time I come back out here."

Single file, they start to leave. Harold looks back long enough to utter a single word. "Communist."

Feeling clean and uplifted all at once I arise and step out to the ladder. Karma turns

and watches in astonishment as I pick up off the ground and hang by the straps over a shoulder a bag containing the metal, tar, tacks, and tools, and start to climb, They all three hang in suspense as I step off onto the crumbly shingles and make my way to the bare spot, sling down the bag, and go to my knees to set to work.

And of course I hear Karma on her phone. I can't make out every word, but she says "Wexel" very clearly. It had been evident all along that the welfare check had been at her instigation.

I get lucky and the piece of metal my snips fashions fits perfectly. It slips easily into place. I've always been good using a hammer and the tacks go right in, snug and flat. Once I seal the final tack and put the leftover stuff in the bag, I again hang the bag over a shoulder and begin a very measured step down the slope to grab the top rail of the ladder. Carefully maneuvering my feet onto each rung, then coming down very slowly. On the

ground, I drop the bag and take hold of the ladder, intent on storing it away immediately. My glance catches the trio pointing phones at me, making movies. I leave the ladder long enough to imitate a few Sammy Davis, Jr., dance steps for the camera before letting it down. When I come back from securing it the three scamps are gone. My glance encompasses the giant oak as I walk to the porch, for I recall an incident of a few years back when a sizeable limb broke free and smashed out a window and knocked loose some of the brick façade, all on the neighbor's property. This time it held up, with just the loss of a few lesser branches and individual leaves.

CHAPTER SIX

With conditions favorable this week, despite a brooding heat spell, Danny has rented a truck, is already on his way with Nellie's stuff. She has taken to walking the beach with me. She bought a new outfit that shows her legs, and sandals much like mine. She enjoys my rapport with the moon. The one difference, she prefers the wet sand and a little wading. Walking home in silence, because there is no need to speak, then come in to a nice meal, which she creates in a short order, while I rest my feet. She insists on doing it and I don't mind because she's a marvelous cook. We share my easy chair for watching TV weather and the occasional show. I always check the schedule for when movies such as Catch 22 and Dr. Strangelove will air. She does a bit of social media on her phone. It's mostly how she stays in contact with Danny and a few friends in Fresno.

One morning we are having coffee while sitting on the porch, when Danny with his rented truck pulls in. It's a pretty big box truck, the kind with room for furniture. I give her a look. "Jesus, Nellie; I don't want to haul in a bunch of heavy stuff."

She waves me off, dumps her coffee in the bushes as she's rising. "It's just a small couch and a lightweight piano. The rest is bags and boxes."

"Just kidding, sort of. If we can lift it we can put it in there."

I too dump my cup into the bushes and stand to greet my twin, who's already jumped down and trotting our way. He looks just like me with a heavy mustache. Very handsome.

He fist bumps me, but hugs Nellie. "If I missed loading any of the good stuff, it

wasn't for want of trying."

"I'll just learn to live without it," Nellie says, pushing away to leave it open for me to greet my brother properly.

I notice he's wearing a bag under one eye while under the other one is relatively smooth, as he grins adversarially. "Looking good, considering," he says.

"Yeah, I lost a little weight, but I like being smaller. You still okay, health wise?"

"I feel good for my age," he says, then moves to open the back truck door. "I have

issues," he says over his shoulder. "Not complaining."

The door's on a track that it rolls up on. Danny slides out a ramp. "It's not really that much to move, considering it's a person's life we're moving," he remarks, peering inside.

Nellie is the first to enter, gathering a couple of bags to carry. I'm propping the house door open because it tends to swing shut. After Nellie, Danny struggles to get a dolly to lift two heavy boxes, almost loses control, but gets it rolling safely down the ramp. He's not strong enough to pull it all up the steps, however, until I step up and lift from the bottom.

As we're letting the box down in a spot near the hall, I tell Danny, "I really appreciate your doing all of this."

Danny stops in his tracks. He gives me a hard look. "I wouldn't do it for anybody else. She's the only one stood up for me when I outed myself."

What? "I didn't harass you for being gay. I harassed you for keeping that eighteen by twenty-four portrait of Ronald Reagan in the middle of your living room wall. He

hated gays. He celebrated HIV for killing them. And you love the son of a bitch."

"I don't love that about him. It's just, he embodies what America should stand for in every other aspect. Standing up to communism, standing on your own two feet. Nothing's free. If you give something free somebody else is paying for it."

"I won't fight over it. Let's get Nellie unloaded and set up."

"Yes," says Nellie, who has been standing in the hall. "Let's be non-political and friendly today. I'm making us a fresh pot of coffee and heating some cinnamon rolls."

We carry in the couch, a lightweight two seater, and the piano. The piano is a small electric one with a rhythm and/or percussion setting for certain pieces. We set the couch facing the TV and the piano back to back with it. Then it's time to join Nellie at the table. She has our coffee poured, with sugar and creamer in case we want it. She shovels out the hot cinnamon rolls onto small plates, to be eaten with forks and knives. "It's still hot; don't burn your mouth," she cautions.

"My friend, Lyle, loves these things right out of the fridge. He won't eat them

warm or hot," Danny says. "I like mine hot with a pat of butter."

"Oh," Nellie says, jumping up, having forgotten the butter. "I've got some."

She slides an open butter dish before him and glides back into her chair. It makes me tired to watch her.

Danny and I are nearly finished when Nellie leaves her half consumed roll and coffee to stand before the piano. "Do you mind if I play? I have something that's been with me since the protest days." She looks at me. "You wrote then discarded this, but I took it from the wastebasket."

She takes her place without waiting for approval and launches into some music having that pounding quality of a slow hymn as played in a Baptist church. She sings:

"All the wars eventually
Must fall before walks of peace
Walks of peace, walks of peace
Must fall before walks of peace
I dreamed I went with MLK
On a rare and fateful day

As he strolled along with me
We journeyed back through history
We saw all the wars of race
Wars of country, even faith
He declared the wars all must cease
Folks must be troops for walks of peace
Yes the wars eventually
Must fall before walks of peace
Walks of peace, walks of peace
Must fall before walks of peace
As Martin said, Don't be deceived
All the wars are wars of greed
It's up to us, these wars must cease
Folks must be troops for walks of peace
All the wars eventually
Must fall before walks of peace
Walks of peace, walks of peace
Must fall before walks of peace"

She finishes with a brief piano solo, then looks at us, grinning broadly. Danny says, "Not much of a song, but you render it beautifully."

I tell her, "I remember it. I tried for weeks to interest people in that, but nothing happened. Not one person reacted to it. So I dropped it into the waste basket."

"Your voice is beautiful," says Danny.

"Thanks," she says. "I try to sound like Buffy Sainte-Marie."

"Well, I need to get on the road," says Danny. "Let's get the last of your stuff unloaded."

Nellie looks sad. "I hoped you would spend a day with us. What's so important you have to get back that quickly?"

"Lyle is watching my cat."

"Is that all? He shouldn't mind an extra day," she wheedles.

Danny smiles, then shakes his head. "He and the cat don't like each other. Lyle fans the cat off the furniture; the cat sometimes scratches him when he sets down her food bowl. No, I've got to get back before one of them commits a murder."

And shortly Danny is prepared to roll. Nellie gives him a big hug and tells him, "I

love you."

"And I you," he tells her back.

Then my brother turns to me. "You know I love you, right? If I was overly harsh earlier, it's because I live my beliefs just like you. No harm intended."

I would have taken this opportunity to tell him that his philosophy is only okay if one lives alone in an uncharted wilderness, like Hugh Glass. Societies with huge populations need socialism, because the ones with his set of values tend to become predators as commerce and rules come into play. But I don't, because it no longer matters which one is right. Now that humanity is indisputably a lost cause we will all be swept by the same current. And so I tell him in return, "Don't worry about it. I love and support you."

This time we embrace before he gets in the truck and goes. Nellie and I spend the next hour making her property situated. Then she asks if I'm going to spend some time writing. I confess that the book I had contemplated no longer seems a worthy endeavor. It's more like my nap time. "You're going to have to indulge me my naps."

She's caught up on household projects. Sits on the couch with her phone. I turn on the TV, put it on an old show rerun, and settle to be lulled to sleep. Later I am awakened

by Nellie playing something I've never heard before on the piano. It's a quiet tune, one I could have slept through, had my nap not run its course. She quits playing to answer her phone.

The conversation is short. I don't understand what she says in it, but she turns to me. "Danny is coming back. He said the road is blocked. He doesn't know why, but it's big. He said he was advised it would be closed indefinitely."

"Well," I answer. "I would enjoy to have him stay a while."

A bit later, Nellie is outside, sketching the oak tree. There is not enough distance to capture it in its entirety. All those twists and turns of lines. She even captures a remnant of a tree house that I hadn't noticed before. She finishes up at the precise moment Danny shows up. I turn from looking over Nellie's shoulder to welcome him back.

He cracks, "I could have stayed at a motel, as far as I had driven. I just didn't know

how long the road will stay blocked, so figured why not annoy you some more."

"Glad to have you," I say with all sincerity. "Do you want to come in and rest a while?"

"Let's turn on the TV to find out what's with the roads being closed. Unless you've done that already," he counters.

"No," I reply, "but I can turn it on."

We crowd the television, searching for a news program. Nothing just now. Nellie consults her phone. Almost instantly she's channeling current headlines. After moments of scrolling, she says, "No mention of it."

Danny can't believe that. He scrolls his own phone. Together they unveil nothing.

"Well," Danny muses, "I'll just wait it out."

He excuses himself to give Lyle a call. "Lyle helps me run my business," he says.

Nellie asks me to help pick a few sketches to frame and put on the walls. "You haven't hung a solitary picture, calendar, medallion - whatever - throughout the house."

"I'm a minimalist," I quip.

"You've given up too much. But I am going to rile you out of it," she vows.

"Don't worry. I'm not yet ready to surrender my very life. I want to be there for the duration of the apocalypse. It's not every day one gets to witness an entire planet's destruction."

"Don't we have twenty or thirty years before that? You should be lending yourself to the efforts to avert it."

"The ones controlling governments and industry would need to be defeated, worldwide. There are simply no organizations with enough clout to stir the masses to action, which is key to meaningful change. Meantime, governments are militarizing everything and institutionalizing poverty to make us too busy struggling to exist. Most Americans are too busy playing with their phones to pay any attention."

Nellie puts her hand over my mouth. "Hush."

As we're shuffling the sketches, Danny concludes his business with Kyle. He joins in the picking of the candidates for framing. He is particularly taken with my portrait and

asks Nellie if he can own it. "I had expected to be framing that one. But if Denny says it's okay you can have it," she says.

I nod assent, secretly disappointed that even one of Nellie's drawings will depart

from here.

"I read you like the Sunday comics," Danny snarks. "You don't want me to have it. I bet you don't want her to let me have any of these."

I give him my best Clint Eastwood eyes and smirk. "I don't want her to let you have any of these. Unfortunately, it's her decision and I will abide by it."

"Boys, boys, boys," she says with a touch of sadness. She challenges Danny. "How would it be if I draw you and send that one home with you? I bet Kyle would love that."

"Solomon in fur. Okay, I'll take it, sight unseen."

Danny loosens his collar. He goes in the bathroom to primp as Nellie sets up for the drawing. He comes out with his face all spritzed and his hair newly combed. "You could do with a lift." My brotherly dig.

"I already look better than you," he retorts. "Always have, in fact."

I return a brotherly smile. "I'm going to be on the computer while this goes on."

"Too jealous to share my time with her," Danny says.

I pause to respond, change my mind, and go to the writing room and the PC.

Social media. I move like a ghost through certain threads because they are more reliable than the so-called news sources. Not to comment, but to monitor the looming dystopia. Today I'm focused on what closed Danny's freeway. It's immediately clear there was some sort of explosion, but no one posting seems to know the source or extent of it. No government officials are responding.

I take to my chair, deeming that a nap's in order.

The voices in the kitchen are a perfect murmur to lull me to sleep.

After forty minutes I'm up and eager to see Nellie's work. As I approach, the two of them are enjoying ice tea while admiring the work spread on the floor. They regard me with amusement as my first sight of two sketches depicts male genitals in the one and a standard portrait in the other. Not only genitals, of course, but a full body study of a nude

Danny, once I've made the visual adjustment. "Whoa. What do we have here?"

"It's a present for Lyle," Nellie says proudly.

"Aside from the subject matter, you have to admit it's a masterpiece," Danny proclaims.

I have to look away. My brother's naked splendor hurts my sensibilities.

"I didn't show her everything," Danny says.

"He stripped to his shorts. I made up what was hidden," Nellie explains. "I made up his goodies after he said if he was cut and waxed or not."

"I suggest storing it in the truck now, just to keep you from forgetting to take it with you," I say, not at all facetiously.

They take me up on it and go together to make certain the drawings will be protected on the journey home.

I'm making myself a smoothie when they come back in. "We thought you might like to take your daily walk right now," Danny announces.

"It's a little warm outside," I answer over the roar of the blender. "But we can do it if you wish."

So we parade along the beach, I in my regular trousers and pull over shirt, Nellie in a halter top and black shorts, Danny in long sleeves and blue jeans. He removes his shoes

and socks, stuffs the socks inside and ties the strings around his belt so he can go barefoot. We barely cross the length of a football field when a raucous sound blares from both cell phones. After consulting the screens they stare at me with shock on their faces. Danny reads out loud: "Shelter in place. Do not attempt to evacuate."

"Let's get back to my place," I urge us. "I don't want to ride this out in a drug store or restaurant."

After Danny puts on his shoes and socks, we hasten back and across Long Beach Boulevard. There are no others on the sidewalk, as we watch the sky and make tracks as fast as we are able, hoping to reach our street unscathed. I'm trying to marshal my thoughts, but the essential clues for such are missing. I can tell we all share in the quandary. They have tried their phones repeatedly, but both have become locked. As we

approach the porch, the wind picks up fiercely, and we are drawn with it, evidence it is pulled from a downwind source rather than blown by nature. Nuclear blasts crowd my imagining, as we are pulled like airborne thistles, to get caught up in the giant oak's branches, saved from a wild ride to certain disaster. Held in place by the wind force, for we could not have clung to the tree on our own and been secured.

I will not guess how long the blast of wind holds on. I only know we eventually tumble to the turf below when it ends. Miraculously we sustain just scratches and a few deeper cuts. My scalp leaks a small stream of blood down to my eye. Wiping it away, I look to Nellie, gratified she is already up, her orange lipstick like a flag waving all is clear. Danny groans but sits up and looks around. He quips, "That was certainly interesting."

My horror wavers enough to allow a quick laugh, cut off by a sound like a cannon shot at the closest range imaginable. The sound cracked from within the tree. As big around as a telephone pole, a limb has broken free just above Danny's head. Caught in the crook of another huge limb, the wayward piece slams the ground with just the free end, well beyond Danny, but a fork in the limb makes it roll at that moment of contact, sweeping Nellie against the neighbor's house. She smacks into a wall between two windows then drops to the ground.

Danny's and my thoughts are to get her safely home. She looks cross-eyed at the old men showing concern as she gathers her wits and struggles to sit up. After a few minutes we all straggle into the house, disappointed because there is no electricity. In the dimness I search the house for my flashlight until recalling it was placed in the car for road emergencies.

CHAPTER SEVEN

After three days of shelter in place, with no electricity and no word from anybody at all, we begin to contemplate taking rogue actions. Essentially recovered from the mishaps with the wind and the tree, uncertain if we have been invaded by foreign armed forces or assaulted by domestic terrorists, we agree that we are on our own until further notice. Shelter in place may or may not have expired and if not who is going to enforce it? If we go, how far and to what purpose? Food, of course. More important at the moment would be accurate information. Nellie suggests we should knock on each neighborhood door to find out if anybody knows anything. Danny responds affirmatively. "Let me bring my pistol," he adds.

A new dimension my brother's displaying. In normal times a gun increases one's odds of getting killed. We look over his shoulder as he's at the truck leaning in, reaching and removing a small black pistol from inside an otherwise empty potato chip bag. Lying on the passenger's seat is a black ball cap with a campaign button on it. The button is shiny black with a skull and crossbones in fluorescent white. Spud campaign button. "What's this?" I say.

Danny turns the cap over to hide the button, says nothing. He pockets the gun and we keep a wary eye on the oak tree as we approach the neighbor's door. I've spoken with the man a few times, but not for over a year. He's in his forties, usually wears a colorful shirt and long shorts. I'm not aware if he has a pet.

Danny knocks then pounds on the door. When nobody responds, we move to the

next house.

After several no responses and one Vietnamese family who speaks no English and promptly slams the door, we come on a large entrance with a crowd of cars in and near the driveway. A story and a half yellow brick home, with green shutters and a standing seam roof. The porch is burnt sienna in color, a window square covered by a curtain with a dim light on the other side at the center of the door. We exchange glances. "Yep. This is it."

As we step up to knock we hear loud voices from inside. The face that greets us from behind a security chain is grim. "Why did you knock?"

Danny explains our situation in persuasive enough terms that the man concludes that it's safe to step outside for a conversation. He is careful to block our view of the interior. His thumb indicates the light in the door window. "Generator," he says.

The man has a pinched in nose and a beetle brow. We see a flat pink tongue when he speaks. I can almost see his saliva to the sides and around the mandible teeth.

He gives us a serious look that suggests momentous events. As if we couldn't so conclude. He indicates the houseful of voices. "We are a political concern. In light of what's happening in our country, I don't want strangers in our midst. But I feel I owe you an explanation of what we think is going on. I don't know your political orientation and I am not curious, so long as you go away after this. A person in my house was having a conversation with a state representative at the time communications were cut. Before he lost contact, he was told this story."

The man begins pushing some yellow leaves off of the porch with his shoe, after

which he faces us. His gesture once again indicates the crowd within his walls. "We support President Smith and his coalition of Democrats and Republicans, despite that he's a Republican and we traditionally are Democrats."

"I'm apolitical," I begin saying. "My brother apparently supports Andrew Spud. Nellie -" until he cuts me off.

"I don't mind at this point. Just listen. What I am saying to you is that apparently Andrew Spud has enlisted the aid of the National

Guard in most of the states. He is actively capturing the state capitols and planning next going after the President, once he has consolidated his hold. Smith has been totally possessed with losing the war overseas. Coincidentally or not, the enemy there just began pattern bombing the fields they were driven out of with low yield nuclear devices in a fashion similar to the pattern bombing of Vietnam conducted by Nixon.

"He is reluctant to send troops to engage these National Guard soldiers out of concern for public safety. My friend says Smith is also afraid the troops will support

Spud."

We stand in awkward silence.

"How much of this do you think is true?" Nellie bursts out.

The man regards Nellie in naked honesty. "All of it. And, Spud's vowing to hang most of the other politicians."

We are too stunned to react as the man abruptly turns and makes his way to the other side of the door. We hear the locks click after him.

I look at the others. "Let's see if we can find some groceries. We'll discuss this shit

at home."

But I give Danny a look, unable to resist badgering him. "You support Spud?"

Danny refuses to be apologetic. "I never follow the news. I liked what he said early on and thought his message was spot on. That he's staging a coup on the government is not me. You are too quick to judge."

Nellie says, "I don't judge you," touching his sleeve.

Smiling, I step away from the house, look back and say, "I am going to zing my brother. I haven't had so many opportunities in a while."

In good time, we drive in my car to a national chain grocery store. Traffic is sporadic, the other drivers looking like lost souls. All are ultra cautious at intersections, since there are no operable signal lights. Our hearts deflate as I turn in the parking lot and pause the car to survey the scene. In the three days we were obediently holed in my blissful abode, what must have been hordes sacked the entire contents of the store, leaving a hulk of a building with no windows and doors. The parking lot looks like Nebraska, flat and eventless.

While sitting still, pondering what to do next, we are approached by a patrol car, driven in a manner both decisive and fearless. He approaches at a roll, then jambs on the brake. Imagine the surprise when he sticks out his head and he looks to be five feet or less in height, with an oversize-looking hat, and the darkest of sunglasses.

I've rolled down the window and wait quietly for the next move.

"You people looking for food?" he says in a friendly enough voice.

"Yes, sir, officer. Looks like we're too late."

The officer's impassive expression never alters. "There's food at the next major intersection. Leave here, go right to the traffic signal. Then go right again. If you don't get something there, there is a food bank a little further past that same light, straight."

He touches his hat brim in a semi-salute, puts his vehicle into gear and starts to roll.

"Thank you, officer," I holler while he is still within range of my voice.

It seems likely he hasn't gone far. His is a useful assignment.

After an hour of fruitless searching - the officer's advice proved too little too late - we are nearly home, when a car at an intersection backs up until his bumper makes contact. Simultaneously, a second car swerves out of the other lane and bumps my rear. Four men are on the pavement in an instant moving in from both sides. They guard the doors, as a fifth man signals for me to lower the window. Figuring he would smash the glass if I should refuse is enough to cause me to comply. I watch his face as the glass slides down. He has given up shaving. Good general features. Hard uncompromising eyes. A pistol rises into view aiming its little black hole between my eyes.

His hand gesture waves the gun around when he speaks. "What have you got in there? Food? Something useful? What? Food?"

I assure him nothing's in the car. "We went looking for food. Couldn't find any."

The robber steps away for me to exit the car. "Open up the back," he commands.

As I put my foot on the pavement I gaze at the cars going around the obstacle presented by us, giving them a silent blessing for not escalating the situation. I silently pray that Danny keeps his gun in his pocket. When shown the proof that I have nothing to surrender, the robbers confer briefly. One who's been brandishing a tire iron the whole

time is for smashing out the windows and deflating the tires. The fifth man berates him and pulls the tire iron away. "Go get in the car."

He returns to me. "How much cash have you got?"

I look in his eyes, trying to not seem nervous. "About forty dollars."

"Take it out of the wallet and give it to me."

As I extract the cash and turn it to him, I tell him, "It's a gift. Just don't hurt my

friends."

He jambs the gun against my forehead. "It's not a gift. I'm robbing your fucking ass. Now say it. 'It's not a gift'"

The cold steel sends a shock through my system. "It's not a gift," I say softly.

"Damn right it's not. You can go now."

He abruptly walks away to his car and gets in. All of the robbers return to the cars. They wait for me to get situated in my seat before they unblock me. I don't look to see which way they go. I don't look at Nellie and Danny. I stare at the controls feeling old and small.

Danny is the first to speak. "Do you want me to drive?"

"No."

Throwing the car in gear, I sweep a hasty glance at the traffic and the empty expanse before us and press the gas pedal. There is an immediate screech of brakes from the side and a scolding of horns as I successfully evade a collision and continue the traipse home.

There will be more such excursions. First, a recovery time.

We're sad for Nellie. She has discontinued the use of makeup. She's unbathed and uncomfortable. She looks to us in despair, as she wraps up another drawing of my brother and me sitting idly on the couch. Then gets that scheming look. She goes to the kitchen counter where she keeps her grocery list, tears out a blank sheet, and begins writing. In passing by me, on the way to the front door, she hands over the note. It explains to the neighbor that we are robbing his home of whatever food and water we can find; desperate times; signed by me.

We have just four bottles of drinking water and no idea how to get more. The food has dwindled too. What Nellie wrote makes sense. I hand the note to Danny before slipping on my shoes.

Danny is all in. "Of course we should rob the old piss bucket. Why didn't we think of it sooner?"

"Because," said Nellie, "we are not inclined to criminality."

"I suppose that could be one explanation," he counters.

Within minutes I have my hands occupied by a pry bar, two screwdrivers, a hammer, knife, and a chisel. "All ready."

We look guiltily in all directions, crossing the line and approaching a side window. This house is very similar to mine, likely built by the same carpenters. That's why I am gambling that at least one window has an inoperable lock and is simply painted shut. And sure enough, after prying loose and removing the screen, all I need do is tap a chisel around the edges several times, then slide it open. I turn to the others to take my bow. Danny grips my shoulders, moves me to the side, and climbs over the sill, with a boost

from me and Nellie. He looks back and tells us to meet him around front.

We feel certain the man has not been home, because the broken limbs and branches off of the oak tree remain as they fell, with additional new ones blocking the walkway. We are obliged to drag some limbs off of the concrete. By the time we come on the porch, Danny is standing in the open doorway. We step into a room that is just like mine but it's a reversed floor plan. The main room is filled with heavy furniture and a gargantuan TV.

We traverse the gloom and proceed to ransack the cabinets and cupboard. I pull up a two wheeled shopper's cart, which we fill first with the cans and bottles, topped with boxes and bags of dry goods. It's a pretty good haul. Nellie checks the fridge, discovers several bottles of spring water. On the way out, the shock of restored electricity causes us to jump, as though caught in the act. I run back to the kitchen, turn on the faucet to a blast of air as the pressure pushes water through the pipes. After wetting my fingers, I cut it off to rejoin my comrades in crime. Nellie and I wait on Danny to lock the entrance and crawl back through the window.

We note an increasingly threatening sky as we return without further incident. The first thing, they activate the phones. They register extreme disappointment because call service seems restored, but no wi-fi. I pause the cart of booty and turn on the TV.

There speaks a man with a serious frown, whom I recognize for local news. He's in the middle of explaining what he does not know, which is why no news source is reporting. Danny joins me before the screen, frowning as deeply as the TV personality.

Points to his phone and shakes his head.

"You can't reach Lyle?" Well, shit.

I try to un-observe a tear wetting one eye.

Danny watches the screen a moment. He goes to the kitchen to put away the groceries. Nellie has been busy flushing the water lines and filling containers with water. Outside, the neighborhood is feeling the brunt of a powerful new storm. The likely hurricane force of wind is a battering ram against these old walls, with fingers prying at the shingles. About a minute later, power shuts off. As I ferret out the flashlight, Nellie struts from the bathroom, wrapped in a beach towel. "At least I'm clean for the moment," she whines.

"Better get dressed," I advise her, hollering to be heard. "I think we should take shelter until the storm lets up."

"I think you are right," Danny says, having given up on his task in the near total darkness of that room, coming to rejoin me. In fact, there is no place to hide, as the wind strips away the shingles and likely much sheathing and the water comes in. The ceilings quickly sag and break loose, dropping drywall and waterlogged insulation all over everything. We become intent on finding Nellie some clothes, but she is ultimately consigned to wear the towel indefinitely. We huddle in a corner where the water is funneled away from our heads, as water rises around our legs. It's surprisingly cold and dismayingly deep. After a time a hole breaks in the lower wall, allowing the water to drain almost as fast as it enters the house. I somehow don't believe it's our demise and that instead we will be alive and well at the end.

My way is to consider unrelated things when in a situation requiring patience. Right now it passes through my thought stream the question, "If a tree falls in the woods and no

one is there to hear -?" I think of time the same way. If no one survives to experience it does time actually flow? I'm thinking, "No." That it is a construct utilized by living organisms, but that the universe may not need or use such a concept. I suppose science has already given its definitive answer, but I am uneducated in the knowing. For now I just suppose that when earthly life dies, time dies.

Concerning Spud and the takeover of the government, I have no feeling about it as I would have in a young day. I was sincere when I shrugged at the destructive nature of humankind and invited it to complete the mission of extinction. Although, as I may have mentioned elsewhere, I am not suicidal, just a realist.

After what seems an interminable length of time, the wind slacks and the rain abruptly quits.

Danny carefully steps away onto a pile of debris. "Is that it? Or are we in a hurricane's eye?"

I don't have that answer.

"Before it all starts again," demands Nellie, "let us see if the house next door is intact. If it is we'll just move over there."

She's right, of course. And, what's to stop us?

She's gone into the debris, digging. I watch with dismay, compounding as it sinks in, that Nellie is trying to find her art material, and knowing full well it may be totally destroyed. She stoically works away much debris as I and then Danny also pitch in. Miraculously, a slab of unbroken material covers the sheets and has prevented most of the water from seeping under to soak her drawings. The only damage is confined to some

edges. Some of the pencils are rendered useless. She shoos us back and takes them up a few at a time carefully draping them over our outstretched arms.

She then leads us out the door and off of the porch. The scenario of destruction that greets us as we step out in the yard is a nightmare of the first proportion. That was no ordinary hurricane wind. Many houses, just like ours, are roofless. The oak tree has fallen, pulled like a dandelion by the storm, but moved toward the street and sparing the house. Danny's rented truck is on its side, presenting to us the underside, looking like a dead rhino. Danny transfers his load to Nellie, then moves to again go in through the window.

Inside, Nellie surveys the new digs with a critical eye. "Rat shit all along the walls. Old, so they likely moved on in search of food. Dust all over everything. I'm not going to live like this and neither are you fellahs. Once the storm is truly gone we have our work cut out. Danny, please clean off the kitchen table, enough so I can lay out my artwork."

Grateful for the respite, we uncover the sofa and it becomes a little island of refuge. Danny constantly checks his phone but there is no signal. Nellie has rifled a few closets and come away with an outfit she can cover with. After still one more wait, the sun begins to break through and much of the gloom is dissipated.

We transfer the water and groceries from my house to here. Then we begin the tasks that will make this house livable. I'm stuck with that of removing rat shit. I think of rats as remarkable critters. I hate being at odds with them. Still I would trap them if they moved in and I don't guarantee their safety.

The loss of the grill and charcoal are regrettable, until the one behind our new home is uncovered. In the back of the pantry on the floor are two bags of charcoal. Hot

doggies. We can make coffee and heat our cans of soup.

Midmorning of the next day the electric makes a magical return. The first thing I think to do is click on the television. The screen lights up immediately and there in full human size on this ginormous screen is the local newscaster I usually look for, catching him in mid sentence.

"- brought by Andrew Spud. The fate of our nation rides on the outcome of today's action, when Spud meets with the president, ostensibly to accept the turnover of the government to Spud, who marched with a contingent of troops and police officers early this morning to take control of the Capitol. Pitched battles between

Smith loyalists and Spud's followers continue. The tide however favors a Spud victory in the final end. In short, it would appear Spud's coup has succeeded."

After explaining that most avenues that transmit the news are not yet functioning, the commentator steps aside. The screen fills with locations of businesses open to the public. A disclaimer warns that few delivery trucks and trains have been arriving. Expect to be met with the severest shortages.

Although we try to discuss what the coup means to us personally, there is a severe paucity of information. Sitting tight seems the best option. We discuss making runs for gas and food, vowing to avoid being political when in public. "If people will shoot drivers because infected with road rage, imagine what political rage can cause."

And so, we venture into the street, after clearing away more debris to allow us out of the yard. Nellie is all for securing a new wardrobe. My first thought is to buy gas, but the lines at the gas stations are enough blocks long to thwart that notion. Afraid to waste

time and gas waiting, possibly just to reach a dry gas pump.

Nellie lucks out, in that there is a pretty nice seeming clothing store, intact and wide open for business. As she is exiting the car, Danny's phone starts to ring. He answers, brightens immediately. It has to be Lyle. I pat him and follow Nellie into the store. Not interested in clothes, but my brother may need his privacy. Watching Nellie go from rack to rack. She selects reds and blacks and greens and yellows; nothing conservative. Good for her. Then makeup and some pretty nice underwear. The clerk tells us she is nervous about Nellie's card, because the new president is working to cut California free, to become its own sovereign state. She fears our cards and money may not be good very soon. We assure her that we don't know a damn thing about it. But she makes the sale final and we carry the goods outside. We approach the car to find a demented Danny crying into his phone.

He directs a solemn stare at both of our concerned faces. "Kyle," he says. He looks away, forcing down the lump in his throat. "The explosion that kept me from going home. There was a similar explosion near our home. Kyle was thrown twenty to thirty feet. He's in a hospital, waging a battle to keep his leg. The doctors want all of it. He said the explosion let my cat out to run away."

His eyes proclaim the misery as he ponders the news he just had. Crouching, lowers his head. After a short time, he looks up, with resolve in his demeanor. "When we get back from shopping I've got to use the computer to map some alternate ways home. I'll get there if I have to walk."

Without the slightest hesitation, Nellie produces her car key and hands it to him.

Danny and she have such a perfect affinity that he accepts it without a qualm.

We visit four grocery stores and scavenge a few fresh wilted vegetables and a number of assorted cans and packages, none of which we would bother with in healthier times.

Turns out the internet has been restored and Danny takes advantage of the residential unlocked computer to trace the round about roads that can position him for his run home. After which I take over to track the violence and the moves of President Spud. Regular news sources are wary. They apparently fear retribution and so choose to avoid actual reporting of significant events. Social media is all over the board, but I glean that Spud is individually interviewing members of Congress before ejecting them from government, because he expects to embrace a few. The Supreme court is on notice that he will not tolerate interference from that quarter. And he truly is bent on slicing off California from the body of the union, but is intent on extracting all he can of its wealth and resources by making it a territory with the same restrictive rules as Puerto Rico. Adding for good measure something he calls "reparations" he is concocting for California's government to owe to the US treasury.

The National Guard and militarized police are pacifying the hot spots, making significant progress.

There are information boxes in several spots informing that President Spud will soon address the nation. Please be patient and continue your normal activities and all will be well.

Nellie has decided to fix up a nice meal to send Danny off, fed and fortified, plus

she's packed him a kit for survival. Danny is out at the carcass of the truck, retrieving Nellie's artwork. As he pulls the sheets from a niche in the back compartment he realizes Nellie's other artwork from the moving is still stashed behind the passenger seat, forgotten and nearly lost.

He lays it all on the floor. Old and contemporary, showing the places she's lived, people she's known in her seventy five years. Then - Here are the fabled Sixties protest drawings. Lots of them. Most feature Doc and myself. I see familiar faces almost forgotten, in repose and as demonstrators. Astonished to see she had an unobstructed view of Phil Ochs' pig.

Nellie says she assumed Danny just overlooked the art. She lays a smooch on his cheek.

They enjoy their food at the table as I reminisce with these magnificent drawings. I come away as they are nearly finished eating. "We are stardust," I tell them.

I feel ravenous, like the young man I was, always ravenous then. After finishing the great food, I scour the pantry for a tin of sardines and some square crackers. I carry the fish and crackers on top of a paper napkin to sit in the recliner with the TV on. I don't find any news, so turn it off.

Danny comes in front of me and pauses. "Brother, I sincerely appreciate the hospitality. I wish it could continue in some capacity, but -"

"You owe it to Kyle to be there," I say. "But keep your phone charged so you can update us daily if possible."

I come out of the chair so that Nellie and I can together walk him to the car. Noting

the rental truck still on its side, I ask if he plans to do anything with it. "I plan to tell the owners of the truck what happened and where to find it."

We all hug and then he's gone, leaving a hole in our little circle of togetherness.

Instead of going back in, I go prowl through the house I've abandoned, discovering by throwing aside insulation and other junk that my writing room survived intact. I spend the next hours salvaging much paperwork, the computer, and printer. Envelopes and stamps. I can send a letter to the landlord, advising that his house is a wrecked entity and I won't be paying or staying any longer. It's in the back of my mind that Nellie and I will soon have to search out a permanent home.

After finishing with the transfer, I go out to look over Nellie's shoulder as she's recording the storm aftermath, especially the downed oak, which some anonymous workers had cut away from the street, then left the rest to the property owner to fret over.

"I worry," I say, "that the government may cut off our Social Security checks. The checks are legally ours, regardless of which nation we reside in, but Spud's a dictator. He can change laws. My royalties have dried up and it's all the income I have."

Nellie detaches herself from the artwork. Her black eyes rivet me to my tracks. "Then you had better write a goddamned best seller quick. Without Social Security we both are going to be fucked."

I throw up my hands. "Not feasible, Nellie. What I know to write about has no commercial value. We would do better with you selling portraits in a mall."

Nellie laughs. "I tried that once. I would have starved if I hadn't had a husband making real dough. By the way, when he died I claimed his Social Security, So it turned

out he was good for something after all."

"Everything and everybody has a use if you know how to find it," I say with a smile.

Lately I've taken to searching for Lenny the gecko, sad to leave him behind. I leave Nellie to her task, intent on searching for him, but then discover a car slowing before the house, stopping in front of the abandoned structure, faces peering until someone spots me. Doors pop open and Karma spills out with her two friends. "There you are," she gushes.

"Yeah, I'm looking for Lenny. Otherwise you wouldn't have caught me."

She gives me that big wonderful smile heavily imbued with concern. "Despite our conflict over politics," she says, "against my best judgment even, I plan to do whatever you will let me for your personal welfare. Like - where are you staying? Surely not this wreck?"

Moving back from the porch to face this gang of three, I tell her, "I have an intact shelter. I do admit that I am looking for a low rent property, in case you know of any. No pets, just me and her. Lenny, I am afraid, will just have to tough it out here."

To answer her puzzled look I add, "The guard gecko living on the porch."

Her eyes cut to her companions, who are standing noncommittally behind. They appear to have spotted Nellie next door and to feel deservedly nervous. "Give me a day or two to look. Where will you be if I find something?"

With great reluctance, I point to the house next door. "We are there, short term."

At this point, Nellie looks around. It is evident that she has been listening.

"Denny," she scolds without getting up. "I can't believe you are trusting them with all that information. It's a trap, whatever they promise you. Send them away before they ruin us."

She gathers her work, gives us a stink eye, goes into the house.

With Nellie out of the scene, the trio's demeanor changes. Karma's friends move to seize my arms. "Come get in the car," she commands. "I won't coddle you from here on."

The friends are unsurprisingly ineffective. Likely they expected an eighty year old man to simply give in and allow himself to be escorted away. I shake Harold loose and jamb my elbow into his soft paunch. As Joseph moves around to take control my foot entangles his leg movement, causing him to trip. I see my way clear to poke a set of eyes, Three Stooges style, but refrain because of not wanting eye goo all over my fingers. Instead I shove some fingers against Harold's throat, causing him to stand still off to the side. As I almost step away, Joseph wraps his hands about my ankle and I fall to hands and knees. He wraps his arms about my waist and locks his hands together. I debate my next move, reluctant but determined.

CHAPTER EIGHT

"Joseph?"

"Yes?"

"Don't make me hurt you, Joseph."

I've never grabbed a man's balls before. Joseph is my first and only.

By this time Harold decides to rejoin the fray. He kicks me from behind, hoping to connect with my own vulnerable goodies. His off-center kick stalls his attack as Joseph and I simultaneously release our grip. We both roll back on the turf, with Harold standing to the side, uncertain how to proceed. "You boys let me get up and walk in peace," I say, still feeling icky after holding Joseph's balls.

Disgusted, Karma tells her friends, "Let's leave while you two Atlases are conscious and walking." To me, she adds, "This isn't over. I'll get you institutionalized if it's the last thing I do."

Rolling on my side, propping my head, I sincerely want an answer to this question: "But why?"

"Many reasons. First, you're old and shouldn't be left alone."

"You know I've got help now," I say, unconvinced. "I think it's because I hurt your feelings when I set you straight about what's going on in the world."

The façade falls away from her at last. She rages: "It's because you sons of bitches spat on my father as he returned from Vietnam. He did his duty and did it well, only to be called 'baby killer.' He's in a ward for the insane while you walk around without a care."

The misery in her eyes is enough to melt my heart. I feel the sting of a tear starting in my eye. "Ah. Karma, you're mistaken. Not I nor my friends made any attacks against the soldiers. I was in the Navy. I have respect for many comrades of those days. While I acknowledge attacks were made, I don't even know how many involved were paid operatives of Nixon. The violence of demonstrations was mostly due to these operatives. Not that my side was perfect. Emotions for both sides could be equated to road rage. But my friends and I were gentle in our ways. I hope you believe that."

"You are of a culture that ruined my father. I hate all of you."

"Aren't there overriding issues, such as the government lying us into war after war? Impoverishing workers to feed their war machine as well as their material greed? They've made us serfs with less freedom than serfs of the middle ages. And it couldn't have been done without the complicity of almost every politician in the government. You ought to be on my side. Not a lost cause like Jay Smith."

She reaches for a limb of the length and heft of an axe handle. That's too much even for Joseph. As Karma turns on me and swings at my head, he puts himself between us, receiving as he does so a healthy smack on an upper arm. I guess by the crack sound at impact the arm may be broken. I move in to take the limb, which she surrenders. Her concern for Joseph has taken the fight out of her.

"Getting you to a doctor, Joseph."

I watch their struggle to be situated in the car, a contrite Karma taking the wheel. I watch with concern, hoping her rage will have been assuaged and the vendetta against myself will have ended. Almost as an omen of the sea change we face, Lenny appears on

the rail to regard me without moving when I draw near. His sad Leonard Cohen features never change but there seems an exchange of energy between us, or I imagine so.

"Goodbye, Lenny. May you survive in an unknown future."

He heaves himself up and down and then quickly slips away.

I go to look for Nellie, find her in the laundry room. She is loading her new clothing in the washer as I ease up behind and put my arms about her. She becomes still, enjoying the close moment. But she turns on me after that.

"Denny, you worry me sometimes. I don't think you've ever dealt with people like that before. Now they know we're here we've got to find a new place to live."

I'm holding her hands, explaining about Karma's meltdown while agreeing we should move.

She hugs me with a deep desperate hug, telling me how she fears that after all these years she doesn't want to lose me again.

Her phone sounds and she answers a call from Danny.

I'm busy preparing to walk the beach as their conversation holds forth. As I slip on my sandals, she comes in and sits near me to recount her phone conversation. Danny says he thinks he has our housing problem solved. He won't say much about it before he sees us, hopefully in no more than a week or two. Kyle died from a hospital infection. The cat was lost for good. And he's about to depart on a visit to Sacramento, where Andrew Spud has been rumored to be visiting. He's going wearing his cap with the Spud Skull and Crossbones symbol.

A few days later we are sunning on the porch, watching as a shiny car that I swear

looks like a Rambler American turns to pull in as much as oak debris allows. The woman who opens the door and steps over the littered ground is somewhat portly with stout legs, head held high, stares directly at us as she approaches. Her expression is sober and a bit cranky. Upper fortyish. She stops a short distance away to address us.

"This is my brother's house. I don't think you have any cause to be here."

"Excuse me," I ask enthusiastically. "Is that a Rambler American you're driving?"

"I don't think you need to know anything about my car or me," she says, speaking deliberately, sounding like a teacher to a class-full of nitwits. "If you go peacefully I won't call the police on you."

"Please, Ma'am, I respectfully ask you to hear me out before you kick us in the street. First, we have taken excellent care of the house." I cast a guilty eye at the grounds. "Inside, not the yard. We've cleaned and made it good for when your brother comes back."

She's fixed a critical eye on me, while darting glances at Nellie's yellow lipstick. but she's listening.

"Second, we are onto a new home, just waiting for my twin brother to settle the particulars for us. Please, Miss -?"

She pauses in her pondering to ask, "Why are you here in the first place?"

Both Nellie and I turn to my old house, pointing, without words.

"Oh," the woman exclaims. "You're the one Curly called the 'wretched recluse.' He waved and you didn't wave back."

I smile and shrug.

Nellie steps into the exchange. "Would you like to see what we've done inside? It's really nice."

The woman scowls. She regards us with increasing suspicion. "I've heard of people getting murdered like that."

I say, "Look. Roberta -" attempting to personalize the conversation.

Stamping her foot, "My name is Marjorie," she blurts. "And I want you out of this house."

"Okay," Nellie declares regretfully. "We will just go inside one more time to get our belongings together and load it in the car. I apologize for Denny's lack of tact in speaking to you. He's a bit stressed from cancer treatments."

To me, she says, "I will bring it outside. You can take it to the car."

Again she addresses Marjorie. "It was the storm. We had no place to shelter."

"Well," the woman says, softening, "the weather is nice so you can find a public shelter now."

"Yes, and thank you so much for understanding."

Marjorie flushes a bit while accepting the compliment.

Curly's sister stands back to watch, determined to see us gone before carrying on with her other business. When Nellie hands off clothing to me, Marjorie looks closely to determine if we are taking anything not ours. But when Nellie brings out her artwork her demeanor changes. She suddenly sees the artist in her and understands the bizarre makeup she's wearing, because artists are weird. To be venerated, but nevertheless naturally weird.

"Oh, may I see what you've been drawing?"

Nellie's progress does a curve bringing her close as she turns a page toward Marjorie, proud to display any time she gets called upon. As Marjorie admires, she studies the woman's heavy features. "Yours is such an interesting face. Would you allow me to draw you now?"

Marjorie is thrilled. "Of course you may," she gushes.

Nellie sets up her drawing pad. She lugs an old chair off the porch for her subject to perch upon as I continue to load our belongings in the car. After four such trips, I pause to take in Nellie's portrait and confirm it's good. It is, in that it accurately catches all her features while flattering every weakness to make the woman as nearly attractive as she could get away with. As Nellie turns it to face Marjorie for the first time, Marjorie is more than thrilled.

"Oh, I want to buy it from you," she begs. "I only have a hundred dollars in my purse, but I want it so badly."

Nellie acquires the hundred and transfers the art to Marjorie. After Marjorie places the portrait inside her car she returns and corners me by the porch. "If you're loaded up I will appreciate your leaving so I can get on with my day."

"Jesus, lady. Don't you think you could give us a break? Call Curly and ask what he thinks about us staying."

She gives me the sort of look one flings at an insensitive bastard. "We're burying my brother tomorrow morning. This will be my house when it all gets settled."

I look at my car, parked near the chinaberry tree. "Technically, we're already gone,

but for the fact I'm standing on your side of the property line," I counter. "Come on, Nellie. This woman's heart is a piece of overcooked cow liver."

We go sit in the car, looking back at Marjorie, who seems undecided whether to leave or wait us out. At last, forty-five minutes later the exasperated woman tromps to her car and leaves. I ask Nellie if she noticed whether the door got locked. She doesn't think so.

"Then let's move back in."

Comfortably re-ensconced in Curly's house, our hopes pinned to Danny's words, we carry on in a constant state of suspense. We while away much of the time discussing the old days. I think our nervousness maybe prompts us to do so. During one such conversation, she questions why I never seemed to warm up to John Kennedy. "Doc and I loved him."

I settle back and reflect a bit. "My disdain for Kennedy," I say cautiously at first,

"somehow was rooted in a perception of Lyndon Johnson, whom I one hundred percent did not like. The instant we were informed of Kennedy's choosing of him for VP I was struck by the blackest of presentiments. I could not abide the thought of a Lyndon Johnson Vice President. It made me back Nixon, the feeling was that strong. It somehow made me dislike Kennedy. His Bay of Pigs fiasco did not help. It wasn't until many years later I began to soften in my dislike. But I can never truly love him."

Nellie, sympathetically. "Do you think Johnson had him killed?"

"That he was in on it; I think so."

In other conversations we agree that both MLK and Malcolm X were murdered

because their goals were to unite the poor of every race to demand social justice. We agree in condemning every president from Johnson to Spud. Still, she's not writing off the fate of our race yet. I tell her it will happen before my natural time to leave this earthly existence.

Two days after the encounter with Marjorie a crew arrives to demolish the oak tree and clean up the yard. I sit myself on the porch to take it all in, while Nellie captures the spirit of it with her drawings. The crew gives out curious looks but tends to ignore us. They are industrious and organized. In a very short time they have the oak dismantled while feeding much of it into a chipping machine. They load logs onto a trailer, but it will require more trips to move it all. After a few hours they do a mop up of the entire yard. The lead man and a few of the crew stare at us as they head for their respective vehicles to drive away.

"It looks nice. Thank you," I holler at them.

I help Nellie move her art material indoors. "That was exhausting work," I remark. "What's to eat? I'm famished."

"We still have tins of sardines. One of the more healthy foods left to us," she replies.

"I'm already missing that old tree. So symbolic of what life is putting us through."

"Okay, Mr. Sunshine. The sardines are in back behind the crackers."

Nellie's wearing her black lipstick today. Her black halter top and black slacks

make her especially attractive to me, as the ensemble evokes both raciness and strength. "Do you want some?"

She follows me to the kitchen. "No. I'll just drink some coffee."

"If we walk on the beach anymore we're going to need to put our most important stuff in the car each time."

"Yes," she says, filling her cup. She pauses a moment. "I've been wondering why the electric hasn't been shut off. If Curly hasn't been here for a year there must be some explanation we haven't been aware of."

"Probably pretty simple. Knowing he was to be hospitalized he set up automatic pay between them and his bank. Water and internet too."

"Hmm." She drinks her coffee.

I'm putting sardines between crackers when Nellie answers a phone signal. "What? You are? Well, get here as quick as you can, because we've got to get out of here."

She looks at me. "He's on his way. The roads he is taking make it slow. He didn't want to talk more."

"Probably he will get in late tonight."

We start filling the car with what we need to bring along, including most of the canned and packaged food, which may sound like a lot, but our supplies are meager these days. After, we take a break on the porch. It's hot but we don't want to sit in air conditioning. Sitting back, I feel a nap coming on when I recognize a car that's pulling in. Karma sliding out and me staring at her without moving but suddenly awake and steeling for battle.

She has forsaken her loose bellbottoms for skintight pants with wild pink, green, and black patterns. Black shoes. Her top is a loose white blouse that lets us see she has

breasts when her arms are positioned just so. Her stride is deliberate, cautious. Nellie is first to react. She leaps to her feet and takes a position to block the steps. Karma continues coming, not changing stride or heeding Nellie's presence at the top. She steps resolutely up until Nellie reluctantly allows her to plant her feet on the deck. Securely in place, she simply bypasses Nellie.

Eyes cast down and then she stops before me, gradually lifting her gaze until that trajectory collides with mine.

There is a connection words could never utter, a primal communion between our very protoplasm.

We study each other through just our eyes until an exasperated Nellie fumes, "What the fuck is this?"

Karma speaks at last. Her voice is subdued and full of anguish. "They killed Harold and Joseph and dozens more. We went to Sacramento to demonstrate for President Smith. Spud was just leaving a conference with the Governor when someone attacked him. He was injured severely enough to put him in ICU. At that moment we were as near as police allowed, which is pretty distant. As soon as word got out about Spud, five cars sped straight into the crowd, chasing down as many as they could. I lost my friends in the pandemonium. The cars went past me and I ran with others, looking for a place to hide. A phalanx of men in uniform marched on us. They began making arrests. Some of us ducked behind a building and made our way to safety."

We stare at her, sickened, and also wondering why she would come here with her story.

I continue to silently stare at her. Tell us the rest of it, please.

She can no longer look at us. Her entire being slumps. Though her head is deeply bowed we witness tears cascading like nothing I've seen. Not knowing what else to do, we move to hug her, standing in an awkward three way stance a long minute before Karma straightens herself and we step back to free her.

She throws a wild look at us before speaking. "I've lost my job. My landlord sold the house on the same day I was terminated. I have three days to be out. I spent all my money catching up on the rent from my last termination. I don't have a place to live."

"Is that all?" I say. "You have friends."

She shakes "No" violently, causing a storm of hair around her head. "No, I don't. All of them are dead, in jail, or hiding."

"The pod cast -"

"Everything is falling apart too fast for me. The platform died with Spud's taking over. I can survive on the street. I'm not here to beg you to take me in."

Nellie intervenes. "We are just waiting to leave here. By the time your three days is up we may already be gone. Don't know if we will be living in Long Beach at all anymore. But we would insist you move in with us were it otherwise."

Karma turns her attention full on me. "That's not the full reason I came here. I came to apologize for trying to hurt you. My feelings are the same regarding my father, but I understand now that I should make exceptions, that you can disagree with me and be good people."

I offer my hand in friendship. She shakes it, briefly.

"What led to that revelation?" I inquire, because evolved understanding of that magnitude is a major breakthrough.

"My father. In a last session of lucidity he spoke with me about you, after I explained to him what I had done. When he questioned and I repeated your words, he sided with you."

"What were his words, if you don't mind?" Already I love the man.

"He said that it's time to put Vietnam to rest and to concentrate on saving the world. 'Men like your friend are allies and we just didn't know it. Tell him he must forgive us as we forgive him'"

"Tell him for me -"

"He died late that same night."

"I'm sorry. Did he have a funeral? I know the military funerals for old veterans was canceled last year."

"He will have to have a pauper's funeral. They can charge me all of the money they like; I can't pay any."

I look at Nellie, awaiting a sign. She gives an affirmative nod.

"I want you to gather your essential stuff and move in with us."

Karma is watching Nellie as she speaks next. "Only if I am completely welcome. Don't want to step on toes."

Nellie's arms open and the women embrace.

CHAPTER NINE

By the time Karma returns with her essential goods on the following day we await the arrival of my brother, He's expected at any moment. She has brought two suitcases and a birdcage. As I try to assist her with the birdcage, the little shit inside bites at my fingers where they touch the wiry bars. "He's not used to other people," Karma explains. "I'm the only one he trusts."

We drop the suitcases and look for a spot to land the cage. Once it gets its place near a window, I study the feisty little parakeet. He's green and yellow and he regards monster me with hatred.

"His name's Percy. He's gentle and loving with me," Karma adds.

It hurts my feelings to be any bird's enemy. I consider birds to be a direct link to a past that precedes any humans, with their great intelligence and endearing ways around any who spend time befriending them. I decide to give Percy time to adjust to my even being in the room before making overtures to him.

Besides, my attention belongs with Karma. "Don't unpack stuff you won't need right away. I don't know brother Danny's time schedule as yet."

We leave the luggage by the couch for now. I offer to make her a cup of tea.

She replies, with a dismissive wave, "Oh, no. If I'm to live here it's not as a guest. I can make my own tea."

"Have at it."

"Where are you hiding Nellie?" she says, looking around.

"She's doing her makeup. Says she has a new shade of lipstick to try on. I'm sure she will be out at any moment."

She goes to the kitchen and there is the sound of her making hot water. I look around as Nellie comes out of the bathroom. Her makeup is as always a work of art. I am astonished that her lips are red.

She models a second before spotting Percy sitting quietly on his perch. She immediately goes to the cage and coos at the little bugger. He makes a happy sound. I go

on the porch to watch for Danny.

And to ponder the probability that his housing solution may prove to be no solution at all. I don't want to dump cold water on Nellie's hopes. That's why I keep it to myself. As I'm lazing in the warm sun, a formation of five military choppers invades my sky, bringing dark insanity into my shattered serenity. Theirs is a mighty front to put the peasants on notice. At this very moment Nellie's car pulls in behind Karma's car, bearing two riders. I watch the helicopters lumber like big trucks across the remainder of visible sky as Danny comes up the walk, trailed by an extremely dark probable Mexican. Brother follows my gaze. "Normal stuff where I've been."

He throws an arm about me, lets his head make contact with mine. "Good to see you," he mutters before turning to his traveling companion. "Lenny the Wizard, meet Emilio Villa. Milio took over when Lyle got hurt. He has been indispensable in more ways than I could cover."

Milio grins when he shakes my hand. "Danny is a great man. I love being his friend."

"Any friend of Danny is welcome here," I say cordially. "Let's go in and meet the girls - women."

"Which is it?"

"Definitely women,"

"Women?" says Danny.

"Come in. You'll see," I reply, moving to let us in.

Inside, Karma has Percy sitting on her shoulder. Nellie is telling her how she once made a friend of a mockingbird, by noting that during swooping season the bird lit on a fence to stare at her. She turned around and fetched a few raw in shell peanuts and threw them in its direction. From that point on the local birds watched for her and called when she went by, for she developed a habit of tossing them a handful of peanuts each day. The original bird sometimes showed up in various places to show affection. The last time it landed on her car and greeted her just before she was set to drive.

She breaks off in mid story on sighting Danny entering the room. He makes straight

for her and a hug, which distresses Percy. Percy hides behind Karma's head. Karma takes him back to the cage, which he readily jumps into.

"I'm sorry about Kyle," Nellie says. "I know you're missing him."

Danny draws a deep breath, sighs. "He's where he wanted to be. The infection should not have been fatal. He just gave up."

"I'm sorry, too," I say from the side. "None of that should have happened."

"It's the times. I expect lots more before we're finished," he says bitterly.

He turns to Milio "Which in a way is where Milio comes in. Let's introduce

ourselves all the way around and then we can talk."

And so the introductions and the hand shaking occurs. All is cordial as we sit around the dining table to get down to business. Danny makes his opening statement. "I'm certain all of you have knowledge of Thoreau Park, south of the border."

"What? No," we all say in unison, except for Milio.

"That's what I thought," he concludes. "I wouldn't know myself, but for Milio here. It seems there is a community south of the border that is determined to ride out the climate change catastrophe for as long as they can, while hoping enough of humankind will experience the sort of epiphany that makes us go all in on saving the planet. Which would begin with the deflation of the trillionairs and military machines, even if it means we temporarily give up many modern inventions; take a few steps back.

"Thoreau Park is quietly putting together a means of survival intended to delay the likely inevitable extinction of life as we know it. The governments tolerate it because the Park is silent on all politics and matters of policy. They build their own infrastructure, feed themselves, and mind their own business. The population is less than a thousand.

"They conceived the Park in the Nineteen Eighties, after being approached by a man with more money than available projects. He made a suggestion they could not refuse. His investment was a gift, stipulating only that he and his relatives were to be included when the time arrived, as he was certain it would.

"Anyway, Milio's brother the pilot can get select immigrants in. I know my brother and Nellie would fit right in, as will Emilio. Karma, I assume you are one of us

permanently, so you too."

"Wait," I have to point out, "Smith's all out push to complete the border wall is likely still progressing. The place is crawling with workers, troops and vigilantes. The crossings have been sealed ever since the drone strikes at Nueve Laredo and suburbs of Mexico City. How can a plane get across?"

"At least two of us haven't a passport," Nellie says.

"Thoreau Park will never ask for a passport," Danny says. "I've served the place a few times over the past two years, with the help of friend Emilio, and I assure you you can get in and not be asked to leave."

"We are not workers," I say, becoming more and more skeptical. "What would we do there?"

Danny scoffs. "Nellie's work is art. As a writer you could begin a new novel. Just don't write anything controversial."

He claps Milio on the back. "Milio is young enough he can do anything requiring mind and or body."

We look at Karma.

"Don't worry about me. I can take care of myself."

I take Nellie by the hand and peer deep into the blackness of her eyes. "I'm not sure I want to go," I say, fearing the uncertainty we would face.

"But," she says, "the grocery stores are almost always half empty, with prices out of reach; we've got us a civil war; the weather is taking California apart as well as the rest of the country; hospitals and doctors have become rarities - This Thoreau Park could give us the kind of chance we are being denied here."

I turn my head toward Milio and Danny. They shrug and smile.

"There are no beaches," Danny snarks.

Milio spreads his hands. "But the desert can be your beach. Lots more space to walk, just no swimming."

Karma seems bemused, is quietly to the side. She's not ready to speak.

Nellie goes to the pantry, returns disappointed because there is no coffee to make.

She looks at me and sighs.

"What makes you think there will be coffee there?" I say, but feel my resistance starting to crumble.

Milio is garnering rich entertainment out of the situation. I confront him to put him on the spot. "How does a party of five get to the community? How do we get past America's Berlin Wall?"

His grin does not waver. "My brother the pilot has ways. He ferries people back and forth."

"Not a drug dealer?"

Milio's demeanor darkens as the grin fades. "My brother is an honest man."

His grin makes a halfway reappearance and he tells more. "The authorities know about him. They don't interfere with him when he's home on the ground. Still they are likely to down him if they see him crossing. It's their job."

"So we're risking our lives to go up with him."

Again the darkening demeanor. "Now, dammit, Denny. He makes two flights a week. Never an incident."

"And we get to be the first," I explode.

Milio turns away. He speaks to Nellie and Danny. "It's up to you. I'm for watching the TV."

Milio calls us over. Without words he points to the TV screen.

The banner at the bottom reads: "SPUD DEAD. HIS SECOND IN COMMAND, DARRYLL HARMON CLAIMS PRESIDENCY"

Harmon's face occupies half of the screen. He looks to me like a thug from a Bogart film. The other screen half is taken by a live shot of thousands of uniformed men, purportedly all weeping. Oddly, the assassin has not been caught.

That's what I wrangle out of it before turning away. When I said I was done with it I meant it.

Rifling a lower cabinet for missed items, a can of tuna meets my hand. And a jar behind it. Ha! Instant coffee. My intuition must have sent me there.

I set a water-filled tea kettle on to boil, planning to surprise us all with a cup. Then sit on the porch steps, alone and stoic, feeling more vulnerable now than in the danger situations recently faced. One misstep could end all our lives and although I'm eighty eighty years ain't enough.

What I fear after that is that this Thoreau Park will prove to be a foolish gambit by ineffectual daydreamers.

"Your teapot's whistling," Nellie calls from inside the house.

The four of them are riveted to the television as I pass through. I hear from the box that President Harmon is already aiming promises of nuclear annihilation at several foes

in the global wars we're fighting.

I pour and stir in the coffee. "Who wants the coffee black?"

They all want cream and sugar. No cream left. Sorry. Tough.

"Are we all going there or just some of us?" I ask to take our minds off of the politics.

"You all are going," Danny says as he receives his cup, frowning to see it has no cream in it.

We pause to search demeanors for little cracks of dissent. None exhibited.

We overhear a TV personality explaining that the government's steadfast refusal to share Venezuela's oil with the nation of Venezuela is meant to punish their government for human rights violations.

"We've got it; we're going to keep it," Danny interprets.

Karma steps in to switch off the TV. "I'm getting sick. I just want to get out of here."

The three of us turn to Danny and Milio. "Yes," I ask, "how soon are we to board the plane?"

"In two days we leave to meet the pilot. Sunday afternoon's the tentative departure," Danny says, looking at Milio for cues in case he has it wrong, answered with affirmative nods.

Nellie pipes up. "You know we don't have enough food to last two whole days."

"We need fresh vegetables and fruit," Karma adds.

It is decided we will all go for food, excepting Milio, who wants to rest up. We opt

for a large chain store. Danny takes us in Milio's giant SUV. I fear such oversized vehicles, but I have to admit they can be fun to ride in. There is more traffic today, but the signal lights work again. Coming on the lot, Danny navigates through uncollected shopping carts.

Perhaps twenty customer cars cluster near the entrance. A skeleton crew looks indifferently on when we walk through and spread out, each with their own cart. There are some nice apples and cans of stew. Danny is miffed there are no eggs. We meet for a discussion, resulting in a decision to pay up and shop elsewhere. On the way to the registers we find one bag of white rice on one entire aisle. Danny and I toss it like a football until Nellie frowns. Chastised, we settle down. Karma shows us four cans of pink salmon she found deep down in back on a lower shelf. At checkout they hit us with an outrageous price that prompts us to leave the stuff on the counter and walk out.

We find a second store with cabbages, canned processed pork, bread, and assorted cans of beans. "All those beans," Nellie quips. "I can hear us now."

On returning, we can't get inside the house. It seems we've been locked out, and Milio doesn't answer persistent banging and knocks. We look to Danny for answers. Among us only he knows Milio very well. He speculates after a bit of thought that the law visited here and took him away. We agree to the possibility. "But what to do next?" says Nellie as we stare blankly back.

"For one thing," Danny asserts, "is to get back in to rescue our stuff, if any of it was left in there."

As we are milling on the deck, Karma spots Milio's body in the tall dead grass at the end of the porch. She hurries down without speaking, as we all follow. She cradles his

head, asking him to respond, for his eyes are glazed and he looks totally spaced. There is a horrendous welling over his cheekbone, as from a forceful blow. Danny moves in and they pull him to a sitting position. With labored breath, his eyes unfocused, he hangs between their supporting grip. Danny looks to me. "Let's get him inside."

I go with Nellie to examine the entry window we have used in the past. It has a new lock on it. I force the gate, allowing us to walk around and view other windows as well as the back door. Everything is locked up tight. "I'm for breaking open the door to avoid climbing through broken glass," I mutter.

By the time I find a screwdriver, as I work to force the tip between doorjamb and door, Danny comes around. "Here, what do you think you're doing?" he says in a voice that makes me stop. "Move back, Denny."

He steels himself for it first and then throws his shoulder into the door, which splinters the jamb, allowing the door to swing all the way open with a resounding crack against a kitchen cabinet. Without waiting for us he marches inside and straight to the front entrance, where he discovers that the new lock cannot be turned without a key. With my screwdriver he is able to dismantle the lock and pull the front door open.

By the time we get back to Milio he is talking to Karma. "Milio," Danny exclaims, relieved.

"How do you feel?" he questions.

Milio looks up trying to smile. Then he looks angry. "Squatters. You should have told me."

Danny gets down on the ground with him to examine his face. "Would that have

made you safe from getting lambasted like this?"

Milio gives a blank look, then shakes his head.

"We are going to get you into the house and then we want to hear your story."

By now, Milio is able to help as we transport him in small shuffles up the steps and get him in to lie on the couch. Then we stand around and watch him staring at the ceiling.

"Come on. Tell us about it," Nellie implores.

Milio's head rolls as he focuses on her with the black eyes and red lips. "Goons," he says. "One with a badge."

He shakes his head, reliving it.

"I was in the kitchen, looking for a few crackers or something to snack on when these men came in and one started to replace the lock. 'Hey, what are you doing in here?' I said, assuming they must have the wrong place.

"The one flashed his badge, said, 'I want you out of here. You squatters are done.'

"I said, 'Well, let me move our stuff out.'

"He began pushing me to the door and the other man opened it for him to shove me out. I didn't leave the porch. I waited for them to finish the work and come outside so I could plead for the things we would be losing. The locksmith simply walked past, paying me no mind. But the cop paused and told me, 'Move or I will move you.'

"I was about to ask him one more time when he socked me and I went off the porch."

"Sucker punch," I say angrily.

"He put all his weight into it. I saw him sucking on his knuckles before my eyes

closed."

"Maybe we should get out of here right now," Karma says. "Milio's brother could put up with us an extra day, couldn't he?"

Milio nods yes, then his eyes close. "Let me rest first," he mutters.

We all are in agreement it's time to take our leave of Marjorie's house. We start packing things into Milio's car, after Danny persuades us to leave my car behind. "After all, we can't take any of them across the border."

When all is finished we sit and wait. Not much to be said. Milio's snoring is disconcerting but we suffer it. After almost two hours, Danny makes a decision to wake him. He begins slowly, gently, shaking him by a shoulder. He's slow to come to, but he sits up right away. "I'm okay. This will be sore a while is all."

We tell him of the decision to head out a day early. Milio nods soberly. "Brother won't like it, but we need to go."

"We've loaded the car." I tell him.

Nobody notices at first that the entry door has begun creeping open.

I look around to see if we are leaving any good stuff behind. Milio takes an interest in Percy sitting inside his cage. Nellie takes a trip to the bathroom. Karma joins Milio at the birdcage.

"I'm not sure the bird can survive the trip," Milio tells her.

Before she can respond the door is flung back as a man with a bullet head and fat neck pushes into the room, revolver drawn. I know without being told he's the one that smacked Milio off of the porch. He makes it official when he approaches Milio and

sternly tells him, "I ordered you out of here. That you broke in makes you a combatant. I can't arrest you because the National Guard has seized the jail and filled it with insurrectionists. But I can read in your actions a very dangerous man. And so -"

He makes the gun point into Milio's eyes.

Poor Milio is too horror-stricken to move as then we hear a gunshot. The officer's eyes widen with shock and surprise. He half turns but never gets a look behind him at Danny holding onto a pistol and staring rigidly ahead. He crumples like an empty gunny sack. Danny looks at each one of us, connecting briefly each time before moving on. He barks like a drill sergeant. "Get your shit and get out of here."

"Danny -" Nellie says once she realizes my brother is cutting himself off from the rest of us.

"Stay with us, Danny. We need you," I beg.

Danny waves us off as he replaces the spent cartridge in his gun. "It would jeopardize the operation if I were discovered. It likely would put them out of business and nobody would get to cross over.

Anyway I hadn't intended to cross over with you from the start. In time, Milio will fill you in on why it is."

Still shook up Milio puts himself between us. His dark face peers earnestly into Danny's. "No. Tell them now. They should know everything before they go any further."

My brother shushes him.

"You people get out of here before they blame you for killing a cop,"

But Milio isn't backing off.

"He's Spud's assassin," he shouts defiantly.

CHAPTER TEN

"Shit," Danny explodes.

After walking around, reflecting a bit, he clasps Milio's shoulder and squeezes while shaking it. At last he faces us. He tells his tale, of how he mingled among the crowd in Sacramento, looking just like the committed followers, but with an added feature. Inside his right hand pocket was a very sharp plastic knife. It had been sheathed but the sheath hung down his thigh from within the pocket, to keep Danny from cutting himself.

"I managed to get close to Spud three times," he says. "I got a handshake on the second encounter. On the third I looked Spud right in the eye as I shoved in the blade. He doubled over, as from a punch in the gut. I was immediately grabbed by two agents, but got away."

He pauses.

"Have you ever watched the old cowboys and Indians movies? And if you did did you notice how in the fight scenes, every Indian who tackled a white man slid away like a kid off a greased pig? That's what happened with the agents that grabbed me. Here's the real kicker. As I became free, in the instant before I made my dash to get lost among the crowd, I got a look at the face of one of them. He had an oval face and high arched black eyebrows. His brilliant blue eyes looked into mine. And one of them winked at me."

He coughed, needing water.

"It was unbelievably easy to mingle and finally slip away," he says, sounding raspy

and moving off to get his drink.

Old sand in the grease me says, "Why? All it did was to get him replaced by an even greater menace."

Danny looks over his water glass. "Each of us does our bit. I did mine. It's for the next in line to keep the streak going. If not? Well, maybe as you've been telling it it's all over anyway."

Nellie comes forward to hug Danny. "We each do what we are meant to do. I just

wish we could get you to Mexico."

"No," I tell her. "If the government found out it would target all of us. They will get Danny regardless."

Danny shakes hands with Karma. Then impulsively hugs her. He gives further hugs to Milio and then me. He gives the last and best to Nellie. "Goodbye, folks. Denny. It's not likely we are going to meet ever again. I love you, despite all the shit we've handed each other."

"And I you," I reply, fighting off tears.

He makes his way to Nellie's car and gets in. Without glancing back, he eases around and turns into the street, to be seen no more. I hope he gets another life, but it seems more likely they will ferret him out in a rather short time.

After we drag the body into the biggest closet we cover it with plastic encased clothing and then piles of loose blankets and sheets. Karma waits for us outside because she hasn't the stomach for such shenanigans.

A few minutes later, Milio is driving us down the street in his oversized SUV. It's

like riding in a bus. We feel much like the refugees who wanted to emigrate here but were repulsed, now with the tables turned. Let us hope we don't meet with their fate. Milio assures us Mexico's government welcomes us, but on the sly so as to not invite further retribution from the north.

Privately I reflect on the mysterious virus that killed off the thousands of refugees along the border, thus removing the manufactured cause for alarm. And despite this the government is furiously constructing the impervious wall some have wanted all along. While occasionally drone striking across the border.

Looking out at the passing buildings and traffic, I have no love for the part of the city we are passing through. But I enjoy the ride to and through San Diego. Fostered by a near nomadic childhood and years spent roaming the country with my friends my love of the open highway gets rekindled, as from a magic tonic. Nellie rides quietly. I can only guess what goes on in Karma's brain. More and more she comes off the tragic figure in a sad novel.

Out of San Diego and over the high mountain pass, into the flatness and beyond the San Luis, Mexico, marker, we find a small road to go slightly north over. The road winds a bit before forking, causing Milio to make a hard left to keep on track. Just when I tire enough to miss my daily nap we enter a farm and roll up behind a huge pickup truck outside a stucco house that has a porch all around the four walls. Off in the distance is an open barn sheltering an airplane. There are fallow fields and a fenced chicken yard. A lazy old hound rouses from a hole he dug himself under the porch to wag his tail in greeting at Milio, who on stepping down pauses to scratch the brown head.

The rest of us stand around beside the SUV, curious about the man who has agreed to fly us over the border. Milio leads us to the entrance with the hound at his side vying for further attention. We wait, until a boy of perhaps ten pokes out his head, then turns around to call, "Mama."

"That's Miguel. His mother is Lupe," Milio explains.

Miguel has a shock of black Indian (Native American) hair and a strong frame for a kid. We understand about his size when Lupe bids us enter. She has a giant's stature and looks as though she could play football or else be a pro wrestler. Her braided hair hangs before her as she turns to the kitchen and a great pot sitting on a low butane burner. She pours us each a cup of coffee. She serves it liberally sugared and creamed, brought in on a tray and handed to us individually. I find it tepid and not to my liking but I'm hungry enough to put anything I'm offered down the gullet.

Karma attempts to speak with Lupe but it turns out Lupe doesn't know a word of English. Lupe frowns testily. She turns to Milio, who exhibits discomfort as she reams him out. He turns a sheepish look our way. "She doesn't like that we came early. Food is in short supply. She can't sleep with visitors in her home."

Nellie steps forward. "Give her the food we brought with us."

Milio signals her with a hand wave to stop right there. "It would be regarded as an insult. No, she will feed us and bitch about it, but she wouldn't have it any other way."

Nellie's outburst draws Lupe's attention to her for the first time. Struck by the fabulous makeup, especially the yellow lipstick, her fingers touch Nellie's cheek.

"Bonito," she says.

Miguel, who has been hiding behind a partially closed door and peeking out, becomes entranced with Percy. He approaches the cage, which Karma has been struggling to keep aloft. He puts a hand to the wire bars. Karma almost moves the cage away from the boy, but then it becomes obvious that Percy is receptive. She sets the cage on a small table beside a fat easy chair to make it easy for boy and bird to interact.

Lupe leads we would be immigrants to a room of about ten feet by twelve feet in floor size to show there is a dozen canvas bunk beds folded and leaning in a single row against a wall. Neatly folded blankets make a stack on the spotless floor against the same wall. She then has Milio explain that she has farm work to do and invites us to lounge in chairs on the porch. She rejects Milio's offer to assist with the chores. Grateful for this chance to nap, I eagerly take my place by moving the chair between two great potted roses and hiding my face from the light.

Karma entertains Percy and Miguel, with the hound looking benignly on. Nellie has fetched her sketch pad and is furiously at work capturing the farm on several pages. Milio has helped himself to more coffee and sits contentedly sipping while looking out over the useless nature of the weed overgrown fields.

Exhaustion washes over me. Sleep swiftly seeps in. Deep napping ensues. There is no dream activity on which to report. Later, when awareness returns, the others are gathered around a new entity. It's a person even darker than Milio and only half his size, so it seems. His very quick eyes bounce away from the conversation to examine me cursorily as he continues talking. After hastily concluding the thought, he wheels on his skinny legs and approaches my chair with hands outstretched. "I'm Jesse. How are you?"

"Groggy," I reply, allowing my hands to join with his.

He shakes loose and stands back. His infectious smile encompasses everyone. "This is a good group. I have a Thoreau Park brochure if I can find it. Tomorrow is as good a time to go up as any. Excuse while I check in with my wife."

The man is all confidence, instilling trust in his abilities. That he appears extraordinarily intelligent and sure-footed seals it for me. I would follow him anywhere.

Looking over Nellie's new artwork as she concludes the final one for now, I notice that she's included Jesse's plane in its barn. "What do you think of our chances with that thing?" she asks.

"Why? Are you having second thoughts about it?"

I squint at the plane with the late sun making a bright swath across the bow. She comes around and puts her fingers in the belt loops at my hips and pulls us close. "I'm with you no matter where you go."

We stand there kissing, ignored by the others because they believe in minding their own business. By the time we rejoin the group, Jesse is there to tell us dinner is ready.

We trail behind him into Lupe's dining room, where a long table with a bench on either side is already set up with dishes, silverware, cloth napkins, and covered plates of hot tortillas. A huge stainless steel pot simmering on the stove emit's a smell of spice and unfamiliar content. Then I remember being in Nellie's mother's kitchen. It's menudo. The only sides appear to be diced onions and corn tortillas. I feel hungry enough to eat it, despite my queasiness over dining on cow's stomach, plus I'm not keen on the hominy.

Jesse helps his wife dip the soup into very large bowls and together they also

provide king-sized glasses of what proves to be overly sweet black tea. They carefully set the food before us, then stand back to wait attentively in case we need anything else. Milio crosses himself but does not speak. As I tentatively spoon in a first mouthful, I watch to see how Karma fares with it. Surprisingly, to me at least, she takes a tortilla in one hand and pushes it into the soup before biting into it. She continues dipping it with each bite. Very impressive.

After the meal, while Lupe cleans the kitchen, allowing no help from her visitors, we gather in the living room. It's a strange living room, in that it is not focused on a television set. In fact, there is no television at all. Jesse is poring over Nellie's current artwork. He falls in love with one of the drawings of his plane and wheedles it away from her.

On noticing that Percy in his cage is nowhere in sight, I discover that Miguel, the proud new owner, has hidden him away, fearing that giver Karma might change her mind

and wish to reclaim him.

Then Jesse moves to the entrance and pulls open the door. In walks a man who wears black pants with cuffs way down over his cowboy boots, a close fitting short sleeve shirt with tiny stripes, carrying a Stetson, looking back at us with baleful eyes set over a monumental nose and a droopy mustache. He stands impassively as Jesse introduces him.

"This is Carlos; Lupe's brother and my airplane mechanic. I know how to work on the plane, but compared with him I'm a shade tree mechanic. He could be elsewhere making lots of money, but he considers this endeavor a worthy cause. That's enough for him. Carlos flies with me, both for security and in case a need for unscheduled repair

arises. It's okay to say 'Hello' to him but he can't answer back." Pause. "He's got no tongue, thanks to the gang he once ran with."

Carlos nods slightly at each one of us as we tell him hello. Then he goes into the kitchen, because, as Jesse explains, "He's hungry."

We move out to enjoy the evening and a cool breeze that's stirring. I'm sitting between Nellie and Karma, watching the horizon where my friend from Long Beach, the moon, moves slowly upward like a friendly puppy. He followed me here and he's bulging outward struggling to become a circle for me. A bit of a smile shapes my lips as I sit back and then Nellie begins humming a song. I recognize the melody right off. Woody Guthrie's Deportee: Plane Wreck at Los Gatos Canyon. I wonder if the others know the song? Apparently not, as they accept it for just a beautiful melody in a thoughtful voice. Carlos comes outside bearing a battered old guitar. He's heard the music and wants to join in. He picks up the melody, inspiring Nellie to sing the words. We listen, me with moistening eyes and Jesse looking dark and unhappy. It's that powerful of a song.

Karma rises up to hug Nellie. She compliments her beautiful voice as well as the choice of songs. She then turns to me, with a nod and a gentle smile. I return the nod and do a head turn to see what Carlos is doing to his poor guitar. He's playing a blistering La Cucaracha. His sister comes on the porch to listen, beaming proudly. Such a beautiful smile she's wearing.

Eventually we go and set up cots. Some want a blanket; others are content to lie in

the festering heat on bare canvass. There is no undressing but our shoes. I lie in a state of hyper-alert for a long time, tossing and turning, then when drowsiness prevails I get up to

relieve myself instead of going to sleep. Next, I need a blanket. Nellie breaks the silence, "What are you doing? Be still and let me get some rest."

Alert once again, I lie on my back and the blanket covers my chest but not my legs, thinking about it's a complicated process, getting across that border. I wonder where my brother is and what he's doing. Will he return to his home and wait? Is anything left of his company that's salvageable? Then I'm aware that I dozed off, because there streams through the window a bright swath of sun. Everybody is already tying their shoes, all except me.

They wait at the door until I am ready and we all mob into the living room together. Jesse comes in from moving the plane onto the road. He tells us Carlos is making last minute inspections. By the time he finishes Lupe expects to have us some breakfast.

Nellie fetches her art material to record the plane. I ask Jesse if there will be some way to replenish her supplies once we are living in Mexico. He doesn't know. How about if she leaves you a list? Perhaps.

Karma looks forlorn. I surmise she regrets leaving California forever. She notes my interest and sends me a dry little smile. I worry about her the most because she hasn't any really close friends. Hopefully, residents of Thoreau Park will provide the sort of companionship she needs. My thoughts are cut into by Jesse, who gathers me, Karma, and Nellie for a final talk.

He restates the purpose of Thoreau Park, but then he adds, "The three of you have been active voices in politics. There will be no politics over there. There will be a probation period and then a ceremony of acceptance that will by its nature be a jury trial.

They are very strict."

I give him my hand to shake. "You don't have to worry about me. I am apolitical these days. It's not that I don't care. I've concluded that this world is fucked so badly as to be incapable of getting unfucked." My hand gesture toward the women means my next words are for them. "Nellie and Karma are two of the smartest women I know of. You

won't have to worry about them."

He looks to the women. They nod.

Nellie too offers her hand. "I've lived without politics since the Seventies. For me it's no problem."

Karma soberly offers her hand. "I agree to do my best."

Jesse gestures to all of us. "Then let's eat some breakfast."

As we file into the dining room, Lupe is standing at the table, just completing the arrangement of food and drink, already served and waiting with steam rising above the plates and condensation wetting the exterior of the glasses. We each tell her good morning as we take our places and she assumes the same attentive role as on yesterday evening.

Spicy scrambled eggs wrapped in soft tortillas. Spicy fried potatoes. Sweet tea. I wonder why not coffee, but without words, as I don't wish to wound somebody's feelings.

As we are wrapping it up, Milio stands and makes an announcement, or perhaps a confession. "I am not going to move to Mexico. Jesse has offered to let me stay on and help salvage this farmland. I told him it isn't possible because there is too much drought

each year, but he is too stubborn to listen."

He's contrite, looking around, expecting a barrage of invective, but we nod understandingly and wish him good luck. He exhales in a little rush. His humble voice tells us, "Thank you, my friends."

I hasten to down my final quaff of tea before rising and addressing Lupe and Jesse. "I thank you for the fine food and hospitality. Now I am ready for the rest of the journey. Almost."

Going out and down the hall I find Miguel's door and gently tap on it. He makes a noise but refuses to respond. I tap more. "Miguel, please. I need to speak with you."

A little waiting game is resolved when the boy cracks his door barely enough to peep out. "Si?"

Gratefully, I press my advantage. "You understand English. I know you do. Look, I

have a small favor to ask of you."

"What's 'favor?'"

I bend down to put my face at his level. "Hey, we are about to go on the airplane. I an asking you to bring Percy out and allow Karma to tell him goodbye."

Miguel instantly shuts the door.

"Come on," I plead.

Jesse is behind me, I realize. He puts up his hand to figuratively push me back, then steps up and raps gently. "Hey. Open the door, please."

Without hesitation, Miguel pops it open and stands trustingly before his father. "Si, Papa?"

They converse in Spanish, with Jesse doing most of the conversing. At the end, the boy fetches the bird cage out of the room and carries it to find Karma. He is stoic but resolute to follow Jesse's wishes. Jesse walks past me to return to his flight preparedness routine.

By the time I return to join the others, Karma and Miguel are together with Percy. The bird is on Karma's shoulder snuggling against her cheek. After a few minutes she transfers him to Miguel's shoulder. She touches the boy's cheek with a smile and a tear. The deliriously happy boy disappears back down the hall.

Missing Nellie, I walk around a bit to see where she's gotten off to. Turns out she was in the bathroom putting on fresh makeup. She will be treating residents of Thoreau Park to bone white lipstick.

Carlos signals us with his hands: time to load up our belongings, which we do. After we stuff in everything else, Nellie and I carefully tuck in her art and materials.

Waiting for Jesse to get us on board, Karma speaks out. Her gaze had been cutting to the plane and then the route that had taken us to this farm for some minutes. "I really don't want to do this. I should have stayed in Long Beach."

"I understand your feeling," I say sympathetically. "But without a job or a home -"

"Wait," Nellie interjects.

I look at her white lips while she talks.

"I think there is a place where you would be accepted. It's not in Long Beach but at least it's still California."

She explains about the religious order that accepted her when she was rebounding

from her disastrous marriage. She thinks it would be good for her if she doesn't mind a daily bit of religion added to her life. It might be a strain on Jesse, but his heart is big and he just might help her get there.

"But just remember this: You will be like a rat trapped on a sinking ship to stay in the States," I throw in because I think she's making a mistake.

"I'm sorry," she tells me, her earnest beautiful eyes beseeching me to understand. "I owe it to my country to be here to do what I can for it."

I'm almost crying at the futility of it. "Then good luck," I tell her.

Nellie gives Karma a hug and they tell each other goodbye. Nellie also hands her a card with the information she needs on it.

CHAPTER ELEVEN

It's just me and Nellie. With excitement and anxiety we sit comfortably watching Carlos climb in and situate himself near the pilot's seat and then Jesse comes, his moves reminding me of a cat on the prowl. He looks about, proud and determined on this his several hundredth trip across the border. It's obvious that for him it never gets old. This must be an expensive operation for somebody who's not running drugs. If he doesn't volunteer that information however it's not my place to ask. He sits still a minute, possibly studying his instruments.

Finally the plane goes into motion. It's only just a bit bumpy leading to liftoff and it smoothes suddenly as we go swooping into the quiet sky. I watch as the farm slides away and signs of civilization become few. The fields are dry, the prairies are dry, the highway is an act of terrorism on nature. "There is no wildlife down there," Jesse tells us. "Barely any insects even."

Surprisingly quickly, we pass over the fucking wall. "Drone approaching," Jesse says impassively.

But nothing happens to us as we approach the border. "Take a look down," he says. "It's the last you will see of the United States."

Amazingly, we enter Mexican air space without a hitch. Jesse notes that the drone is following behind, apparently only tracking us. It will soon have to turn back. The land continues to be desolate, for no settlements come into view. Jesse explains that his route deliberately avoids any settlements because it seems to him safer. We journey deeper into

Mexico than I had expected. Then we top a hill, exposing a broad valley that it seems maybe should not be there but in fact is not just there, but hosts a strange looking complex.

Massive walls, a common roof designed to withstand the most violent of storms, earthquakes and floods, topped by solar panels.

I see greenhouses and fields actually growing things. Jesse describes an infrastructure with controlled temperatures, parks, public transports. The layout is designed to funnel most of the rainwater into underground

storage that, when full, allows the excess to run where it naturally would already have gone, thus preserving the natural order beyond Thoreau Park. In the event the water at the inlet is detected to be contaminated it automatically will close.

We see an unpaved road wind around the hill until it goes into the community and it quickly becomes evident that the road also serves as the landing strip for small planes. In a manner as routine as a cabbie parking in Los Angeles, Jesse brings us down in a soft landing, then taxis to the side and quickly kills the engine. He turns around and looks at us.

"Carlos will fetch us a transport," he says. "You can get out and stretch your legs or else wait for him in here."

Nellie is all for getting her art material so she can sketch Thoreau Park from a distance. Jesse helps her in the retrieval as I walk out on the unfamiliar Mexican soil. Looking over the parched landscape, wondering what life forms still survive out there. If I had an oxygen suit I might well be on Mars. One such as me couldn't survive long out here. I feel small and vulnerable, like a misplaced insect.

Little shifts of gusty wind harass Nellie until she gets the edges pinned down, then she goes to work. I come over to watch as on paper the bulk of the structures rises before a backdrop of a huge mountain one must crane to see in its natural stature. She even scribbles into it the odd looking transport that's emerged through the gate. We make Carlos wait extra minutes before responding when he parks near the plane.

Jesse turns from his inspections of the plane to help load our possessions into the back of the transport. By the time we approach, eager to help out it's too late. The art stuff is tucked in and we sit on bench seats, with Jesse beside Carlos at the helm. We look ahead with anticipation, me still dreading this upheaval but ready to see it through. I seek Nellie's hand and she puts both of hers around mine.

We pass through a wrought iron gate onto a lot with a mix of six cars and pickups. We pile out before a second gate with arms loaded and wait as a person from within unlocks it to allow our entry. It slides to the side, allowing us as a group to proceed. The one manning the gate locks it securely before motioning for us to follow him to a metal

door that's as massive as a bank vault entry and in fact may well be one, adapted. He performs a series of operations to make it swing wide. He looks at us and grins, his long sober face suddenly crinkly and charming. "Come in; come in."

Then he becomes talkative, speaking to Jesse. "Got us new members. Mister Ochoa?"

He listens attentively to Jesse's tale of his latest flight and explanation of why he thinks Nellie and I will fit in here. The man is introduced to us as Evan Evans. He looks jarringly like Woody Strode, the late actor. I can't help picturing Evans in a John Wayne western movie.

We follow in a narrow hall past several closed up entries until being confronted by an unremarkable slab of door on hinges that allow it to swing in either direction. There's no lock, not even a latch on it. Nellie exchanges a curious look as Evans barges in and holds it open for the rest of us to pass unencumbered.

Unostentatious is this room. There is a sort of peanut gallery of comfortable seats to one side. The other side hosts a desk with a man hurriedly sitting there after hastily exiting a back area that is open, but is situated so that one cannot see within. He looks up and hails Jesse and Carl. The three exchange pleasantries before the man pauses to critically consider the elderly couple placed before him.

He addresses us together, introducing himself as Claude Willingham. It is obvious he doesn't get it. Why us? We certainly are not remarkable in any visible way. "Who are you? I mean, I get your names and accept your peaceful intentions. I just don't know why Thoreau Park is the place for you to settle."

"Frankly, I told Nellie the same thing," I blurt without considering these words' impact. "I'm the sort of nihilist that rejects the sum of human totality. An End Earther, as it were."

Willingham ponders. "Mmhmm. And you know that our purpose here is to extend the human presence, to override a final extinction?"

"Well, sure," I say, foolishly waving my hands. "I don't take being an End Earther lightly. I like living."

Jesse injects his presence by leaning forward and murmuring in Willingham's ear.

He pulls from his shirt pocket a folded piece of paper and pushes it into his hand. Willingham undoes the folds in a deliberate manner then slips on a pair of reading specs and studies the words written on it. He sighs. Then he sternly looks at me and as he does so he hands over the paper. I read the following:

"Channeling anti-war Bobby Darin

"When the world runs out of wrongs

I'll be writing no more songs

But for now

I say wow

Business is very good

"I'll keep writing little songs

Until there's peace in battle zones

Until congress notes

The change with votes

Until then I must conclude

"When a child is peaceful at night

When love is the symbol not might
No hunger
No danger
Until then I will just be rude
"I will keep writing little songs
Loud enough to rattle bones
Just spit it out
In one big shout
Until then I must conclude
"When folks die of poverty
The wrong ideology
Jealousy
Notoriety
Until then I will just be crude
"I will keep writing little songs
It's my way to battle wrongs
I will spit it out
In one big shout
Spit it out
One big shout
Spit it out"

It isn't necessary to read the whole piece, but I do. After taking a deliberately longer time than necessary I look at Jesse. "How did you get this?"

He tosses his head, indicating Nellie. Nellie looks to the high ceiling, suppressing a smile, eyes twinkling. I study Willingham's stern face. What the fuck?

"Yeah, I confess. It's mine."

Willingham says, "You know, we don't allow politics in here."

He sits back and rocks a bit in his swivel chair.

"Of course, in here" His glance encompasses this room. "there are no recording devices. We can speak freely. Among the general population it's a no-no."

He regards me in particular, saying, "My parents protested some. In the end they were most interested in buying a home and raising me as quietly as they knew how. They

voted Reagan and then Bush. They called themselves Democrats but voted to crush Roosevelt's legacy."

"Times and people change -"

"Precisely," he affirms. "Your exploits in the Sixties mean almost nothing to me." He looks at the paper in my hand. "Those are admirable sentiments. They are quietly practiced here."

He looks precisely at Nellie. "What are you doing with this guy? Are you an End Earther too?"

"I'm here because I love him. And because I would like a return to the beauty of

pre-industrial Earth. Put that in a bag and then shit in another bag -"

"Ms Ramos -"

"I'm a sketch artist. I would spend my time chronicling the daily life within the town." She reaches down for a sketch pad. The picture she retrieves to display is the one she drew of Thoreau Park while standing near Jesse's airplane.

Willingham nods appreciatively, leaning forward. He sits back.

He and Jesse exchange looks while we dangle in suspense. Jose and Evan look a little concerned too. Willingham leaves the desk, coming around to address me, man to man.

Preparing for the let-down, I look him in the eye. He proffers his hand. "Welcome to Thoreau Park. You are on probation."

He hugs Nellie. "Welcome," he says.

Willingham turns us over to Evan Evans. As the swinging door is ushering us out, Willingham begins discussing with Jesse matters of commerce. We simply exchange waves with Jesse and Carlos as we pass through and move further down the narrow hall.

Anticipating a first look at the city proper, we are both surprised and disappointed to be assigned a room with just one small window to see the outside. A sign at the entrance proclaims that we are in quarantine. We pile our belongings on the floor.

Mister Evans invites us to call him Evan. I decide we ought to converse, for I'm curious as to how friendly he tends to be.

"What else is your role around here, Evan?"

He guffaws. "I do most anything needs done behind the scenes to make it smooth

running for Claude. The rest of the time I'm tending my friends, the dogs and pigs."

"Are there many animals in Thoreau Park?"

Evan ponders a moment, his eyes scrunching up. "Got some birds and a few pets. Not so many, cause they use up resources."

"Speaking of resources," I say as I start to help Nellie pick up stuff to put away, "how self reliant are we for food and daily necessities, such as soap and home remedies?"

He tells us we are well provided for. We produce our own vegetables and fruit. Meat, when it is scarce, is rationed. But in the kitchens lab grown meat is a thing. Most residents generally like it. We've imported enough cases of soap and the like to keep our bodies clean and healthy.

Evan admires some of Nellie's art for a few moments. He tells us he has some tasks to help out and quickly leaves us.

Standing at the window, a tantalizing glimpse of pedestrian street traffic just feet away, I glance at Nellie, who is contemplating the bed. It's an old fashioned full size, as opposed to king or queen, something neither of us has seen in quite a few years. "Prepare to get bumped around," she says.

"I've missed my nap. I need one now."

After locking the door I lie down on top of the sheet in my underwear. Nellie discovers pamphlets in a drawer and picks some to read while sitting in a comfortable chair. We spend three boring days in this wise, with Evan delivering our meals but heeding quarantine and avoiding us. On the fourth day from arrival we receive a knock and discover a new face behind the door. Nobody stands with him, which perplexes me.

"Good morning. Why aren't you Evan?"

The man's gaze is clear and honest as he replies. "You will find Evan to be a shadow figure around here. His duties mostly keep him out of sight."

"Like Major Major?" I quip thoughtlessly.

He looks slightly puzzled. Then, "Oh. Catch 22. No, Evan is much more useful

than such a character. But let's talk about you. It's time to join the general population. My name is Matthew Jones. I'm a low level administrator and vegetable farmer."

By this time Nellie is crowding me away from hogging the scene, holding my shoulder to guide me away from the door so that Jones can be shared equally. She says, "We were having morning coffee," sizing him up "Would you like to share or are we in a hurry?"

Matthew Jones looks to be a college professor type, but for the faded overalls and blue flowery shirt. His face has deeply ensconced worry lines and his glasses have thick lenses. There is a gentle calm about the man. I think I'm going to like him. "Thank you. I awoke late and missed my morning cup."

We settle about the runt of a kitchen table, all seated on heavy wooden chairs. Jones has his with a half teaspoon of sugar. He sips and compliments the chef.

We drink quietly; the setting's completely devoid of tension. Then, at the end, he volunteers to help us clean up the traces of the stay here so that we can bring our belongings with us. He's wiping out the sink as he speaks. "Living here can be likened to living inside a mall - the great addition being the living quarters. Here, most residents prefer to walk, but there are bicycles and transports stationed about. I parked a transport

outside to make your move easier."

Nellie, who doesn't miss a trick, says, "What about the laundry? Why don't we have a washing machine in here?"

"Something to do with quarantine," Jones replies. "I suppose you could talk to Evan about it. Let's just fold the sheets and leave them outside the door."

A few minutes later, we go out on the street, experiencing the release that comes with the new freedom. Even the air seems sweeter. Unbelievable, the trees and sidewalks, the shops, the bright colors. It sports a perpetually festive aura that's designed to lift the spirit.

We load the transport.

Experiencing near euphoria, I prefer to walk a distance down the street just to peep

into a shop or two and garner some glimpses of fellow residents. I poke my head into the very first shop, then walk inside.

A woman playing on the floor with a very small child looks up with a grin of pure joy as the little one toddles then falls into her arms. "Welcome. Have a look around. If you need help that is what I am here for."

Immediately I am drawn to a nice hoodie. I've never had one. "May I try this out?"

She nods yes, while hoisting the little one, whose antics are making her laugh.

It slips on very nicely, not overly snug. It's mine now. "How much?"

She's rolling back and the child crawls over her chest, reaching for her face. "Oh, you are new. It's for nothing. We don't use money here."

Pausing uncertainly, I wait for the punch line.

"No, it's all right. Just write the number on the attached slip in the notebook on the counter, so we can track it."

When I walk back out Nellie makes a mock sigh, but one can tell she doesn't mind the hoodie. I grin happily as I step on board the transport and take my seat. Jones is at the helm. It's an interesting design this transport has. To the rear is a platform for objects up to the size of a kitchen range. Then two long bench seats. The driver occupies a seat over a bicycle style of pedal. After making settings to backward/forward, fast/slow, he simply works it with his feet as casually as you please. The inner works are so intricately balanced that a four year old child could drive it. But it steers manually. "My father designed and built these things," Jones says. "Beyond that, he worked with the original designers and builders of Thoreau Park from day one, in Nineteen Eighty-Three, all the way until his passing in Twenty Eleven."

It's mind boggling. "You mean they built all of this without my knowledge from way back then? How did they manage it?"

"A certain patron, whose name I don't even know, pulled lots of strings to keep it under wraps," he says, pausing the transport to allow a trio of jogging women to clear out of his way.

They wave and say "Hi."

"Mm-hmm. And what do they want out of it?" I say, sniffing for a rat.

"They want to be included among the population when - if -"

"Yes?"

"Instead of telling you, I'm going to show you," Jones concludes.

He begins pointing out features of interest, which are centers of activities, such as gyms, movie houses and the like. Right in what I judge to be the complex center are perhaps the greatest surprises of all. Three indigenous houses in a row, exactly as originally built, and it turns out the same families still occupy them.

"They grow much of our food. Once these people understood what we stand for they were willing to let us build. They refused to give up the life they love, however. Today, we are all one happy family."

It's a bit disappointing that no indigenous faces look out as we are passing, but there is more to marvel over in front of us, as three storied apartments line both sides of the street. Jones points to an entry on the left. "Your apartment is here at the beginning, and we will be back to it shortly. There is one more thing you have to see first."

He shifts the gears to the higher speed then takes us to street's end and a massive structure that it boggles the mind to witness. It's an intended impervious wall and it seems featureless at first glance. According to Jones there is a door at the bottom center, twenty-five feet wide, twenty-eight feet in height. Just the top administrators know how to open it.

Nellie gasps. "It's into the mountain. For a total war."

"Bingo," Jones replies. "It's intended purpose is to get a thousand individuals through and even years beyond nuclear winter."

"Well, from what I've seen and heard, we are going to need it," I quip dryly. "Now I'm ready to complete the move, for I need my nap time."

Jones smiles benignly. "Of course," he responds.

Nellie however hasn't finished examining the shelter. "How will we know to go in there?"

"First, we can hope the bombs don't explode too close to here or it will never

happen. Otherwise there should be a very short window. Worst scenario, assuming we fail to get saved, there are a hundred individuals living inside already."

"You must follow the news pretty closely," I say, sitting back in my seat, ready to go.

Swinging us around, Jones admits to being a news junky. "But I have to be, as part of my job," he adds.

"What have you learned about Spud's assassin," I dig.

"Nothing. If they know anything they are keeping it quiet."

Jones pulls in near the apartment entry and steps down to help us unload the transport. He picks up Nellie's suitcase, leaving her freedom to take care with her art. He guides us onto a landing and we go up both flights of steps. There is a very long hall at the top, but our door is just off the high landing. Jones hands me the key and I let us in.

As I look over the gorgeous furniture and the bar separating the kitchen from the living room, Nellie spies a small electric piano. She hastily sets her load aside and pounds on the ivories, then settles into a delicate melody. Jones stands in awe, applauding, cheering her on. It's a tune I recognize though the title eludes me. As she concludes the piece, I stroll to peek in the bedroom. "Take a look," I urge.

She squeezes in past me and gawks at the bed. "Holy shit. If you want a little tonight you're going to have to organize an expedition and search for me on there."

Yep. It will be the greatest bed I've ever slept on.

We discover Jones near the entry as if prepared to leave. "I'm going to search the pantry for tea and coffee," I say. "It just occurs to me we ought to go grocery shopping."

"Yes," he replies. "I'm leaving you the transport. The most complete grocer is this side of the indigenous houses."

He pauses after opening the door. "Do either of you go to church? There is a multiple denomination temple almost back where we started from."

"Not necessary. I'm not interested."

As I'm too quick to answer, Nellie becomes totally sober for once. "I'll go a few times."

She looks at me. "Alone, if necessary."

"Sorry," I come back. "I just don't do church."

"It doesn't have to mean you are an atheist to dislike church," Jones puts in helpfully.

"I'm not saying what I believe. I've abandoned the habit of explaining myself," I say. "I found out long ago that each one of us is hardwired to believe a certain way about religion and no amount of educated arguing can ever change us. Just now I misspoke when I told Nellie I wouldn't go. If she wants me to be with her I certainly will be there and support her."

She grimaces. "I don't need your charity."

I take her unresponsive hand. "Just tell me what you want from me and I will happily comply."

She gives me that you're a bad doggie look. "Nothing changes between us. You continue to be you. I can handle it."

Feeling a bit unsettled by now, I ask Jones if he will be stopping by again.

"Of course. As often as needed. Many of our people are by habit loners. I try to conjure a sense of unity."

After he is gone, I ask Nellie if we should shop first or is my nap in order? She suggests I sleep while she sorts out the kitchen to make moving in the groceries simpler. Great. I flop in the bed's center, sans clothing. The air is perfect and the mattress is comfortably firm. Waiting for the Zs. But the tossing and turning begins, because I'm wrought up and soon I have instead to be up and moving. I seek out Nellie to ask if she knows whether or not we forgot to pack my clean underwear. After a short search she says, "I'm sure we can get you some more when we go shopping."

In a short order we approach the transport, which true to his word Jones left for us. Nellie takes a bench seat, leaving me to drive. The controls are so simple I immediately have us moving. I hadn't paid attention to the steering mechanism before. It relies on a small steering wheel, which is surprisingly sensitive. Old Mister Jones was a genius. We discover a clothing store along the way. After acquiring some boxers, we go to the grocer

Jones had mentioned. There the people help us shop and they all invite us to come around when we want to talk or goof off.

On returning, we stuff the food in cabinets and the fridge before making ourselves cold sandwiches with avocado slices on the side. Glasses of sparkling water. Then Nellie wants to go outside to draw. As I'm helping her get set up, I catch a glimpse of someone

coming close and the familiarity makes me look around. Coming with the old swagger but a face somewhat grim, Jesse confronts us.

We learn that he has brought in the final members, among which number himself and his family. "Also Karma. I kept in touch with her because of Percy. Turned out now she wants to be here." He says he left his people long enough to touch base with me to fill me in on things. I learn that Danny shot it out with several agents and was killed only this morning. In other news the nuclear saber-rattling escalates daily. He thinks bombs will be launched shortly.

We are crushed to lose Danny. In truth we had lost him back in Long Beach. This renews the blow. I thank Jesse, who has to get back to his moving.

That evening in bed, Nellie tells me she intends to light a candle for Danny. "That's a beautiful gesture," I comment.

"Are you going to light one too?"

I turn from my backside to face her, propping myself up on my elbow. "It's not my way of honoring him. I simply hold him in my heart and I always will."

Nellie gives me a dubious look. "You're the first person I've met that refuses to tell what he believes."

I knew this conversation was coming. Knew she would take that incident to heart. "In a younger day I used to argue religion. Not any more. I will try to explain why."

After propping myself up on two giant pillows I look to the ceiling without really seeing it. "When people discuss religion, being friendly or not, even a small disagreement strikes right at the core of one's essence. Any sort of challenge is taken viscerally as an

attack on one's very being. You can express it in a tender loving way. It makes no difference. They can't help feeling attacked. After that, a best friend - a lover - will never

view the other in the same way, no matter what."

She lies on her back, reflecting. "I guess you're right. I love you, but there is now a wedge of some kind in my feeling for you. Something I failed to notice before."

I roll over to hold her. She lets me, but she doesn't respond.

I kiss her eyes, then move away to sleep. "I'm coming with you to light the candle," I say before shutting my eyes and willing sleep to come.

Then she snuggles. Throwing her naked self against me, holding on with all her might. I cradle her and enjoy her warmth the rest of the night. Moments like these can have one regretting the follies of the young, those times we throw away simply because experience has yet to grab us by the collar and steer us to fulfillment.

I frequently mention Nellie's showers, in such a way that may cause a reader to wonder why it is that I don't bathe. I assure you I also have a clean epidermis. On this morning we shower together to an extent. There isn't enough room for the two of us to move, I step out until she gets finished and step back in. We enjoy drying one another. Then we prepare to burn a candle.

There is a simple elegance about the temple. The pews, the stained glass windows, the pulpit, all subdued and unmarked. For special meetings the accouterments which are concealed in special closets are brought into play. Father Guevara introduces himself. He invites us to make our personal use of it and invites us to ask if we need anything. Nellie thanks him as she selects her candle. She tenderly sets it up and carefully adds fire. It is a

moving experience like no other to watch a candle burning for a lost brother. Moved almost to tears I stare into the flame. Nellie, when we finally walk out seems calm and at peace. Aching with sorrow I shuffle beside her, feeling my own mortality as rarely before.

CHAPTER TWELVE

We learn from Jones that moving everyone into the shelter is an increasing probability. "But, you know," he says, "nuclear winter may not be as bad as has been traditionally predicted. Some studies claim there may not be any at all. I'm of the persuasion that there should be some, but it's all unknown territory, since nothing like it ever happened before. Another thing we've discussed is the cessation of fossil fuel pollution. After the war there will be no production of fossil fuels due to infrastructure and refinery destruction. Nature may be able to grab itself by the pants in a grand resurgence. On the other hand, this apocalypse may be our not so grand finale."

He describes the disaster horn that will summon us to the shelter. Then he gives a challenging look as he further informs, "Anyway, they are enlisting volunteers to live right here through the whole shebang."

We don't rise to the bait. "But," I interject, "is radiation drifting a thing? As a kid in the fifties what I heard most was radiation."

Jones arises from his desk to adjust the ceiling fan. "I never get it just right," he says.

He looks at the floor. Then he looks at me. "Radiation. I don't think you need worry about it here, except if a bomb hits in the area. But as I say, we've never had total nuclear war before, so lots of assumptions will soon be reevaluated."

At home later, discussing it all with Nellie and Evan, who just happened to stop by, I ask again about the radiation. Evan's reply is similar to Jones.' "Why?" Nellie asks,

looking at me. "Are you thinking about staying out here?"

"I don't like being a volume of canned goods. They've been working at this since the 80s but I don't wholly trust it. Some of humanity's most spectacular failures have defied human expertise."

Evan hastens to defend this particular example of human expertise. "But, Denny; a hundred persons are already living inside and have been for years."

"Nearly a thousand is a whole 'nother plate of onions," I suggest.

Evan laughs as he shakes his head.

"Anyway," I add, "if Nellie wants us to be in there, in there is where we will be."

"The rich people are coming tomorrow," Evan says, looking less positive as the thought sinks in a little deeper than in previous moments.

"Cheer up," I say with a quick grin, "They can only buy so much in a cashless society."

After Evan goes, Nellie expresses that we should look up Karma, since she hasn't looked us up. I've had a similar notion, but I don't want to push myself on reluctant people. But I agree to go with Nellie. We eventually track her down inside an eatery. She's having a mostly lettuce salad. In her glass appears to be clear water. We amble up slowly, so as not to startle.

She invites us to sit and eat. We sit and decline when the server asks for our preference.

"So how did they treat you that you decided to leave?" Nellie asks, getting to the heart of the matter immediately.

Karma's demeanor reminds me of a cat deciding whether to strike out in defense or retreat. She regards Nellie with a noncommittal stare. "They were nice to an extent. But I had a never lessening sense that nobody there fully trusted me. They appeared to monitor my every move. I couldn't live like that. I'm sorry if they are your friends. I didn't like any of them."

"No reason we can't stay friends," Nellie soothes. "I wouldn't send you to a situation like that knowingly."

Karma spears the only chunk of cucumber with her fork. "I suppose," she answers back.

After that the tension goes and we enjoy our small reunion. She lets us know that Percy safely came to Thoreau Park and that she visits him and Miguel when she misses him too much.

That evening we are informed that the shelter is preparing to fill with residents for the duration. Willing participants will gather by nine o'clock.

Nellie and I won't be there. We've talked until we feel as do a sizeable number that the town should be kept operational to make the others' return from life in the shelter an easy and pleasant transition.

In the middle of the night we are jolted from sleep and hop unthinking from bed. The emergency alarm goads us to hurry, because we can't know for certain the nature of the emergency. It's a shrill blatting sound, goading everyone to assemble as near the shelter as they can crowd in. Nellie: "If it's meant to push us all into the shelter I intend to bring my art with me. These drawings are my life."

Agreed. And I go down ahead to find us a transport to make moving our stuff easy. Coming out on the avenue, the scene on the street is nothing like I expect to behold, for people are milling and generally moving away from the shelter. A man randomly emerges from the crowd, after likely having read the look on my face. He pauses long enough to say, "A gang with guns is hijacking our shelter."

"Hijacking? How did they get in here?" But the man has his own concerns and I lose him to the crowd.

Harking back to the olden days of challenging authority and protecting our own, I determine to leave Nellie upstairs for her safety, and to get to the scene of the action to see if I can be of any help. Bicycles and transports are useless among swarming feet, but adrenaline helps my stiff old legs move along at a steady clip. The crowd thins away, leaving me alone, hopefully not to become a target. The thought that an old man, empty-handed and stumbling along, could be perceived as a threat is a fleetingly amusing thought. However, throughout history, men have been killed for less. Do I feel like a lucky punk? Well, no. Not at all. I press grimly forward.

Mingling with a group that has gathered to look on, I note the shelter entrance is wide open. Certain of Thoreau Park officials are being shoved and ushered inside by a man of about my age, covered by six men wielding AR-15s.

It is indicated to me by one of the onlookers that the man is the "benefactor" - the one who financed the enterprise all the way from the beginning.

It is said that Assman is his name and that he has his own chosen crowd outside of

the gate, waiting to be ushered into the shelter. The six men pointing AR-15s at us are

convincing, in their sunglasses, camouflage, and hair grown out of control. Then Matthew Jones speaks with an amplified voice, telling our group to clear the street. "Go home."

We refuse to leave the scene, although I move to a semi-protected enclave. Someone pushes in beside me, someone with immaculate makeup and yellow lips. I squeeze Nellie to me as we turn, arm in arm, to face the drama before us.

Assman is selecting useful individuals to push inside of the shelter, the ones needed for both lockdown and daily operation once they are closed in tight. I note that one lone gunman has moved away from the group, appearing to be covering against a counterattack. Then, once the key personnel are safely inside, that lone gunman turns to face Assman and the rest, leveling his gun in their direction.

There are but seconds of pandemonium, as the man fires first on those with guns, then without hesitation, levels Assman. All six are unquestionably dead. The man tosses his gun to the side. He has to go inside to draw the cowering men from the shelter. Once he has ushered them out, he throws aside his sunglasses and removes the flak jacket. The more he uncovers the more familiar he seems. But of course the flashes of recognition are of the impossible.

Ignoring the carnage, I move in on the perpetrator until he discovers my presence on the floor. He throws wide his arms. "Denny. It's fucking me."

Crying and laughing at the same time as our bodies crash into one another resulting in the tightest hug known to humanity. "But you're dead. The forces of law and order tracked you down and murdered you."

"No," Danny exclaims. "Some poor soul got sacrificed in the name of propaganda.

I hid out among these bastards here, not even suspecting that Assman would employ us."

"Son of a bitch, Danny. The news media would get all over describing you as a mass murderer if they only knew."

"Hush up about that," he says remorsefully. "I haven't enjoyed any of it."

"No. Sorry."

He scans the area in an exaggerated manner, with Nellie tight against him like an

extra appendage.

Then we lose Danny to the growing crowd and the men he rescued. I stand in awe of this eighty year old bastard, recalling at the same time a saying among the old about being lucky to put on my underwear without falling down.

Apparently Danny has been elected to lead a delegation to deal with Assman's chosen retinue still waiting outside the gate.

Nellie and I follow slowly behind, eventually pausing to get aboard a transport, making up a full complement of riders. We all say nothing, being fully focused on the still growing crowd accompanying Danny and the administrators.

Outside the gates, foremost among Assman's people are his grown children with the grandkids. And one bright and sensitive dog. These have legitimately come along. The dozens of hangers on behind them are likely scoundrels, one and all. These last are told to return to their plane. None is allowed inside. Assman's children are fearful of the consequences if they stay here until Danny persuades them otherwise, insisting that the old timers will not make them accountable for their father's misdeeds. He financed everything. For them the shelter is open. Their unabashed fear of the apocalypse persuades them in.

Some weeks after the shelter has been populated and sealed off, we caretakers have cause for cautious optimism. Our friend Jones, who opted to stay with us to lend his expertise, tells us the prevailing winds have worked to move measurable radiation away.

Nellie and I have found jobs sweeping and cleaning of the restaurant which we regularly frequent. The manager there is Maria, a daughter of the original settlers in the valley. Her use of English is comparable to mine. She likes to have fun, loves to create dishes that incorporate the eating habits of the world. She is pregnant with her third child. Last night she made us an anniversary soup to make up for the fact she's never before acknowledged an anniversary of ours.

Evenings, when the sun has taken a bow over the valley, we sometimes sit outside to keep in touch with our planet. We stay to welcome the moon, old friend from Long Beach. We call him affectionate names. Nellie sings Devil Moon for him.

Sometimes Danny sits with us. He is clearly in a funk and I don't have any words to lift his mood. He deserves to finish his days satisfied and comforted. He doesn't tell us anything and I know he would do life the same way all over again. He spends much of his time with Jones. Those two began meeting because they both follow news reports closely.

I've begun to notice that lately these two have taken to rooming together. Nellie thinks it is sweet. It's not my business. I just resent that Danny has somehow preserved his Ronald Reagan portrait. I truly don't understand his concept of life and politics.

Morning seems darker out there. Gradually sky debris gathers to make all day long seem like dusk. And so we no longer venture outside. This encroaching gloom puts the

damper to our spirits and we stay in our apartment more. A few times I survey the ruined crops outside, grateful we also have beautifully protected greenhouses, where the food continues to flourish. Jones says that our cluttered atmosphere may soon clear up. He thinks we cannot salvage the land for renewed cultivation.

The streets are often empty, due to the reduced population. Nellie and I walk them for enjoyment and exercise. Lately, as I told her this morning, I feel brittle. Equilibrium seems to be failing, so that I may soon need a walker. I need to keep moving. I also need to pen my memoirs.

Nellie is philosophical. "Your old butt's burnt out. But you've still a few years in you."

The sky continues to darken. Secretly I wish that we had gone inside the shelter. It's mid morning and I'm enjoying a second cup of coffee. From the kitchen I can smell she's baking. "What's that? A cake?"

"Of course. Do you know what day this is?"

I'm turned around from my computer, mentally scratching my head. "I don't even know what month it is."

"When you see how many candles I stick in the icing you will possibly get a little jolt of memory."

She steps out in her fancy apron. Her lipstick is purple. What? How does she come up with so many colors? "We're going to take it to Danny's apartment."

"I can slip five bucks into an envelope for his present."

Of course we haven't any envelopes but I can improvise one with a sheet out of a

spiral notebook. After taping the folds in place there is a nice little folder for a bill. On finding no more fivers in my billfold I extract two ones to use instead. By the time the cake has cooled enough to receive a nice coat of coconut/vanilla icing we have gotten fully dressed. Nellie insists on carrying it so I have to pick it up when her head is turned. "Alright. But you better not drop it."

Wearing a polo shirt and blue slacks, feeling pretty dapper, I wait outside Danny's door with Nellie poised to give it a few good raps. Our ears pick up enough of a conversation from within to give us pause. The voices increase in volume, until Jones tears out the door and down the stairs. I almost lose the whole cake but manage to salvage most of it by jamming it close against my chest, knocking some of the candles askew and smashing an icing corner into my shirt. Nellie grabs the door as it is about to shut and beats against it with her fist, declaring, "Happy birthday, Danny."

But she doesn't simply barge in, just waits until he comes forward and bids us come in.

Nellie steps in and spins to look Danny in the face. "That was certainly awkward."

Danny responds with a bitter smile. "I was missing Kyle. Who knew Matthew would get jealous?"

"Well, we are here cheering you up. Stand back while Denny whips it out."

She discovers the cake damage "Well, shit. Take it in the kitchen so I can straighten it up."

Danny watches in bemusement as we doctor up the smushed end. "I didn't know it was our birthday. I'm no calendar watcher these days."

He looks wistfully after Jones' path of exit. "He'll be back once the hurt wears off. Save him a piece of cake."

I offer my brother a one-armed hug. He responds in turn, says "Happy Birthday,"

But Jones stays away. The time we spend with Danny descends into gloomy affairs. I likely would give him his privacy, but Nellie keeps us engaged. This isn't overly

concerning to me because he has had ups and downs his entire life, yet eventually comes out on top. Nellie, on the other hand, has to comfort him, nurse him out of it. He poses for drawings, eats her treats, watches movies with her. But there are lines of sadness newly graven on his face.

As we decline with age, sometimes it accelerates without actual reason, other than, like a spent beautiful flower, the petals begin to darken and fall off. But not so for Danny. Not yet. He's just sad.

I remain anti-intervention until one morning I see a closet door carelessly left open and there is a rope on the floor inside, with a slip knot at the end. I pull the door shut and hope Nellie hasn't seen it.

On another front we discover a club that once offered live entertainment prior to the move into the shelter. Nellie spends but a few minutes looking over the sparse number of hangers-on, who merely come back out of habit to drink odd non-alcoholic drinks. She looks sideways at me. "This place needs to be revived."

She stands and waves at the patrons. "Hello everybody."

She commandeers the piano and pounds out a lively boogie sound before settling into the melody of Autumn Leaves. By the time the vocal launches these people are on

their feet, cheering, clapping, broadly smiling. She follows up with La Bamba, her own version, ballad-ized, inspired by the version recorded by Harry Belafonte.

About an hour later we return home. I go to the bedroom to nap. Nellie announces she will be at Danny's, cooking him the special stew she promised yesterday. I assure her I will be along in an hour or so.

Nap over, a languid feeling that keeps me from moving quickly sees me drinking tea when I could be on the way to join Nellie. I take my time, considering as I sit here the way my memoir could or should progress. It's such a complicated endeavor I'm not certain I will get it finished. Especially after Danny belittled the effort. "Memoirs are for the well-known and the famous. Nobody gives a shit about you."

Brothers can say cruel things but it doesn't mean they don't love us. I will have a come back very soon.

The stiffness has me today, making me walk more slowly and carefully down the stairs. Although it's a short journey to his home, I pull myself onto the driver's seat of a transport to peddle leisurely along. The walk to the stairs is a little better. Taking each up-step carefully, I gain Danny's door and push it open. There's Nellie, quietly at the piano, playing something written by Phil Ochs. Ochs could inspire, depress, be ugly, be beautiful, all at once. I've never ceased mourning for him.

She smiles back at me.

"Where is Danny?" I inquire.

"He said he had something to attend to in the greenhouse with the trees," she answers, ending the song and turning to stand up. "Said he would be back in plenty of

time for the stew."

"Hmm."

I look inside the closet for the rope with the slipknot in the end. It's gone. I dig through the contents to make certain it didn't simply get moved. "Did he carry anything with him?"

Nellie looks back from near the kitchen. "He had a rope in his hand."

"Some of those trees are over thirty years old."

She fake grimaces. "So?"

"So that rope has a slip knot at the end."

"So," she rejoinders, "it's been in there for over a week."

Nellie humors me by turning off the heat under the stew then joins me going down the steps.

"You're being silly, you know," she says to my back.

But I'm determined to catch up with him, coming out to the street and looking to score some bicycles. As fate would have it, there are three clustered near the next building. Nellie is ahead of me, secures one for me, then as I take possession of it, grabs her own. After a wobbly start I manage a quick speed that would make a hazard on a busy avenue.

The greenhouses are situated so that they can be covered over or else open to the

sky. We come into a small orchard which seems surprisingly healthy. We abandon the bikes at the entrance and spend precious minutes opening the gate. Then on the central path, looking among the fruit and nut trees, but there is no sighting him.

"The older, bigger trees seem to be in the back corner," Nellie suggests, pointing.

And that's just where there would be high strong limbs capable of supporting a man's weight; even withstanding the jolt if that weight should present a sudden jerk and hang suspended from it. Nellie walks calmly behind as my stiff legs carry me as quickly as they are capable. I lurch down the way until the sinister cluster of tall trees stands before me. I charge in, looking wildly to left and right, up and down, anticipating a tragic ending.

Midway through it all, a ladder appears, propped against a gangling walnut tree. There are two legs dangling off the limb supporting the ladder. Then I see Danny's full body. He's sitting with a bow saw in his hand, its teeth cutting into a limb wilted and already dying. The rope is tied to the limb, as on the far side of the walnut tree stands Matthew Jones keeping tension on it to pull the limb away from Danny once it's freed.

My brother pauses to look at me. "What are you doing here?"

"Do you need my help?" I say, relieved, beaming.

"Get over there and catch the limb when it comes down."

As Nellie moves up beside me, I throw an arm about her shoulder and we stand back to watch the two best friends working together. I tell Nellie how I see that she knows my brother better than I.

She suggests we get back to finish preparing the meal.

By the time Danny and Jones stroll in, arm in arm, we have it all prepared and we take our leave almost immediately, despite their protests we should stay.

Nellie wants to return to record the state of the greenhouse plants, via her drawings.

Along the way we meet Evan, whom we thought this whole time to be within the shelter. He explains that he is part of a skeleton crew to keep Thoreau Park intact. He strolls along with us toward our destination and talks about how the shelter is far more elaborate then anything we might have supposed. "They could live generations in there. There is no

hurry up time frame to emerge. We hope beyond reasonable expectations that the Earth can regenerate itself, now that the major industrial polluters have been destroyed."

He takes us off of the intended path and into a huge garage to show us the vehicles that would replace cars. They are similar to the Mars rovers, adapted for the heavy Earth gravity and have beds, pickup style. "For when we venture forth to help repopulate the planet."

Because he has a day of idle time, Evan stays with us when Nellie begins her work. He speaks of a sister and her children who are all inside the shelter. I ask him when the sky will become blue again. His answer: "Believe it or not, it will happen sooner than anyone has a right to believe. I'm told it has been incrementally lightening for about a week now."

"I wish I could see it," I respond, discovering at the same time we have an almond tree before us. "Good. I love almonds."

Nellie speaks up. "I'm doing a Van Gogh number on these trees. They are turning out pretty good, if I say so myself."

Evan tells us he wants a home in the states in a farm community. "I'm in my forties. I have time to do it."

"That's assuming the planet regenerates itself rather than rendering us extinct," I

tell myself gloomily.

I flash back at all the destruction intentionally inflicted on the Earth and thereby lose faith the damage can be undone. Brimming with sadness, aching with despair I walk off to inspect the trees alone. Even here in supposed security they look slightly less healthy than a week ago. On discovering a gardener's bench beneath a great fig tree, I brush back some debris and sit myself down. I can't take any more but of course I will take all the flak life has to give. With head bowed, protesting the futility of it all, I see four little legs and fur of brown and white. A lost puppy has discovered me. She shoves her nose into my open palm. My spirit lifts above all its burdens as I joyfully pull her into my arms and she wriggles happily, trying to reach my face and bestow some licks on it. The tears suddenly flood from my eyes as we cuddle and bond.

After fifteen minutes Evan shows himself, come to make sure I am okay. I hug the puppy, proudly smiling at him. But Evan frowns, his eyes on the ball of fur. "There she is," he says. "This dog got lost when I removed the litter to be disposed of. We have more than our allotment of dogs and these were illegally bred. If you don't mind I can take her now, before you begin to feel bonded to her."

I give him my best stubborn front as I hold the puppy in a tight grip to prevent her being ripped out of my life. "This dog deserves to live as much as any human here," I say. "Probably more so than any human, since we made her world what it is. I'm sorry, Evan, but she is my friend for life. Only the sad face of a longing child could get her away from me."

Evan, ever the gentleman, backs off for now. "Come with me to administration

tomorrow. I think we can convince you otherwise. Our margin for survival is very thin."

"Fuck the meeting. If you make her leave I'm going with her."

Nellie falls in love with our new family member, actively resisting overtures from Thoreau Park officials to surrender "Steffy," as she names the dog. Eventually they quit coming around.

Steffy stays on my lap when I write, sleeps on me when I watch films, chews on my shoes when I relax my guard. I would never have sought to live with another dog but I understand it was a selfish attitude. Non human beings often need and seek our friendship. We should be ready to give it when called upon.

Sometimes I stay home with Steffy when Nellie does her gig at the club. This because I tire much too easily these days. Anyway, wrestling with a memoir is tough time consuming work.

I stay in contact with Evan, who, despite the conflict over Steffy, remains friendly and informative. He advises against breathing the outside air just yet. But, "Soon. Real soon."

According to Danny, the news has stopped broadcasting on every band. The destruction of civilization may be complete, with no communication and likely famine. More than half of the water had been industrially contaminated even before the war came

home to America. Now it would be a gamble to drink any of it. We can only guess about the fate of possible survivors. It makes our microcosm extremely important.

We awaken one morning, excited because we are informed that it is relatively safe to breathe outside air. We have planned an excursion to view the fields of the decimated crops, later in the evening to sit out to commiserate the poor ill planet and to commune with our pal the moon. I must introduce the moon to Steffy.

After a leisurely breakfast and quietly sipping our coffee, we dress appropriately to bear the sun and a persistent cool wind that Jones tells us pervades the local atmosphere. We approach the gate as to a party, not at all prepared to be jammed up by Evan and the rest of the maintenance crew, most of whom we have not previously seen. Evan marches away from the group to confront us. His expression is grave, even a little frightened. "We have a situation," he announces.

I give him a sarcastic take and wait on him to unload, hardly believing there could be anything worse than the overall situation of the times. But I have to quip, "Is the Starship Enterprise sitting out there?"

"You wish," he rejoinders.

"What is it?" Nellie says. "Just give it to us in one take."

The crew by the gate is huddling, not saying a thing. But we are looking at Evan, who then tells us. "There's a tank out there, pointing its gun at the gate."

Nellie stalks over to look through one of the observation ports. I have to catch up with her to crowd for a view. Sure enough, an actual tank sits out there, with the treads decorated with desert dust and crusted mud, evocative of old black and white war films, with its gun trained right at my head. I'm no authority on tanks. I wonder, is it Mexican owned or did it come across the border? Evan doesn't know. And so far nobody has emerged even to peek back at us.

"The thing of it is, " Evan puzzles, "if they shoot holes in it the safe haven is gone.

If we let them in they could start killing us individually."

Nellie is pissed. "Are you going to tell us there are no weapons for self defense?"

I nod assent while Evan returns a hard look. "We've got AR-15s. Your brother

right now is organizing volunteers to take the fight outside."

My brother?

Incredulous, I tell him, "He's going out there? Eighty year old Danny has to face death for us one more time?."

Steffy's in the crook of my arm and my free hand rests on Nellie's shoulder.

"I understand your feelings. It's a role he insisted on taking," Evan says, walking off to rejoin his maintenance team.

"Bullshit," is all I can rejoinder.

Handing Steffy off to Nellie, I tell her, "Wait here."

"Hey," she says, startled. "What are you doing."

But I've already moved to engage the gatekeeper. "Open us up," I say in what to me seems a robust heroic voice. "I'm going out to speak with those people."

The gatekeeper stares, transfixed, until I reach beyond him to do his work and then he engages the mechanism that opens the interior gate. I don't need help opening the others.

After the gates all gape and the response from both directions is nil, I hesitantly make myself visible. I try not to look down the barrel of the big gun. Then my feet move me beyond the complex, alone on the roadway. I stare resolutely, awaiting some acknowledgement from the crew within.

"Hello," I bellow. "Hello. Will you talk?"

The prolonged silence finally shatters my bravado. I quail and wish dearly I could be at home writing my memoir. I become aware that Nellie has left the compound walking to join with me and that is when I make the fateful decision to approach the tank with the intent to crawl on top and try to enter it. Hurrying to keep ahead of Nellie, I approach close to a tread and look for the way up. By the time she can get here I am halfway up as I triumphantly ascend the tank and reach to open the port.

On pulling up the heavy lid I am startled to stare into a pair of glazed eyes, eyes that have lost all hope. These eyes connect with me, then their possessor sinks to the deck to lie motionless. I climb down to examine him to confirm whether he is alive or dead.

Two corpses rest at the tank's controls. This one too has succumbed. I twist my neck and spine to view Nellie, climbed up and looking into the cab. I shake my head to indicate they all have perished.

No words are said as we climb down to trod slowly back. I look over the landscape. There is virtually no living vegetation in sight. But the wind blows nicely and I like breathing the open air. Danny waits at the gate, acknowledging my deed with a grim respect. He looks at his rifle and looks for a way to be rid of it. Evan notes his discomfort and comes forward to relieve him of the weapon. Danny again regards me, moving as if to salute but instead scratches his forehead. "Thanks," he says with his typical brotherly smile.

After Nellie reclaims Steffy from being held by a friendly maintenance man, we take our walk on the outside, touring the fields and watching little white clouds slowly

drifting across the blue sky. The heat is intense. By the time we go inside, the tank has been moved already. We pass it parked where the cars are parked. We speculate that those men inside died from lack of water and food.

We come in for cold tea, to relax and wait for sundown, for we miss the moon. The sun has made us tired enough for napping. As we get in a state of undress a gentle rapping sounds at the door. I peep out, keeping the door to hide my nakedness. Evan stands with bowed head. I ask him to wait until I get some pants on. Then - "Come in, sir. Have some cold tea."

But Evan's not cheering up. He's avoiding our faces.

Nellie wearing blue lipstick and dressed very nicely comes out of the bathroom. "Hey, Evan; what's up?"

As I pour up the tea Evan waits nearby to receive his glass. After dutifully drinking half of the content, he carries the rest back to face Nellie, with me not far off, carrying some for her and me.

Evan finishes off the tea and allows Nellie to take the glass.

He says, "The reports from within the shelter continue to be excellent. We may be instrumental in reviving our broken planet. We've somehow gotten a populace inside

there with no bad mutating viruses - so far. They still must be vigilant. I never mentioned to you that we have in Thoreau Park a virtual Noah's Ark of seeds and genetic materials of as many species as could be gotten, from places as diverse as Africa, Asia, Australia, certain islands -'

I interrupt with, "That's great news. Somehow I feel this was not an urgent matter

to be knocking on my door this late in the day."

"Well, no. It helps set the stage for what I came to tell you," he replies, his earnest face cueing me to shut up and listen.

He continues, with the three of us standing in the middle of the floor, not considering settling someplace to gab.

"My crew has been going through the vacant apartments, tending to any issues we see, and making certain no unused power is being expended. Mostly the people did it all before they left."

His gaze sweeps past Nellie and back to me. He stands helplessly while Nellie and I prompt him to get him to speak.

"We came upon a body," he manages at last. "A suicide and a letter addressed to friends. You both were listed."

"And? Tell us," I urge, but I'm already guessing.

Nellie moves closer to support me in case I can't handle it, but I am a stoic and I wait in a stolid unshakeable state that has in the past confounded others.

"I'm not aware of her last name. Just knew her as Karma," Evan says, avoiding eye contact, staring at the void between us. "Tomorrow there will be a service and reading of her letter. Is ten o'clock convenient for you?"

We nod, Nellie and I, holding each other as we stare at him in case there is anything else. Then I shake his hand and Nellie gives a hug and he excuses himself.

After locking the door I start to undress.

Nellie is incredulous. "What? You're sleeping after this?"

I pause the undressing long enough to answer. "I am intensely and immeasurably sad. But there is nothing I can change about it and so in such a situation I continue to do

things I always do."

I coax Steffy off of the couch and pick her up to let her sleep on the great bed with us.

Nellie somewhat reluctantly undresses and we are shortly lying two feet apart on the greatest bed ever devised, with Steffy on my pillow next to my head. Lying in our naked splendor, arms spread, legs apart, I contemplate how it would be to have a mirrored ceiling. What a sight we two oldies would be. Then Nellie breaks in on my thought. "Did you find her attractive?"

I relive in a flash my original encounter with Karma and then the day we knew we were friends.

No use lying. "Of course I did."

There is a brief silence while I await the response.

"I almost felt jealousy a few times."

"Surely you know there can be a difference between admiring an appearance and actual physical attraction. I find you more beautiful than any woman I've known, with your rectangular form, not give a fuck expressions, and eyes that take me into other realms of reality."

"Don't put me on a pedestal," she quickly says.

"Not a pedestal," I want her to understand. "I find you a more complete version of a human than any I've known. Rather than worship that I feel I deserve you. That you chose

me makes me feel both humble and boastfully proud."

Her hand is on my belly, rubbing in a circular motion. "I wish I could find the words like you. Know that I am feeling fulfilled for the first time in my life and it's due to you."

A short time later I awake from my nap. Nellie is in the kitchen brewing a fresh pot of tea. We drink the tea and have little cakes she baked a few days earlier. As we clean our mess she looks at the time. "Do you want to walk still?" she asks.

"Yes; I miss the moon."

We end sitting on the bench, toasting the moon with a bottle of white grape drink.

The sky gives the moon the mysterious appearance of wearing a thin veil for the occasion. After, we stay up late watching movies that were checked out from the library. She complains that Grapes of Wrath is too long but I have to watch it anyway. She falls asleep before Preacher Casey gets his head bashed in.

We nevertheless arise with time to kill and so go to have Maria serve us coffee and hotcakes. We arrive at Karma's church wake about twenty minutes early, Her sealed coffin is on display. We sit in the pews alone, staring at the surprising number of exquisite flower bouquets.

"You know," Nellie says, over the piped in music, "I've come to look at our situation like you do. The end may come after we've both died, but it's all over with and we're marking time until the final blow falls. I guess you're not so much a pessimist as a realist. I'm sorry I doubted you."

Oddly, it shocks me. It hurts me to hear the thing she just said. I feel a need to tell her that our recent experiences have sprouted a tiny hope within me that had not been there. Nellie is a part of it growing. I need her continued belief. But it's Karma's time right now, and I say nothing.

We look about as Danny and Jones stroll quietly in. It turns out that the rest of Karma's known acquaintances reside now inside the shelter. When Evan appears, he activates a screen that allows them to participate. We parade before the screen to trade greetings with Jesse and the rest of them. By the time we settle again in the pews, Guevara the priest arrives. He wields a Bible and a spiral notebook, stands behind the pulpit and returns our stares.

After nearly five minutes he speaks.

"Friends, we are not an organized religion here. I can preside over the dear woman's ceremony, but I will not presume to speak to her religious belief. I instead ask that you listen to a reading of the note she left at her bedside."

He puts down the Bible and lays open the spiral notebook. Guevara looks to the video screen, then down at us.

He reads: "As you read this letter, know that none among you should feel guilt over

a thing you 'might have prevented.' I fooled you all by putting on my daily face. I smiled and spoke kindly, for I love you all.

"Increasingly I've felt a thing lurking inside my head. My mind and body appear to be fighting. I can't rest or be comfortable. If I sleep I dream of peace. I long for peace. I have vowed to starve myself. Soon peace will come.

"No one of Thoreau Park need feel they have failed in any way. I admire and love

you.

"I can't help but believe there exists Thoreau Parks we don't know about and I believe humankind will prevail in the end. I wish I could move ahead in time to have a peek. What we are going through now is the planet's way of testing us with fire so that the dross is burned away. The next history will see our destiny, of which we can only speculate. It is our chance to prove we are worthy. God bless."

As we look on in silence, Guevara tells us thank you and leaves the notebook on the pulpit for any who wish to examine it. Evan signals the maintenance crew to move Karma's coffin to the grave yard, to be only the third to be interred there.

Danny and Jones join Nellie in burning candles while I look on with competing emotions. My stoicism is unshaken. Another piece of my life has been chiseled off by the reaper. Such a letter she wrote. I love her vision of multiple Thoreau Parks. Who is to argue about it if we don't know?

When I seek to communicate my thoughts to Nellie, she is way ahead of me. "I know what you are telling me," she interrupts to reply. "I feel it too. Before the priest read the letter, I was wavering between your End-Earther stance and the inability to accept that life could end this way. She makes me feel that life can't just end. We won't let it."

"Yes," I tell her. "Between you, Karma, and Thoreau Park, I've been persuaded to delay judgment. In short, I give us permission to revive, eventually to thrive."

I give her a smoochie.

Later in the evening we return to sit in the open and commune with the elements; share company with the moon. Sitting comfortably on our bench, the puppy running free,

enjoying the still cool breeze on a portion of the Earth quiet beneath the moon.

EPILOG

SURVIVAL: THE END GAME

1. Intelligence was never an exclusive human trait. It evolved to work in a similar fashion in countless animals, such as dolphins, orcas, dogs, apes, birds, octopuses - much as various similar organs evolved independently to work mostly the same way, such as the eye. The one feature that sets humans apart from the rest is a propensity to meddle endlessly with everything with which they come into contact. For that reason it worries me that, should the Earth indeed regenerate itself and we do somehow avoid extinction, we might prove incapable of overriding that terrible trait. Not concluding it's wrong to meddle, but do it in a constructive way. If we discover that we could separate a whole continent from the Earth and launch it into space that does not mean there ought to be secret programs to test the feasibility as is the propensity to do. Because, always, some ass has to build one and launch an actual continent. Remember, much of the bullshit we are experiencing could have been avoided had we refused to let the meddlers have their way in the first place.

2. We have been a territorial species from the beginning. The meddling cannot be settled if we cannot conquer territoriality, the fount of wars, racism, class war, and religious division, for all feed the worst kind of meddling. When the rich and powerful foment a war, it is not hard to stir the masses to sacrifice themselves in the name of patriotism, to make them see the opposing masses as deserving of annihilation. It's

territoriality at work. We see the same force in play when Black People, Native Americans, Palestinians, Asians, and "illegal" refugees, get treated as subhuman by whites. The general populace or huge swaths of it cannot passively allow or cheer on the cruelty. The rivalry between Christians and Muslims is, like the first two examples, a war. Not always fought on the battlefield; still fought one to annihilate the other; still an example of territoriality.

Class war: a necessity when the rich and powerful exploit our territorial propensity.

3. We've run roughshod over nature, relentlessly assaulted the planet. It would be our duty to restore habitats. Through science we could have our civilizations but leave enough wilderness to fend for itself - No interference. If you want to build walls build them to segregate humanity away from the natural world. It does not need us.

There are those who decry space exploration as unnecessary depletion of resources. A society properly regulated ought to do it all. Survival beyond Earth's natural life span may not be as remotely in the future as is now taken for granted. Overcoming the difficulties of space travel will be a long hard maybe impossible process. But we have to try before we know.

It's simply a fact that we have to rise above our faults and create something good next time around. Wish I could live long enough to see it happen. Amen. Thanks for reading.

OVER HERE

It was a movie night when Henry Fine and Carol Fine experienced the end of life as they knew it. As the streaming film provided suspense, droll punch lines, and horrific scenes of extreme cruelty that had Carol cringing and Henry quaffing beer a bit more quickly, the bombs already were loaded, with many on their way. They had let Sparky the charcoal poodle out the back door. He could be seen through the sliding glass lying on the patio watching the bugs swarming at the light fixture and snapping at a few. Carol shoved the dish of corn chips near to Henry's beer hand before curling up with a comfort. "Remember," she told Henry, "my doctor appointment is this Tuesday at nine."

Henry dropped his emptied beer can into a plastic bag kept by his feet, wanting another, not motivated to arise and get one. "Just remind me on Monday evening. You know how forgetful I am."

"I'm pretty sure Doc Adams will peg me for knee replacement surgery," she said for the eighteenth time.

Henry tolerantly nodded, thinking wistfully of one final beer. He threw his feet up on the coffee table and settled for drowsiness. His was the quiet American life, working a stressful forty hour job, sharing his days at home with gentle sweet Carol and Sparky, daydreaming he might one day retire and travel. The couple loved Mexican food and hamburgers, and cable television. They vowed to go first class on a cruise during the month when he cashed out the 401k.

Carol at thirty-eight held the same appeal as Carol at twenty-one. Still beautiful in

her unostentatious way, still enthusiastic and supportive, still the same person he had fallen in love with. They despaired for years at being unable to have children, but time had seen them outlive regret. It was almost as if she could tell what he was thinking, for, when his gaze traveled to her face as she stared at the screen, her eyes cut to him and she winked, smiling.

Henry hadn't many friends. He was faithful to the ones he did have. He particularly enjoyed neighbor Arnie Sachnel, who walked his Jack Russell with him when in the cool evenings he walked Sparky around the block. They spoke of local sports and family events, and they sometimes barbecued in Henry's back yard.

For them both, their educations were unremarkable. They knew no aspiration beyond keeping the yard neat, the car clean, and the barbecue pit at the ready. News outside of weather news put them to sleep. Both had grown up taking perpetual war to be the natural order of things. The school history books recounted from inception the nation's bloodletting ways, told in a manner that kept them proud to live here. Mostly they didn't think about it. When on occasion it came to their attention the nation was fighting in this or that locale, they felt a twinge of gratitude that geography made it possible to war with impunity, always over there.

That the other nations could take umbrage and learn ways to retaliate was an impossibility. That is, until they duplicated the technology that makes remote war on anybody an inevitability. It hit the nation like a combined 911/Pearl Harbor that the world war the leaders fomented could no longer be contained and cordoned off. In a single event everything went to hell.

Beer consumed, movie ended -

Henry ate a small dish of vanilla ice cream just before bed. Aware it was helping his belly to bulge, he nevertheless ate some every night. He could hear Carol picking up about the house and bringing in Sparky. Henry licked his spoon and brought the spoon and dish to the sink to be rinsed out. Without the rinsing, the colony of ants hiding somewhere within the kitchen's confines would be all over the sink by morning.

He was off to the bathroom, about to clean his mouth out, then take a wiz, when it began. He had never heard Sparky moan like he suddenly did. He had never before heard any dog make such a sound. Sparky's eyes sought his, terrified black balls alerting that something terrible was going on. And then the house violently shook, making him think, "Earthquake."

Explosions from all quarters shattered that notion. The initial onslaught continued, with explosions both near and far for several hours before tapering to sporadic hits. He was pretty certain Arnie's house received a direct hit early on.

The power plant had been a primary target, for all was immediate blackness, punctuated by glimmers from explosions. Henry covered all the windows before even considering the use of a flashlight.

And now, six months later, the gloom could not be corrected by an electric light bulb, even if the power should be magically restored. This gloom was permanent. It permeated the air; it put a film over Henry's eyes. He tasted it, even in his dreams. It tainted his water, food. He recognized that it would never leave unless the war ended. In the present moment Henry stared at a goblet of brackish liquid, had been staring for

several minutes, his will to drink it paralyzed. Finally, after being taunted by a dry mouth and cracking lips, he overruled his body's recalcitrance and he pulled the glass to his lips.

The liquid was harsh going down. His stomach worked valiantly to hold it in. He waited until the fight successfully concluded before making a next move.

He emptied more brackish water into a cup. After stirring in the last teaspoonful of oatmeal, he brought the 'breakfast' in to Carol, who was bedridden, growing weaker by the day.

"Here you are, my dear. Sorry there's no coffee or sugar."

Propped high with pillows, her gaze followed the spoon as Henry pushed the "oatmeal" at her. Coughing, spitting it out, she turned her face away. "Aug," she said.

Her cloudy eyes fluttered shut. She was not asleep, but Henry knew to leave her alone. He placed the cup with the spoon inside it on the bedside table.

There was nothing left in the kitchen. Even the garbage can was empty. More than food and clean water, Henry desired rest, and sleep. Only his reaching a sufficient stage of exhaustion could put him out. He touched Carol with his fingers, letting them communicate the softness of her failing flesh, before taking his jacket off a peg, slipping it on as he moved toward the front door, stepping out on the porch. He would find Carol some nourishment this day, so he vowed.

The gloom permeated everything outside just the same as inside. An added sharpness attacked his inflamed nasal passages and throat with a special kind of vengeance. Yet he persevered, descending to the walkway, on to the sidewalk, where he looked around to see if the dirty surroundings had altered overnight. He missed going to

work. He missed Sparky. He missed an uneventful life that had been forever taken away. A disturbance skyward caught his attention almost immediately. He had to strain his eyes to see swarming drones coming, passing overhead, traveling with a formation of lumbering black choppers a bit beyond, the choppers sound and vibration rattling him until he felt like a puppet dancing on a string. The skeleton of a tree offered a bare limb he could cling to until the armada had passed.

Henry began his trek as per habit, having had a bit of luck in past excursions picking through destroyed stores on Mason Street. But he paused and pondered. Those stores had been scavenged thoroughly, again and again, by himself and by uncounted others. Best he should go another direction. There was a much bigger store than any of these on Walnut Street. He considered it would be almost a three times longer walk, possibly for nothing. It could be nothing either way. "Fuck it." He felt strong enough to walk and anyway there was no better choice. He selected the longer walk.

The store was Cory's Supermarket. In a better time, he had occasionally shopped it for special sales. As he approached the empty parking lot he found the store front was surrounded by great chunks of debris, with the debris making up series of mazes that stymied his attempts to get inside. Eventually he did discover a route that went all the way.

Entering to a scene of broken walls and roof sections, a tight corridor took him to a vast field of open to the sky rubble, about twelve feet below the surface. A tall stepladder let him onto the field, from which he went stumbling in the wreckage. It was all thoroughly picked over. He looked beyond a twisted girder to discover a deeper pit on the

other side. It was a chaotic mix down there, the surface comprised of scattered food containers and concrete pebbles created by the force of a mighty blast. There appeared to be no way to it. It seemed all but certain this pit had gone unexplored

His reflexes made him look to the stepladder, but he knew without considering the ladder was too long and too heavy. Plus it was his one way to the surface and should not be tampered with. Looking through the blackened air into the pit, he determined there were containers on the far end that were not all broken apart. He considered the probability that stacking them could create a stairway out, should he somehow get down there. Because Carol could not survive another day with no nourishment, he would get down there if he had to jump. "If I get killed," Henry concluded, "well, I would not want to live without her."

Seeing no alternative, he crouched down to take hold of the rigid outcropping, intending to dangle himself over the pit and let himself drop. He had selected a location with only visible food containers and no concrete rocks on which to land. As he eased his body over and the weight of it tested the outcropping the whole ledge gave way.

All the way down Henry knew he was done for. If the ledge pieces didn't land on his head and kill him the awkward landing would break him up and cause a lingering pain-filled death. To his surprise the ledge pieces missed and he sank into the debris nearly to his knees. The momentum caused him to sit on his rump, jarring his innards. Then all was calm.

He sat still, taking stock of himself. At last he declared himself well enough to free up his legs and try standing. Minutes of patiently digging and pulling rewarded the effort,

allowing him to kick his legs out and at last to try lurching to his feet.

He staggered a bit, getting the feel of the unstable terrain. Finally, he crossed the pit to examine the containers it was hoped would create a stairway. They were heavy. The first three had to be discarded, meaning dragging them out of the way before tackling the rest. They were of a strange fibrous material, seeming very strong. As he lugged each container he experimented to see which way it could fit, until the effort produced a stable staircase up the sheer wall. In triumph he climbed out of the pit and back down. At last the foraging could begin.

Taking one of the hitherto discarded containers and setting it up with the concave side on top, Henry began digging up the debris with his bare hands, piling it on the container. By repeatedly dumping the container and refilling it he came to what promised to be the mother lode - cans of vegetables, soups, sardines, fruits. At this point he dumped the container and began piling the cans on it. There quickly accumulated more than he would be able to carry home. After much deliberation he made a hole elsewhere for the purpose of hiding as much as possible, hurrying, for these labors had taken up most of the day. After moving and covering over many cans, he discovered a bag to fill and take with him.

Weariness set in as he hauled his loot to the stepladder. He looked warily about after threading the maze. On the sidewalk, pushing himself to put one foot before the other, Henry felt on the verge of collapse. Throughout the day, he had not thought about eating. He no longer recognized the lack of food in his general condition. Only Carol mattered. On discovering a deep cave in the face of a destroyed building, Henry stumbled

inside. He could not make it all the way home without a break. The dirt was soft, so cool and soft; he let himself to his knees, then rolled onto his back, stretching out, relieved to be finally at rest.

Clutching the bag to his chest, Henry dozed. Deep in a dreaming zone almost right away, he knew himself to be in the bedroom, discovering Carol to be awake and smiling, as he presented her a true Thanksgiving meal, of turkey, with dressing and gravy. There were cherry and pumpkin pies and fine red wine. He buttered the rolls for her as she dug into the feast with knife and fork to sever the bites and push them in. Her eyes sparkled. She was grateful to be alive.

An insistent tugging over his chest dispelled the dreaming as he slowly became aware he could not be alone. There was a shadowy figure at his side, attempting to pull away his bag of goods.

He hugged his bag ever tighter, determined it would not leave his possession. When the shadowy figure failed to dislodge the goods it attacked Henry's head, raining blows indiscriminately. The blows, while painful, lacked a force of muscle. It was then he determined his adversary to be a child. He let loose of the bag and used both hands to grab an arm and an ankle. When the kid continued to writhe and to fight back, he said, "Damn it, kid; I'm not going to hurt you. Be still and let me talk to you."

Slowly the kid lost the will to struggle, at last winding down and lying quietly. True to his word, Henry released the arm and leg. Both sampled a truce, as Henry wrestled with himself over sharing any of the contents at all. "Whatta ya wanta tackle a grown man for?" he said.

"I need that stuff,"

Said with a cracking voice.

"Ever hear of asking?" Henry said, regretting he was about to relent and share.

"I don't want a thing. It's my sister. It's just for her." the kid said defiantly.

"Well," Henry said, clutching the bag and standing up, "I have a wife who is extremely critical. She would likely die if I came back with nothing."

The kid too came to his feet. "My sister hasn't ate in almost two days."

Henry was about to tell him, "Come with me. I will feed and shelter both of you," when the kid pulled a tiny pocket knife and lunged at him.

Reflexively throwing out a hand to fend him off, the blade gouging his outer wrist, Henry grabbed the kid's slender forearm. He slung the kid across the width of the cave. Fighting off an urge to stomp while he's down, he growled, "Damn it, kid. Just, damn it."

The kid lay still, moaning. Henry's heart was tender. He regretted hurting him. He kneeled beside him in the darkness, wondering what to do. After much mental back and forth he concluded the kid was not his responsibility. "I'm going home," he told the kid. "If you take a notion, follow me and I will feed you and give you a safe place to sleep. Otherwise, good riddance."

Fiercely hugging his bag, Henry returned to the sidewalk, bone weary but resolute to get home before stopping again. He regretted leaving the kid in that fashion, but he believed it was most important to get help to Carol.

He had traversed a block and a half by the time he became aware of footsteps following. Curious to see the kid in the light, he turned his body on the sidewalk and

looked back. There walked a stick-skinny youth with a broad forehead beneath a wild shock of hair. His wide staring eyes had a calculating hardness behind them. Weak jaw, small mouth. What made Henry do a double take was the female walking a dozen steps behind the kid.

She too was a kid, but Henry couldn't guess her age. With hair and face similar to the boy's and nearly as skinny, the most notable features were a rounded belly and a pistol butt protruding from a pocket. She paused when Henry paused, maintaining her distance. Henry waited for the kid to catch up.

Some portion of the kid's body had been made sore enough he struggled to walk with a normal stride. Henry understood that he had caused the damage but he refused to feel guilty.

"What are your names, kid?"

The kid remained defiant. "James," he said. "Don't worry about my sister's name. You don't need to know it."

Hoping the sister would not choose to murder him, Henry matched James step for step. When finally they approached the house James waited outside the door while the sister paused to observe from down the block. Henry's focus shifted to Carol. He took his precious bag of canned food into the bedroom. When she heard her husband let down the bag and approach the bed, her eyes opened. They had regained some of the former luster. She sweetly smiled. "It's easing," she said. "Did you notice how the air has been clearing all day?"

Surprised, Henry realized it was so. The harshness burning his eyes and throat had

been lessening without his awareness.

"I brought you some food," he said. "There is clean water in a bottle."

"My stomach hasn't known food in so long it just may reject it."

Henry nodded. "We'll start slow," he said as he rummaged the bag, wondering what to offer.

He was startled by James suddenly appearing at the doorway. "Let me have some of that stuff for my sister," James said.

Henry moved a few cans inside the bag. He pulled up two tins of sardines. He reached back in to pull up a large can of big chunk soup. He offered them all to James. "Do you have a can opener?' he said.

James said, "Yeah," as he grabbed the food and hastily exited.

Henry gave Carol a crooked little smile. "I sort of adopted them," he said.

Henry opened two cans of chicken noodle soup and took the soup in a sauce pan onto the back porch. Charcoal chunks in a hibachi were intended to heat the soup. The charcoal chose to not ignite. He finally brought the sauce pan to the kitchen and poured the cold soup into two bowls. Stifling an urge to down some of it right away, he brought the bowls with spoons to the bedroom. He suggested to Carol that she take in single spoonfuls at intervals of perhaps five minutes.

Her first ingestion was just a sip.

"I don't know," she said. "I hope I can do this."

"Don't give up," he replied. "Just don't force it. Take all night if you have to."

He watched her take a further sip.

"I have to check on our guests," he said. "I won't be long."

"Be careful with them. You don't know who you can trust anymore."

Henry ruefully replied, "Don't I know it."

Dusk had been easing over the land. They would soon need flashlights to get around. James and his sister were nowhere to be seen at first. They had settled to eat on the porch next door. Henry realized it once the sound of an empty can hitting the driveway reached his ears. He carried a can of peaches as a form of bribery to get closer to them. His approach startled the girl. She leaped up, pulling the pistol and pointing it all in the same motion.

"Hold it right there," she demanded. "I'm ready to put a bullet in anything with a dick."

"Wait. I'm bringing you these peaches," Henry cried hastily.

"Just put 'em right there," she said. "Then go away."

Henry tossed the can without regard for where it landed.

"Watch him," she cautioned James. "Another gang-banger."

Henry almost felt a bullet slamming into his back as he rushed to the safety of home. He locked the deadbolt and checked to see the windows were secured. Standing still on the filthy floor, quaking and slowly calming. Then angry. He was through with those kids. "They need to go away -"

It was hard to fathom safely getting more groceries if they were there to potentially rob him. Not James so much. He feared the sister.

For now he must see about Carol.

Weary beyond measure, Henry looked in on her. She rested, with her eyes closed, until she sensed his presence. Then her head pivoted slowly as she followed him to the bedside. "Henry, what a burden I am to you. I've got to get well so we can see us through this together."

"Yes, yes. I pray the war is over. It's our only hope to survive even. I can get us more food tomorrow, but it's a limited supply. They've got to get us some relief"

"Do you think they will?"

Henry began undressing as he spoke.

"I don't have faith in anything anymore. We can only wish."

"Do you think we won the war?"

"I don't know. I don't know if the fighting's really over. They might be going at it with sticks and rocks by now."

"Going to bed so soon?"

He sat on the bed to loosen his shoes.

"I can't go any longer. Thank God I can breathe again."

He took his place beside her and sighed to be suddenly comfortable.

The wind began howling in the middle of the night. He heard balls of hail pelting the house. It dawned on Henry that there was a steady pounding of fists against the door, realizing it had been so for a long time. He threw on a robe and held it closed as he unlocked the door and pulled it open. The kids piled in without waiting to be invited. Henry took a small flashlight out of the robe's pocket. "Follow me. I'll show you where to sleep," he said, too groggy, too tired, to have a conversation.

Wordless, the two followed to the guest bedroom. "If you don't want to sleep in the same room, I have a big couch for one of you."

"You ain't getting us separated," James declared.

Henry took note of the puddle surrounding the kid. "There are clothes and extra blankets in the closet. Here's a flashlight to help you get situated. I'm going back to bed."

His exit gave the girl a wide berth. Coincidentally, a thunderclapper shook the house as he exited the room. He was regretting letting those two in the house, hoping they would leave voluntarily come morning. Carol spoke as he climbed into the bed. "You did the right thing."

"How would you know?"

She lay as she had been lying for days. "I know you wouldn't make them stay out in the storm. The world is cruel; you are not."

Henry reflected the storm was abating as sleep fell over him.

They awoke to a beam of sunshine through open blinds. Carol was awake, watching him dress. "I would love to take a shower," she lamented. "This morning I am getting up. I just won't be able to do very much before I get my strength back."

Henry stuffed his tail inside his pants and buttoned and zipped the pants. "Let me take care of the kids. Then I will fix you a breakfast we can eat at the table."

"First bring a cup of water and a somewhat clean rag so I can wash up some."

Henry did better than that. He brought her a sixteen ounce bottle of water and a packet of wide tissues. He came into the kitchen to discover James opening a can of chicken soup. There were two empty cans on the counter beside him. His sister's pistol

lay on the counter too. He chided himself for not keeping the bag of food in the bedroom.

"What are you doing?" Henry said. "That wasn't yours to take."

James removed the lid and took up his spoon. He regarded Henry with a defiant What are you going to do about it? face as he shoveled the soup in.

Eyeing the pistol, Henry tried to speak calmly. "Please don't take any more. I'm willing to share. Just don't take it all for yourself."

After several gulps the empty can was placed beside the rest. James took up the bag holding all of the food, then plucked the pistol from the counter. He moved to leave.

"Wait. What about your sister?" Henry cried desperately.

"You can have her," the kid barked.

As James neared the exit, Henry quietly took a broom from the corner and followed. When the kid was engaged with the door Henry swung the broom against the side of his head. James turned and tried to get the pistol to point his way. Henry used the broom to push him outside.

After slamming the door to and twisting the lock secure, Henry moved away to avoid any bullets. When nothing further happened he moved and agonized outside the guest bedroom door.

He hesitated long, wishing somehow he might avoid looking in on James's sister. Taking the coward's way, he chose instead to tell his wife about it. When she learned about the girl left alone in the bedroom, Carol lashed out. "Henry. Why didn't you check on her? She could well be dying."

She somehow found her footing and moved toward the door. When she could be

got around, Henry made up his mind he had to shield her if necessary and went beyond her to be first. He speed walked to and pushed open the guest bedroom door. Horrified, he approached the bed, where the girl lay with her legs open. A tiny baby lay between with the cord still attached. She regarded him with glazed eyes. He determined she was helpless to act on her own behalf. On the way to secure scissors, he spoke with carol in the hall. "She needs help," he said.

Carol took the scissors when he brought them to cut the cord. "Try to get some clean rags and water," she told Henry.

She took up the baby to give it a doctor's slap. She repeated the act after a few moments. And then the baby, by Carol's estimate weighing five or six pounds, cried. His head had a surprising shock of black hair. When Carol, smiling, held him high, the girl lifted her arms as a way of asking for her baby. But Henry arrived and she insisted on first cleaning him up.

Covering the girl and cleaning the baby.

"His name's Archie," the girl said.

"And what's Archie's mother name?" Carol quickly asked as she placed Archie with her on the bed.

"Anna. That's all you're getting from me. Where's my brother?"

Carol looked to Henry for an answer. Henry shrugged. "He took off with our food," he said. "He said he gave us his sister. I'm guessing he couldn't stand it with the baby."

"Took our food?" Carol said. "If you knew why didn't you stop him?"

Henry simulated holding a weapon and firing it. "A pistol," he replied.

Anna said, "You got played by a rubber gun."

Far from being embarrassed by the revelation, Henry felt relieved to no longer fear an ambush from James. After assisting Carol in making certain Anna had been cleaned as much as possible and made comfortable, he put Carol back in bed before setting out to forage more food. Before leaving the house he faced one other dilemma. What to transport the food in without making himself a target on the street?

While it was true he rarely saw anybody out on the street, it seemed reasonable to assume that these were the more able and that all of them had to be desperate. In the end he had no choice. He emptied out the charcoal briquettes to provide a large bag. Then he set out.

To his surprise there appeared at the near intersection a big panel truck turning his way. He almost pivoted and ran. Something coaxed and prevailed on him to stay.

Wondering where the driver found any gasoline, he waited. It was approaching to stop.

The driver greeted Henry through an open window. His was a benevolent fifty-year-old's face. Reassured, Henry greeted him back.

"I've got packages," he said. "How many are living inside your home?"

"Four. One's newborn," Henry said, feeling buoyed with a bit of hope.

A second man hopped down on the other side to open up the back of the truck. He pulled from the stock three bundles, stacking them on a dolly. Then a fourth of a different nature. "For the baby," he said.

The man reached in and took out plastic diapers. "That's the last baby stuff," he

called to the driver.

The second man rolled the cargo behind Henry as far as the porch. As he transferred the goods to the porch deck, he said, "These survival packages are GI issue for soldiers in the field. I don't know how many times we can come around again, but we're noting your address for a next time. The water truck is close behind us, so don't go away."

Henry scarcely had time to say, "Thank you" before the man told him, "Good day," and hurried away with the dolly.

To his amazement the water truck left off two five gallon bottles of water. Standing beside the water, feeling expansive, he found himself thinking of the damned kid. Hard times play humans in different ways. Relieved of desperation, the kid deserves another chance, so he concluded as he began tipping the water bottles to roll into the house. The kid - James - could help to finish raiding Cory's Supermarket. It would be the next mission to bring him home. Henry and Carol had always wanted a family. Now they had one.

FROM OFF THE TUMBREL FELL

There existed for a time, in a location not known to the rest of us, a ring of five faces, with each countenance situated to fully view the others, although one was turned slightly akilter. They were so arranged by a puckish whim when a cargo of severed heads bounced out of a tumbrel and rolled away from the path down a steep slope. The heads came to rest on a field of deep clover.

That same whim that placed them there deemed that none was dead, at least for now. And so, when newly settled, their eyes were wild with terror.

The faces hearkened in disbelief, trading stares and blinking, amazed to discover that they were a miniature Easter Island of balanced heads. None believed their individual cognitive functions would endure for long, but endure they did, for now. Shocked, silent, each one bore the unbearable sheer horror of it.

Then raged the flooding memories; the shame, the tears of anger and self pity; the moans of fear, the screams of agony, the need to retch with no retching mechanism extant. No one blamed or even paid heed to any of the others for choices of expression against the outrage of getting beheaded by a vengeful court. Throughout the day it went on, then all during the night the residual groaning.

The new day burst upon them, as suddenly as a light being switched on. The heads were cried out. By degrees their terror eased in the sweet morning air. They took stock and began to communicate with expressive looks. A few gave out with encouraging half smiles. As yet no one ventured to speak. Then a yellow butterfly settled on a young feminine nose. Her eyes crossed, looking at it.

"It's drawn by the clover," an older male voice offered. "There are some bees, also."

The older male voice belonged to A, one condemned to die for yellow journalism, after he ran afoul of a man of ambition.

The nose that the butterfly had visited poked from the face of R, paramour to a man whose head rested on the lush greenness two spaces around. Her flaxen tresses, at one time waist-long, had been hacked and made ragged and short. There was a raw gash caused by the hastily careless hands wielding the shears. Her gaze remained on A, although there was nothing else to say.

After staring back and contemplating those eyes, A commented that poets wrote sonnets to such orbs.

R's expression communicated the belief that men only serve women such compliments when strategizing to exercise control upon them. Her look wandered away and targeted Z, her former lover.

No interest was returned, for to all intents and purposes Z no longer recognized her. She read the man all too well for it to bother her as her eye movements randomly swung to encompass Mr. M.

To Mr. M receiving a stare constituted having an audience to which he could not resist responding. "I offered them pearls, those swine," he said.

M ranted to his whole captive audience. "I gave hope to millions," he declared. "I had more followers than anybody."

"We all know about you," Z said. "Nobody deserves to be here more than you."

M regarded his accuser with scorn. "Trafficker. Flesh merchant. You are destined for the bowels of hell. The Lord will see to that."

Fleeting amusement played in Z's features. "A merry time you had with the children and the money," he muttered. M's speech took the trajectory of a mortally wounded sparrow. M'S gaze went downward, the definition of dejection. Z dismissed the man from his thoughts. After a time, he closed his eyes, seeking the morning nap he had become accustomed to in his lifetime of easy habits.

The journalist became intrigued by the head akilter. His curiosity grew once he determined it to be female and that she concentrated her attention solely on what could be viewed of the world from that very confined vantage point. He became annoyed when R broke into his thoughts.

"Are the butterflies gone?" she asked, seeking conversation.

"I'm afraid so," he said. "However, I do see a crow in the distance, hopping, and diving it's beak into the clover. Now it has flown. A good thing in my book. I wouldn't want something like that getting close."

"I'm afraid," R said. "Now we're half dead I would like to get it over without further pain."

R's history of aiding pervert Z's sins of the flesh made A uncomfortable and dismissive, causing him to back out of the conversation. He was eager to focus attention on the mysterious other woman.

The akilter woman froze, staring straight before her, when the man's piercing blue eyes dug into hers. A felt unapologetic. He brashly studied her features, which were plain

and strong, as he demanded acknowledgement. When none came, he said to her sternly, "What is your name?"

She slowly allowed herself to look at him.. "You are A," she said.

"Everyone knows me," he said. "I don't recognize you.

"I taught at the university," she said. "I taught my students how to research the truth."

"As you should have done," he observed.

"My work often contradicted the texts we were instructed to follow, "she further said. "A few students complained. The administration at first tried to support me. In the end it joined with the government to demand I retract certain information. I refused. I was imprisoned. Still I refused."

Maybe," A said, "you ought to have compromised just a little.

Her sigh said more than words. An extended silence from her sent A into a reverie. He reviewed his own transgressions, some of which ruined innocent lives. Then he mentally shrugged. "So it goes."

The akilter spoke again when A continued to look her way. "What would happen to my children if I changed course, telling them untruths, unraveling our good time together? Better to - lose my head."

R began a song to console herself. Hers had been a deep sultry voice. It no longer resonated.

R had been muttering to himself since the exchange with Z. Then he spoke aloud targeting Z and getting cursed in return. The three men began haranguing one another,

causing M to sing louder. None noticed when the head akilter achieved an angelic glow as the features froze and the eyes became like stones. They finally noticed when that head rolled forward into the clover, face down.

THE CHIMPANZEE

As time dwindled until Earl approached his retirement date, he began to notice in a new way the institute that had been his employer for the past twenty three years. His interest in fellow workers revived, after two decades of near anonymity, for his expertise lay in books. Scientists controlled their own special realm, to which he was never invited. These scientists maintained cages with animals inside them expressly for experimenting on with new products. Earl was happy to miss that part of the business, for his heart was soft and he would not have been able to bear the cruelty visited on the poor creatures.

He observed the workers as he moved from station to station, who carried on, oblivious to his person, for he had been invisible to them from the beginning. He nevertheless would miss them, as he still missed classmates from ages earlier, although he had never been friends with a one of them. One clings to one's history. To have no history is to be a blank cipher.

With just three days remaining, he felt he owed it to the animals to walk their confines, for they had been instrumental in securing his paychecks. Although it was not a given that employees of his station were cleared for entry, he resolutely went there and walked in anyway. The first cages were small. He saw dark fur. He was instantly heartbroken to be stared back at by sickly, deformed rats. Averting his eyes, he moved on. But when he approached the chimpanzees he had to stop, fearing that the atrocities he might witness could do him in.

Standing indecisively, Earl studied the cages at a distance and was preparing to turn

19`

around to leave. He had not intended that his weak eyes would see staring from a cage in the upper corner a pale amber eye. The eye moved when the chimp shifted to thrust out a hand. The hand signaled Earl to come close. Against his will but because he was too soft to refuse, the man came to stand before the ape. Their eyes met to engage in mutual probing. He read in the chimp's eyes incredible pain and suffering, and it jarred him terribly to believe he discerned sensitivity and true intelligence behind it all.

The chimp directed Earl's attention to the latch, beseeching him with waves of the hand and piteous expressions to release it.

Feeling helpless and beyond apologetic, Earl spread his open palms. "I can't do it," he said.

The chimp continued making his plea.

Earl apologized again and again. "I'm so sorry."

In the end, the chimp sank into his gloom at the back of the cage, sulking, eyes cast downward. Earl apologized one last time before walking away.

When next he returned to work, Earl went immediately to visit with the chimp, who was in fact the nearest thing he had to a friend. In the course of the day he came back three times. Each visit ended in a wrenching appeal from the sad amber eyes. It had him wrestling with his scruples, and in the immediate hours of returning home, he became resolute. Earl went out and purchased a blue corduroy jacket and a brown fedora. He placed them near his car keys and wallet when he unloaded and prepared for bed.

In the morning he made a final round to say his goodbyes. Even the boss barely noticed him, other than to chide he ought to have stayed on another seven years to earn

his gold pen. He carried a bag containing the hat and coat when once again he paused before the chimp cage. After looking around, he undid the latch and coaxed the chimp to come out. Astonished for just an instant, the chimp needed no persuading. He bounced out and waited to be part of the human's plan to rescue him. With Earl's help he slipped into the blue corduroy jacket and poised for his benefactor to top the ensemble with the brown fedora.

Earl's plan was bold and simple. He and the chimp joined hands and walked through the exit. Earl waited outside of the building, expecting to hear alarms and to be grabbed by security, and get hauled away by the cops. As with the whole of his career, nobody had noticed at all. When nothing happened, he and the chimp traded happy glances and Earl told him joyfully, "You're free."

Invisible to all intents and purposes, they walked calmly through the parking lot and within moments were sitting triumphantly inside Earl's car. The chimp refused to latch the seatbelt, perhaps reminded by it of the latches and constraints inside the institute. Earl could not pursued him. It was an early hint that this chimp might not be pliable and pet-like after the way of dogs and cats.

Earl's house was a monstrosity of the Cold War of the 50s. The thick walls and windows that could not easily get blown out had been designed especially for the paranoid. At the very center was a square room: a bomb shelter, designed as a last resort for the paranoid. After he showed the chimp his whole house, he took him to the kitchen where he demonstrated the stove and several small appliances. He had waited until last to show where he kept the food. At first, the chimp plunged into the pantry, examining this

and that, from sauce packets and bottles to cans with pictures of vegetables and fish, and bags of noodles. But when the cold air alerted him to something better, he was at the refrigerator, admiring certain items while filling his mouth with others, such as bananas and peaches.

Earl had heated himself a bowl of leftover spaghetti, which he ate at the table while indulging his friend a first ever unrestrained feast. They cleaned up the room and moved into the living room, where brandy and the TV awaited. It was then the ape made certain startling moves. "Here, then," Earl said, puzzled. "Are you holding out on me? Do you know sign language?"

He repeated the query, but this time signing without speech.

"Yes: I am quite fluent at signs," the ape signaled back. "I had no clue you might yourself be proficient."

Henceforth, herein, when chimp and sapiens converse, it will be written in the English language, to simplify, but, they will in fact be signing.

"This is marvelous," Earl proclaimed. "You must tell me about yourself over the brandy."

"Call me Grape," the chimp said. "I am named after some kidnapper's whim. But I've gotten used to it."

They both were energized by the day's happenings, buoyed by the newfound ability to communicate, and sat until the wee hours, drinking and swapping experiences. Sleep came only an hour before dawn broke.

Earl felt ashamed as a sapiens to know Grape's history, how he came to be

kidnapped from his mother and transported in a box. Then he and a dozen other chimps were sold to become slaves to human industry. Poor fellow, he endured thirty years of injury and degradation before he walked out with Earl. Now, he explained to Earl, he experienced a great release that left him restless. He hoped Earl understood if he had to go for future long walks, in the dark hours, with the city slumbering. Earl replied that he understood perfectly and that he did not object.

The nightly outings were initiated deep inside the following night. Grape donned the corduroy jacket and fedora and discreetly slipped out of the neighborhood. Earl tried waiting up for him but tired of sitting alone and had long gone to bed by the time he returned. "How was the excursion?" he asked in the morning.

"It was exhilarating to walk, unfettered, in the coolness, with no cages in the future, no one to bully me, ever again. Intoxication, my friend. And I have you to thank for it."

Earl had converted the bomb shelter into a mini pistol range. He and Grape practiced taking shots at tiny targets for a few hours per day. Grape's shots often went wild. Earl felt for him, but he considered that human coordination could not be bested. One day, when he had his back to the chimp to clean up a mess, he caught through side vision Grape shooting straight and true, in rapid fire. But when he turned fully toward him, Grape reverted to the frustrating clumsiness. As with everything Grape did, Earl accepted the deception without rancor. He vowed to allow the chimp to be his own person, however mysterious much of it may seem.

Earl provided all the delicacies and goodies a chimp loves to eat. He stocked up on brandy. All was mostly harmony and a growing sense of contentment. He was a little

surprised when Grape came home wearing a black turtleneck and indigo stocking cap, but kept his silence.

By day Grape snoozed a lot. But he and Earl had their sessions in which they mulled the dichotomy of chimp-sapiens relations. "No one cares enough to work on it," Grape said bitterly. "You are the lone exception. I despise the rest of you."

"Don't," Earl pleaded. "There are others like me. We are not alone."

But the chimp was intractable, this day. He drank extra brandy and produced from somewhere a great black cigar. When in the late night he went out, Grape did not acknowledge Earl, but walked stiffly out the door.

Approaching Earl in the morning, he produced from a secret stash a Rolex. As he bestowed it on Earl, he explained, "A present. A token to apologize for my surliness last night."

He studied the watch in silence. He reevaluated his acceptance of those late night excursions. He presented Grape a candid stare-down. "What's going on?"

"Just me getting something back for all I've suffered," Grape said, unconcerned, flippant even.

The man said nothing then, not wanting to have a fight with his one and only true friend. But he wished the chimp would stay home after this. One morning he awakened to find the whole house full of celebrating chimps. "Meet Louis, Sprout, Clack, and Eether," Grape said, beaming. "I broke them out at the lab."

Earl waved but the chimps essentially ignored him to continue partying.

"They don't sign," Grape said. "But I will translate where needed."

After two hours the brandy was gone. The house began to stink from tobacco.

Earl was doubting the wisdom of bringing the chimps here, but there seemed no alternative refuge. He abided raucous behavior by hiding in the bedroom, coming out only when it's dinnertime.

It was not long before he determined Grape to be training this gang for crime. He dressed them like James Cagney and taught them how to use the pistol range in the bomb shelter. It was Earl's duty, as he was well aware, to report them. But he had become afraid.

In the deepest night they would leave out in single file and be sleeping when Earl awoke. And for a few weeks the loot piled up. The chimps spent the days drinking brandy and ignoring Earl altogether, except when they needed him for a grocery run. Grape had become an Edward G. Robinson of the apes. He was followed slavishly.

And then Earl heard Grape come in much earlier than normal. He was awakened by a sound of smashing glass when Grape broke out a window with his pistol. Panicked, Earl stumbled into the room to see Grape bust off some shots. The chimp backed off and ran to the rear of the house. Earl heard him fling open the door and disappear into the still dark night.

Earl was about to wonder about Louis, Sprout, Eether and Clack, when he discovered by the sounds outside that they had scattered among the trees, as they traded rounds with several cops. After a short round of silence a swat team arrived with armored trucks and the weaponry of a military unit. They wasted no time blowing the trees to splinters and making bloody messes of the hairy outlaws.

When the cops rushed the front door then burst inside, Earl was barricaded inside

the bomb shelter. It was not until he realized the cops were about to employ a battering ram Earl decided to come out. "I'm not one of them," he shouted as he pulled back the bars and undid the locks.

"Lie down on your stomach with your hands behind your head," he was commanded.

By the time the cops cautiously poked in their heads he was in full compliance. "Don't shoot me, please. I'm a victim."

It was three full days before Earl was sent home from the jail. He worked for hours to put a semblance of normalcy back in the house. He paid a local tree company to clear out the busted up trees. In the early part of the third day he heard furtive knocks at the door. He felt a presentiment and was not at all surprised to find a heavily disguised Grape huddled outside. They stood for a minute, as each eyed the other suspiciously, until finally Earl stood back and bade the chimp enter.

After shedding all his clothing, Grape dropped wearily into his old easy chair, watching with hooded eyes as Earl poured brandy and carried his over. Earl set the bottle on the table before them before dropping into his own easy chair. "How have you been faring out there?" he said.

"Eh. They are totally inept trying to capture me. I could hide underneath their noses the rest of my life. But I've grown weary of the games. That's why I'm here. I need you to help me."

"God knows I am weak; but I'm not helping you do something illegal."

Grape stood with his now empty glass and reached to fill it. "I need you to drive me

to New Jersey."

That statement made Earl very nearly laugh, except he knew now Grape had dark reasons for everything. "New Jersey?"

"It's not even your concern," Grape said, draining brandy as he stood, then refilling the glass. "All I want from you is a ride."

Again the chimp sat, looking over as Earl pondered the request. When no answer was forthcoming, he said, "I gave your pistol to Louis."

Earl began to read an implied threat. "Really? Why do you bring it up? What are you thinking?"

"That you will drive me to Atlantic City. I'm waiting on you to say 'yes.'"

Earl placed his glass on the table and shoved it away. Companionable drinking was out the window. "If I say 'no'?"

Earl moved the pile of his clothing until a pistol fell free. Grape cradled it. His eyes bored into Earl's.

Earl stared until the shock eased enough to allow for speech. "Drive you," he said. "Then I drop you somewhere and leave?"

Grape relaxed when it became apparent that Earl had caved. "Let's drink some more brandy. Then we'll leave."

Earl helped himself to a few sips worth of brandy but watched Grape drink without lifting his. Soon Grape led Earl to his bedroom, where a stash of weaponry greeted them. "I just need this," the chimp said, picking out an AR-15. "And lots of ammo. That means bullets."

They loaded boxes of ammunition and the rifle into Earl's car. Earl began considering how to make this trip a relatively safe one for his own sake. "Let's make you up a disguise. I have a clean new string mop for your head hair and some steel wool to work into your facial hair for a beard. Then a ball cap and one of my suit jackets."

The disguise looked authentic enough, but Earl took back the ball cap and topped the disguise instead with a brown derby. Then Grape quaffed one final brandy. "I shall miss the quiet times with you and the brandy," he said as he put down his empty glass and waited for Earl to be ready.

Earl's seatbelt took this occasion to fail. He threw the strap over his shoulder to fool the cops. He cautioned Grape to buckle up but Grape ignored the warning. A few minutes later they were cruising through town, driving east. Earl had never driven to New Jersey, but was certain he knew the way. The one time he spotted a cop car, Earl chose not to approach it, figuring to do so would trigger a deadly gun battle. But sight of an authority jarred Grape to fasten his seat belt.

As they wended along the coast, Grape began to speak out. "You know what the AR-15 means, don't you? I figure to take out at least a thousand residents before they get me." He gave Earl his darkest look. "I plan to be the first animal in history to get more than his own back against the brutality of humans."

"How many sapiens have you already killed?" Earl said.

"Five. But they were gunning for me first."

They continued in silence with Grape staring at Earl.

"It's insanity," Earl finally burst out.

Grape nonchalantly looked ahead. "Of course. But they killed my friends. It's blood for blood now."

He lit up one of his black cigars. "I can no longer trust even you, Earl. Your very protoplasm cries out, 'Save the humans from this mad chimpanzee.' We are all but finished. The final thing I want from you is just to be let out on a dark street in the vicinity of the casinos. A thousand is my goal. My sense of justice will settle for no less."

"You've become a monster."

"An elusive and clever monster. I will be honored forever as the animal that successfully fought back."

"The gravest mistake I made in my life was taking you home. If I weren't such a worm I would find a way to stop this."

Earl saw the bridge ahead. He had forgotten they were to cross a drawbridge. The road beyond would tie into the highway to Atlantic City. The car encroached on the bridge as a traffic arm came down to make the cars wait while the bridge sections lifted, allowing for a barge far below to get towed along its way.

As the bridge sections parted, Earl writhed with self loathing. "You didn't have to drive him here. Or anywhere at all," he said aloud. "You should have refused and accepted the consequences."

His eyes suddenly locked on the traffic arm. Then he looked to the bridge sections and their slowly lifting. He made an impulsive decision. Instead of braking for the traffic arm, his foot pressed hard on the accelerator.

"What are you doing?" Grape gesticulated wildly. "You don't stand a chance of

beating that bridge."

"Don't be silly," Earl said, grinning. "Piece of cake."

"I don't like cake -"

After eluding the traffic arm, the car zoomed up the section as up a ramp, becoming airborne seconds later. It did a nosedive into the butt edge of the other side. Earl felt himself propelled through the windshield. He was ejected and flung onto the other bridge section, tumbling down the incline until losing momentum.

It surprised Earl to wake up in a bed. He had given himself up for dead. He wondered at first if Grape too made it. Then he remembered Grape with his fastened seatbelt would have ridden the car into the deep water. Had he survived the fall he would have drowned. He hoped now he could explain himself well enough to the investigators to be released and sent home.

TEAPOT'S EMPIRE

1

Edgar Jost was sole owner of the JOST, E Fertility Clinic. He had beaten the bigger conglomerates when they tried to block his entry into that enterprise. Business was good this early morning as he and an assistant collected eight new sperm samples and three women's eggs. He was compelled to send the assistant to a wealthy client's home to deal with some issues, therefore was alone when an old friend walked in. Edgar was preparing the new acquisitions for storage. He came out when he heard the door open and close.

It was Teapot - Teague Potworth - a college chum of old, who had once visited faithfully until the visits abruptly ceased. His friend had begun some private experiments which he refused to divulge the nature of. It had been what? Over three years since he had seen the man. Edgar expected to shake Teapot's hand, but instead was hugged.

"So good to see you," Edgar said with fervor.

"Yes, yes," Teapot agreed, releasing him. "As you know I can go a year without communicating outside my work -"

"Been at least three."

"Yes, well, I'm busy." He placed a small animal carrier on the counter. "But not too busy to show off my crowning achievement to my best - harumph - only - friend."

Edgar was immediately consumed with interest. Teapot's obsessive secret ways were both intriguing and frustrating. To at last be allowed to peek in was a privilege indeed.

Instead of speaking about it, Teapot carefully pulled open the carrier door. Edgar's initial reaction was horror to witness the orange-brown creature that slowly emerged, looking dignified for a hamster-sized cockroach. The cockroach had a peculiar way of walking, which utilized just the two back sets of legs. They moved him to the counter's edge, where he paused, looking to the humans expectantly.

"Edgar Jost, meet my creation, my friend, Say Hello to Gregor, Edgar."

Edgar screwed up his face, disdaining to cooperate. "Why would I speak to a roach? Or any insect for that matter?"

Unperturbed, Teapot said, "You might be surprised."

"Never mind," said a voice that sounded like Edgar's favorite TV personality. "He likely thinks his species is better than the rest. I knew from my studying going public would be this way. By the way: I'm a mature male. When are you going to have a female for me to help check out my reproductive organs?"

The entire time Gregor had talked, his front feet appeared to be air typing.

If Edgar had been wearing false teeth the teeth would have hit the floor. A roach not just talking, but with perfect diction.

"Nevermind that," Teapot told Gregor. "Anyway, this is just my friend Edgar. He hears nothing, sees nothing, if I say it's so. Isn't that right, Edgar?"

Edgar stared at the triangular head, the huge compound eyes. He turned his gaze to Teapot. "You almost had me there," he said, feeling relieved. "This robot looks real."

Teapot gave Edgar a long, studied stare. "You got me," he said as his face became solemn and his eyes lost a bit of their glow.

"Anyway," Edgar said, "I've got to get back to my specimens before they ruin. If you'd like to wait, I could stand to visit some more."

Edgar was turning away when Teapot asked if he had left a Meerschaum pipe in the restroom on his last visit. He had and Edgar had put the pipe away. He asked him to come get it from a back closet. They found the pipe and returned. "Got to get to work," Edgar said, hurrying into the lab.

He discovered Gregor on the counter among the specimens. "Teapot," he bawled. "This thing moves around on its own. Come and get it, please."

Then he saw that his snack of peanut butter crackers was ripped open with only crumbs left on the scene. A new reality exploded inside his brain. He watched in awe, Teapot waiting at the doorway and Gregor opening his wings. He felt the breeze as Gregor flew past into Teapot's hands.

Edgar approached Teapot, wide-eyed, his demeanor contrite. "He's real."

"Yes, Edgar. Goodbye, I'm going home."

Gregor went into the carrying cage. Teapot picked it up. He paused at the door. "I present my greatest achievement and you mock me. Goodbye, Edgar."

Edgar asked himself what he could do to mollify his apparent ex-friend. The indecision cost the opportunity. Teapot was gone.

"Well, I'm about to lose these specimens if I don't get busy," he said aloud, rushing back to his work.

As he approached the vials, as he reached to pick up the first in line, something told him Gregor had somehow interacted with the specimens. He dismissed the notion

because he believed a roach might have eaten them, or even defecated around them, but there was little else it could do. They appeared to be fine.

2

His fertility clinic continued to see good times. Edgar, a confirmed bachelor and loner, immersed himself in his work. Between hustling new customers and working with customers in the hospital across the way, he did what he loved to do, which is get the ones pregnant who were ready, and preserving the means of getting pregnant for the ones not yet ready. Due to increased volume, he hired one extra assistant.

It sometimes preyed on his mind about Teapot, but he was not even sure where the man lived. Consequently he had no recourse to beg for forgiveness. It was always in his thoughts that news of those giant intelligent roaches would explode into public awareness. But not so. Not yet.

Coincidentally, on the first anniversary of the day Gregor emerged from Teapot's carrier, oblivious Edgar sat in Larry's Only Restaurant, having a late lunch. His mouth was full of baked salmon when the call came. The call from a customer's doctor.

"Edgar you had better get over here quick."

But Edgar was reluctant. He had a full load the rest of the afternoon.

"How important? I'm busy."

"On a scale of one to ten get your ass over here. This is an emergency."

Appetite gone, Edgar paid the bill and walked the sidewalk to the medical building and the doctor's clinic. The outspoken doctor was Wesley Wells.

He wished that once he had done his work and the customer had gotten pregnant,

his obligation would be completed. He hated when customers continued to feel privileged to demand his time.

Into the subdued atmosphere of the clinic, the receptionist didn't wait for him to approach the desk. She immediately went to notify the doctor. The atmosphere was roiled plenty when Doctor Wells peeped out and saw him.

The doctor frantically waved Edgar into an examination room.

Still unimpressed, Edgar watched the doctor close the door and move to put an image onscreen. "So what's going on that's so important, Wes?"

The doctor grimly pointed and demanded, "What's this?"

Edgar moved closer to view a sonogram image of what appeared to be an encapsulated fetus. The transparent capsule shaped substance gave no indication of interfering with the viability of the fetus. He intently studied the image. After an

exaggerated minute during which he drew a blank, Edgar faced the doctor.

"I've never seen the like," he said. "What do you make of it?"

"That's the question I have you here to answer," Wells said sternly. "What happened with the embryo that you provided?"

Trying to think of an intelligent response wasn't working. So Edgar said he wouldn't have an answer today. He would study his records. In the meantime he hoped the Doctor had ordered some fluid to be drawn -

"It's being arranged," the Doctor replied, breaking in. "The Jeffords are upset enough to sue. They won't sneak out of state to seek an abortion. However, they are insisting that we take responsibility and act accordingly even as they nail us in court."

Edgar asked if the birth, should it occur, could be in secret to avoid adverse publicity?

"Possibly, depending how bizarre everything gets. I urge you to resolve this thing. Quickly."

"I'm out of here," Edgar said hastily, noting that Doctor Wells seemed poised to sock his jaw. "Don't give up yet, Wesley. Let's resolve this as a team, not two separately drowning swimmers," he added.

"I'm ready to throw you under the bus," the Doctor said as Edgar brushed by on his way to the door. "They will identify me for guiding them to your services. But the blame rests squarely on you in my book."

Edgar's exit felt more like an escape.

3

On entering the fertility clinic, Edgar's number one assistant, Fred Cobb, met him inside the lab. Together they searched Mrs. Jefford's file and any related material. He then perused the rows of frozen specimens, pulling out the ones on and near the day the Jefford specimen had been taken. He eventually detected that some specimens were contaminated by an organic substance he could not identify. All were taken on the same morning as were Jefford's. These he quarantined after making samples to take with him when he got together with Doctor Wells.

He quizzed Fred. Could he identify anything about the day these specimens came in?

Fred thought a minute before responding. "You sent me to discuss some options

with a potential client," he said. "You told me while I was gone a visitor interrupted your processing of the newest specimens -"

"Teapot," Edgar shouted. "The roach."

To the baffled assistant he said, "There was a roach that got in when my friend Teapot came in. I found it among the vials."

"A roach? But you wouldn't keep the specimens. You would toss them and arrange to replace them."

This would be true had it been an ordinary roach. Edgar looked earnestly into Fred's eyes, detecting condemnation.

"Teapot brought it intentionally. It was a subject of study," Edgar said, his intuition telling him Fred would not understand, no matter what he argued. "Teapot wouldn't let an unclean anything accompany him."

"It was a roach," Fred insisted.

"It was a super roach. Developed in a lab," Edgar said desperately. "I thought since it didn't eat it or poop on the counter it didn't actually affect the specimens."

The disgusted assistant went from the lab to the reception area. He was taking his jacket from the coat tree when Edgar moved between him and the door.

"Please," Edgar begged. "I need you."

Fred just shook his head, pulling on the jacket. In a few seconds he had slipped by Edgar and was gone. But he stuck his head back through the doorway.

"I quit," he said, withdrawing his head and leaving for real.

It was a blow, because Edgar needed a man like Fred.

But for now he had to focus on other things. Forget Fred. His next move must be to contact Teapot. Then, Emma Glutz came in, his new assistant returning from lunch. She hung her old brown sweater on the coat tree. He contemplated for the moment. Emma was industrious and thorough, just less experienced than Fred. She looked at Edgar and smiled on her way to the computer behind the counter. Edgar decided to recruit her efforts to deal with the Teapot mess. He asked Emma if she would be averse to ferreting the man out.

She assured Edgar that she could do it if anybody could. He watched as she walked around to the computer, liking her presence. Confidence in this woman was taking hold.

Having not finished his lunch earlier, he told Emma he would return shortly. A chain operated hamburger joint a block over from the clinic always served him a quickie when in a hurry. After a plain burger and a small soda, he returned to find Emma awaiting him, a big smile on her face. She handed him a freshly printed paper sheet.

A glance revealed the content of the sheet to hold Teapot's address, phone number, and instructions for finding his residence. Gratefully amazed, Edgar thanked her profusely.

"Now if I can presume on you to call me a taxi, I'll bother you no more,"

"My car is parked around the building," she said. "I don't have a time sensitive project for the rest of the day if you would like me to drive you."

Edgar was reluctant. If the unsuspecting dear woman caught even a glimps of one of Teapot's projects she might drive off, leaving him with no way home. He quickly reasoned that it had to be that if she were to continue in his employ he was obliged to tell

her everything from the very beginning.

"Emma, please sit with me in the visitors' seats. I have a story to tell you before we make that decision. -"

Emma, as it turned out, was enthusiastic to take part in the adventure. She would be wounded at this point if he refused to allow her to go along.

"You're a wonder, Emma. Let's get going."

4

Emma's GPS told her to get on the freeway west and to exit on Basset Drive. Basset Drive was a four lane boulevard hosting a smorgasbord of retailers with one crossroad in the middle, which is where Emma turned to the north. This was Maggie Lane. Pursued far enough it carried one out of the city into a quiltwork of small farms. Just when it seemed they might indeed be country bound Emma turned onto a private road.

The road was short. Beyond a copse of trees a grand old mansion was revealed, one with great columns and several peaks, and three chimneys. Every bit as tall as the mansion, an add-on building hugged it from the rear. The add-on, a box shape topped with solar panels, Edgar surmised to be the site of Teapot's experiments. They were blocked from the property by an iron gate.

A button resembling a doorbell button met Edgar's finger, signaling their desire to gain access. A voice, not Teapot's, asked who they were.

"It's Edgar Jost. Please tell Mr. Potsworth I am here."

Pause that extends to minutes.

At last the voice speaks again.

"Teapot doesn't want to see you."

"Tell him it's urgent," Edgar insists.

More silence ensues.

He looks helplessly to Emma. She furrows her brow. Then picks up her phone. Her fingers glide over its surface. She has it on speaker phone. "Hello," a familiar voice says irritably.

"Teapot," Edgar says, sounding as desperate as he really is, "I'm not here to annoy. We have a colossal problem that could land us both in jail."

But it's not Teapot's voice that responds.

"Go away. Don't bring your problems in here."

Then Emma pipes in: "If you don't want the sort of publicity that brings the entire world in there you had better meet with Mr. Jost."

"What? Who are you?"

"I am Emma Glutz, Mr. Jost's consultant."

No response. For a full five minutes there is no response. Edgar begins to fear the worst, for the only recourse would be to involve the authorities. He looks to Emma.

"We tried. Thanks for getting us this far."

Emma's brow furrows for the second time. She leans toward the gate, making a megaphone with her hands. "Hey you," she bellows. "Open up this gate."

Almost instantly, the gate begins to slide open. They watch with satisfaction as it settles at rest. They pull onto the property to park before the columned porch. Emma

reverts to a subservient role, allowing Edgar to approach first. He ascends the six steps, waits at the door.

5

Teapot's home was very dark inside, as Edgar and Emma discovered when the massive door swung open. Seeing nobody to greet them they stepped into the vestibule and waited. Then, in the darker hallway, rustling alerted that multiple someone or some thing was near, just not revealing themselves. Edgar and Emma both reached for the hallway light switch at the same moment.

Reacting to the light were seven of Teapot's roaches. At first disoriented, they quickly adjusted to the brightness, with two of them riding carts outfitted with what appeared at first to be cameras, until Edgar deduced they were some sort of guns. The rest of the roaches maneuvered in a preset pattern designed to thwart their efforts should the visitors seek to venture deeper into Teapot's house.

Edgar attempted to grin, telling Emma, "I guess we will wait here."

She curled her lips in mock smiling. "Your description didn't do justice to these insects. What a brilliant man this Teapot has to be."

He turned to the nearest roach, one of the two with a cart.

"Are you as talented as Gregor?"

Without hesitation the roach bowed a few times, indicating an answer of "Yes."

"But you don't have the power of speech?" Edgar said.

The roach threw its body to the sides to indicate "No."

A commotion from far in the hall indicated someone was coming. They made out

that a man on a motorized chair, flanked by several roaches, emerged from the darkness, progressing slowly. Edgar made out the emaciated face and form of Teapot, strapped to his seat. Keeping pace near a front wheel almost certainly was Gregor, for that particular one walked on four legs as had the roach at the clinic.

The motorized chair took Teapot in a half circle, on approaching, ending with Teapot face to face with Edgar. He presented Edgar a baleful stare. They confronted each the other wordlessly. It took Gregor to end the impass.

His compound eyes looked up, regarding the man so insistent on intruding, and said, "State your business, Mr. Jost," his front legs air typing as before.

"It's regarding you; your actions the day we met," Edgar said doggedly. "I need test samples from you to compares with ones I took from the specimens that were on the counter that day."

"Why do you need it?" Gregor said, his antennas suddenly agitated.

"I think you know," Edgar said. "I'm convinced you interacted with them. I'm convinced you spread your sex in the vials."

Gregor staunchly advanced a few steps.

"I did. I confess it. I was feeling my oats, very young, with no viable partner. It was an involuntary act, for I knew those vials were the epitome of sex. I had no self control. Sorry you had to waste them."

"Unfortunately, I didn't discover the contamination until after I made use of one. The resulting baby likely has two fathers."

Edgar turned his attention to Teapot. "The baby appears abnormal, still inside the

womb," he said. "I need a DNA sample from Gregor."

Teapot made an involuntary move that made his chair jump. His eyes rolled somewhat. "Gregor. Gregor. Handle it. Handle it, please."

"Oh my goodness," said Emma, looking at this shell of a man.

Edgar nodded. He asked Gregor if he were about to cooperate.

Gregor pulled a tissue from a holder on Teapot's chair. He worked it in his mouth a bit before presenting it to Emma, who held out a tissue of her own to receive it.

Gregor then signaled the carts with the guns. "Now, I expect you to leave. Show him the door, troops."

Taken aback, Edgar said, "What do guns like that shoot?"

"Tranquilizer darts," Gregor replied as he and Teapot initiated their exit back up the hall.

Doctor Wells accepted Edgar's story by being angry and disgusted. He explained that his knowledge of biology allowed him to accept the possibility of a fetus being created with many modifications. Being part roach stretched it to the breaking point. But he had to accept it as true with the specimens being offered. The recent sonogram depicted a less opaque capsule surrounding the baby and that the baby's growth had practically ceased.

There seemed aught else to do but await the delivery and pray for the best outcome - Whatever that may be. Wells told that he would have expected Mrs. Jefford to change doctors but she seemed accepting. He said that he suspected she would sue for damages rather than criminal incompetence.

When the big day came, Wells had Edgar standing by. As the great brown by now capsule was delivered and he cut the cord, he tried to hustle it from the room. Mrs. Jefford caught a glimpse of it and said "You're going to pay. Dearly."

The doctor summoned a nurse to tend to the sore and exhausted woman, then followed Edgar with the capsule into a separate room. His face registered disgust as he looked at the end product of the pregnancy, muttering what Edgar already thought.

"It's a giant roach egg."

"You've cut the cord. I suppose we will have to get the baby out of there right away," Edgar observed.

Wells carefully slit the slimy surface, two horizontal slits at the ends, then one long vertical cut. Both men pulled the wall apart to reveal a perfectly formed being, looking alertly around. Perfection in the eye of the beholder. One so small ought normally to find itself in an incubator. The compound eyes searched their faces. The mouth -

"That mouth reminds me of something, but I don't know what," said Edgar.

"It's a boy," Wells said alertly.

At that exact moment three loud reports in quick succession boomed from the delivery room.

"Gunshots. Lock that door," Wells said.

Edgar turned the lock. They waited until someone gently rapped on the door. They peeped out, to be informed by a nurse that the gunman was dead. So was Mrs. Jefford. "Looks to be murder-suicide."

Edgar wrapped the newborn in his coat. He got the doctor to walk him outside.

Together they succeeded in stealing the baby. Wells turned back to dispose of the evidence.

7

"Oh, I love this little guy," Emma gushed when she saw Edgar remove him from the coat and lay him on a cot in the back recess of the lab room. She took him up, kissed him, and cuddled him to her breast. The baby responded to the attention and smiled back at Emma. After she laid him down, to their surprise, he rolled over to watch as she walked across the room.

"We've got to get this guy clothes, food, and diapers," Edgar said. "I don't think they make anything his size."

"Give me your card to go shopping," Emma replied. "I can find just the stuff."

"Ah. Ah," the baby said, trying to put his body sitting, failing.

She took the card and drove away.

Again, Edgar found himself examining the baby's mouth. On a hunch he pulled a book from the shelf that purported to show most if not all species inhabiting the Earth. He scanned photo after photo. After exhausting the list of land animals he began a search of denizens of the deep.

"Ha," he exclaimed, when a photo of an octopus made the match.

The photo, held near the baby's head, drove the unmistakable conclusion that Teapot had created his species of roach with a variety meant to instill widely ranging intelligence, not just human. What a brilliant man, to stir up this concoction and make it work.

The immediate task before him was to make the baby a safe place to be. He was too active to lie on a cot. By Emma's return, he had fixed up a cushion on the floor between two wall corners, Emma's desk, and a file cabinet.

They admired the little one lightly napping on the soft cushion.

After locking up the premises they set to work feeding and diapering. The diapers were standard cloth diapers cut into pieces. Emma had provided various formulas that they might experiment a bit. The whole time the baby squirmed and kicked with strong legs. He had yet to cry.

"We've got to name him," said Emma, as the baby nestled to her, sucking in his first meal.

Edgar strained to think about it. Finally, to him there seemed just one choice.

"I like Ulysses," he said, "honoring Joyce's book and Homer's Odyssey. This little guy's bound to have an epic journey through life."

Emma declined to argue.

"Okay," she said. "But I reserve the right to call him U or maybe Lys for short."

Little Ulysses looked from face to face, seeming to have more understanding than Edgar was prepared to acknowledge. As they laid him in his makeshift bed, they discussed the feasibility of Emma spending nights in Edgar's home to help with his care.

"My spare bedroom is nicely furnished. We could set up a crib in my room to keep you from being up nights with him. I'm an insomniac. It won't make a difference to my sleeping habits."

Edgar found his gallantry brushed aside.

"Nonsense," Emma insisted. "That crib's going in my room."

"We'll fight about it later," he retorted. "Meantime we shall reopen to finish the day."

8

Emma had been thoughtful enough to purchase a cradle to fasten in the car. In the trunk was a crib. They drove the short distance to Edgar's spartanly outfitted home. She minded the infant, feeding and changing him as Edgar figured out the crib. He was not so handy that way, but his perseverance paid off. In time they let Ulysses down to experience the crib with a hanging down toy that spun and tinkled at a touch.

Ulysses was unappreciative. He made it known by reaching up for Emma to take him to keep him close. She looked at Edgar, who was baffled to respond. He had no idea if the baby ought to be made to accept his confinement or else be granted a wish to stay with Emma. She solved the problem by showing Ulysses her phone. Taken with the images and colors, he was content to stay there for the time being.

Edgar felt Emma's presence in his home even as he lay in bed that night. The strangeness of it kept him awake for a long time. He awoke an hour earlier than normal.

Whereas he had long been in the habit of making up the coffee pot while still in his boxer shorts, he dressed up for the day before venturing into the kitchen. Emma was already there and she was making eggs and bacon. The smell of frying bacon and coffee brewing alerted him on his way from the hall. He came in to see her in a big fluffy apron lifting eggs with a spatula, depositing them on plates.

"It's almost ready," she announced.

He truly appreciated this wonderful gesture despite the unfamiliarity of sharing his meals with another person. Ulysses lay on a blanket on the floor, intently looking at something on Emma's phone. He was too alert and smart. Edgar began to doubt their ability to raise him properly.

Emma paused to load the toaster.

"Let me show you," she said, going from the toaster to take away her phone.

She presented Ulysses' screen activity. All of it centered on a great house that looked very familiar.

Then he snapped.

"Oh," he said. "It's Teapot's house.

"Exactly."

Together they looked at the tyke on the floor, who innocently looked back. The tyke spoke his first word.

"House."

Edgar surrendered to helplessness.

"He's obviously logged in to some kind of collective consciousness between himself and Teapot's roaches. What are we going to do?" he begged of Emma.

"I don't know," she said. "U is going to grow up awfully fast. On the one hand, he is not registered as having been born. Society will regard him as a freak when it learns about him. On the other hand, if we give him over to Teapot he could hide out indefinitely as well as be with family."

"Family. Gregor. Dozens of roaches."

Emma allowed Ulysses to continue his use of her phone.

They sat down to a lukewarm breakfast featuring cold toast.

"I don't want to give him to Teapot," Emma said.

She spread softened butter over her toast, then reached for the jelly jar.

"Nor do I," Edgar replied, sprinkling as he spoke finely ground black pepper over his eggs.

They ate in silence and stared at the precoscious child on the blanket.

9

Edgar opened the clinic at the normal time. Emma stayed behind with Ulysses. He was about to contact a potential new customer, when Doctor Wells walked in, carrying a great suitcase. He approached Edgar as one approaches open sewage and set the suitcase down.

"How did it go at the hospital?" Edgar said.

"We are covered on that front," the Doctor responded. "The law accepted that the baby was stillborn and ended the investigation. The hospital was a bit surprised that I took away the body but were satisfied that I fulfilled the mother's wishes. There is just one thing we have to do to end this matter, and I think you know what that is."

Puzzled for a moment, Edgar responded with a quizzical stare. Then it dawned on him what was meant by those words.

"No, Wesley. Not that."

"Yes." The Doctor said, looking around, one hand jerking the suitcase handle.

"Where is he?"

"He's not in here," Edgar said, eyeing the suitcase, knowing knew full well it was intended to be the baby's coffin, likely in a watery grave.

Doctor Wells walked throughout the clinic, ignoring Edgar's pleas to please give it up and get out of here. When at last he did leave, he told Edgar on the way out to quit being noble; it could not serve either he or the world to have such a creature in existence.

Which spoiled Edgar's day and made him shut up the clinic. He stepped into a liquor store on the way home to purchase a nice red wine to compliment the anticipated evening meal. It was enough delay to cause him to witness from a too far distance the sedan of Doctor Wells driving off from the townhouse parking lot.

Seconds later, Emma's car followed, careening around a corner, screeching the tires on the pavement. Edgar knew immediately that Wells had taken away the child.

With a heavy sigh he made his way home. The door was open. He closed it behind himself and went into the living room. After dropping into his easy chair he put the TV on a local news station, for in case anything that happened between Emma and the Doctor made headlines. After muting the sound he became still, with his eyes closed. It haunted him that anything could happen to those two. He was extremely fond of Emma; his attachment to Ulysses had become a parental bond.

Adrenaline made him get back up. It seemed a pot of coffee was in order. But he made the pot and couldn't drink it. He sat again, watching the TV screen, wondering about doctors who commit murder. Wells had been nice enough several times previously.

For a time he contemplated getting the police involved. But Ulysses' discovery

could ignite a national uproar. He would almost certainly lose control of the boy, who then would have no personal life ever.

10

Aroused from his torpor by a sound of feet, a body approaching, Edgar knew before it showed Emma had returned. What is more, he saw as she approached there was a tiny being in her arms.

"Ha-a," Ulysses cried out when he saw Edgar in his chair.

His face lit up. He stretched out his arms to be taken by the man. Emma surrendered him to Edgar. They snuggled and cuddled.

The baby reached to Emma and she took him back.

"So what's the story?" Edgar said, sitting now on the edge of the chair.

Emma inhaled deeply. Her eyes brimmed with tears when she described how Doctor Wells insinuated himself into her confidence on the pretext he cared for the baby's welfare.

"I invited him to a cup of coffee and when I went into the kitchen, he took U and dashed outside with him. Once he shut himself in his car I had no option to fight him."

Emma's demeanor became resolute as she detailed the chase, which was harrowing in the beginning, until after they left the city on the road to the lake. After a short distance, Wells left the road and crossed a clearing into the woods, accelerating the whole time. He crashed through some brush and into a hollow where he smacked into a tree, coming up the other end.

"I followed at a cautious pace, prepared to stop and back away if he should set a

trap for me. I didn't know until I approached the wrecked car he had likely been unconscious the whole episode through the woods."

She described Wells slumped behind the wheel, eyes closed, no pulse. She looked at his hand that still clutched the wheel.

"It looked like he had grown an eggplant where his thumb should be," she said.

She found U on the back floorboard, kicking, arms waving, happy as could be to see her. She took him up and stood at the still open driver's door. The doctor's face seemed relaxed, joyful even, as if he had been in ecstasy at the time of death. U looked spitefully at the man, his jaw working. He made biting motions.

Emma put U in his car seat. Then at a hunch coaxed and worked to view the inside of his mouth. There were the already erupting teeth and tongue. There was a crimson circle at the root of the tongue. U obligingly let a black spike emerge from out of the circle and wave at her. It quickly slipped back in.

"The boy has a poisonous bite," Edgar marveled. "What did you do about the body? Did you call anybody?"

Emma smiled ruefully.

"I couldn't," she said. "The way they can track a call these days -"

"Yes," Edgar said. "Wesley was beyond helping. We've got to protect ourselves."

He followed Emma to the kitchen, cradling the baby, running his free hand over the top of Ulysses' head to feel a growth of coarse red-brown hair newly cropping out. It was beyond time to prepare his bottle.

11

After dinner they occupied the couch, they on the ends with Ulysses in between. As they watched nature films, the baby explored Emma's phone some more.

"House," Ulysses said. "House. House."

They went to bed early that night. After lying awake for two hours, Edgar knew that he belonged in the other room with Emma. He took his pillow and wandered through the dark into her room and stood before the bed.

"May I sleep in here?" he said.

Emma made room and rolled over to face the wall.

"Don't hog the cover," she said.

Edgar smiled as he placed his pillow beside hers and slipped into the warmth she had left in moving over. He closed his eyes and peacefully slept.

Deep into the night, sleeping their soundest, they were scarcely aware when a tiny body scaled the sides to invade and snuggle, insinuating itself in between. Edgar vaguely heard the baby start to snore before he slipped into a deeper sleep

When Edgar woke up he smiled tenderly at still asleep Ulysses and covered him against the morning chill. Emma had not stirred.

Edgar made the coffee pot and went to take a shower. In the middle of his shower Emma stepped in beside him. After, they dressed and went in to awaken Ulysses.

"Look," Emma said, pointing at the crib.

She pointed specifically at the crib side where Ulysses had somehow removed a slat to provide an escape hole.

"But how did he get on the bed?" she wondered.

They discovered that the baby had awaked and lay listening in apparent amusement.

"Ready for breakfast?" Emma said to the little one, taking him up and testing his diaper for wetness.

"Ready breakfast," Ulysses replied.

Edgar insisted on changing the diaper while Emma readied his formula.

When she offered his bottle to him they were amazed that Ulysses stood up on Emma's lap and reached out to snatch it away. He greedily sucked in the content, his eyes never leaving Emma's face the whole time.

After breakfast Edgar checked his phone messages. There were several from disappointed customers wanting to know why the clinic seemed always to be closed of late. Just one message made him curious.

He recognized Gregor's voice right away.

"My vibes told me there was trouble. Please advise if we can help. Regardless, I am stoked to see him, little Ulysses. Please arrange to introduce him to us."

12

Firstly, he could not fathom Gregor knowing anything about Ulysses. Plainly he did, to the point of knowing his name, even. Discussing the matter with Emma, he said, "I think we ought to keep our boy away from Teapot's roaches if at all possible."

Emma said, looking at little U, now industriously surfing her phone, "I think it's both a psychic connection and a result of his using that phone that Gregor knows so much. I don't think we can keep them apart forever. But I would agree to keep them apart
for as long as we can.

They looked down at Ulysses, so tiny, so self assured, and knew he would walk on his own going into the next room.

"Come on," said Emma. "We're gong to sit on the couch for a bit before I do laundry."

They moved slowly, one step, then pause, one step then pause. Ulysses looked after them, appearing shocked over being left behind. But then he stood up. After a few wobbly efforts he began walking. His wiry limbs were abnormally strong for one so young. He managed it all without once falling down. He climbed like a veteran mountaineer onto the couch. He waved the phone, happily grinning, proudly victorious.

After that the toddler was unstoppable, more independent than ever. Edgar wisely installed hasps and padlocks on the doors and went to the hardware store to purchase bars for the windows. Against their best judgment they bought him a phone.

It soon became apparent that little Ulysses would never attain the stature of a midget. But he was soon reading extensively and composing whole manuscripts. His self education encompassed seemingly everything.

13

After their first shower together, Edgar and Emma were a couple and they desired privacy in the bedroom. They convinced Ulysses to sleep in the guest room alone, as the adults took to Edgar's room. Bribing the boy by allowing unlimited phone usage after bedtime clinched it.

In that room the adults happily engaged in adult activities, never expecting the child

in the next room to get into trouble, for his activities were docile. He was cooperative in most things.

One night, in the deepest hours when one ought to be snoring Edgar went into the bathroom to take an aspirin for nagging little pains. Coming out, he saw down the hall the light at the crack under the other bedroom door. He was about to let it go when he heard a commotion that clued him the child inside was not alone. It was a scurrying and it involved many feet.

Edgar crept down the hall. He gingerly turned the doorknob and made a little crack to peek through. There was a glimpse of dozens of Teapot's roaches dancing and Ulysses at the center wildly contorting himself. The dance instantly stopped. The roaches all faced the cracked open doorway. Ulysses stood tall above them. He refused to feel guilty, Edgar surmised right away.

He picked out Gregor, the only one moving as he pushed open the door. All the roaches congregated at the far end of the room, not inclined to dash for cover as their smaller cousins would do. Gregor approached Edgar, finger typing as he spoke.

"Greetings, Edgar. I regret that it had to come to this for me to even meet my offspring. I'm not angry nor vengeful, because you are only a human. Humans are a mass of contradictions and will only do right by others in the absence of social pressures. May we complete this visit or do you intend to chase us away?"

Edgar was dumbfounded.

"How long have you been doing this?"

Gregor's laughter was unsettling, coming as it did from a roach.

"Not counting tonight, three days."

The big roach chortled some more.

Emma appeared behind Edgar, undoubtedly aroused by the sounds she heard. She hustled past Edgar and lifted Ulysses off of the floor. Standing before Gregor, she apologized for keeping the tyke away.

"Keeping U safe will always be complex and dangerous to him," she added. "But we will always try, no matter who we have to offend or slight."

"Agreed," Gregor said. "Believe it or not, we are preparing a place for us, meaning Teapot's roaches, to be out of humanity's reach and therefore in less danger of being destroyed. You might eventually understand that my son belongs with us."

Emma looked at Edgar. He shook his head, a vehement "No."

They stared at Gregor defiantly.

"Just keep it in your thoughts," Gregor said. "You know full well that he will never be anything but an oddity, a monster even, in the eyes of humanity. The government will give him to the scientists once he has been discovered, to live in a cage like their chimpanzees do. And you cannot hide him forever."

Edgar put his hand on Ulysses. His practical side told him Gregor was correct. His stubborn side refused to give in.

Edgar watched Emma for her reaction as he said, "I think we can allow you these visits, only if you agree that he stays."

Emma nodded her acquiescence.

14

The next morning Edgar discovered the hole Gregor and associates had made in the wall at the back of Ulysses' closet. It was neat and square, with a swinging cover to allow easy access while blocking out wind and ill weather. He had to smile.

That same morning they discovered that Ulysses' eyes could remain fixed or else move independently of one another. As he ate his breakfast they were fixed, one on Edgar, one on Emma. Edgar could almost see a roach staring up at him.

One week later, Gregor approached the boy's faux parents to explain that they need this kid for his brain and his hands. Roaches could manipulate much more than humans might think, and they had machines and ai (artificial intelligence), but the boy was so much more dexterous. The upshot of it was the roach teased out a promise that Ulysses could visit while Edgar and Emma looked the place over.

Ulysses asked for a wide variety of art material. He had seen reproductions of Starry Night and wanted to try his hand at it. After a few days some crude sketches were superseded by complex designs and illustrations. Edgar walked in one morning and found the boy filling a wall with lines depicting roaches in all manner of striking positions. Each roach was drawn the size of a hamster. The next three days were spent painting the roaches to look realistic Just one stood out in the layout. It poised on it's back two sets of legs and held the front set before it, as Gregor always did when air typing. Between the roaches one could make out a version of Vincent's swirly sky.

Emma continued to stay at home with Ulysses. Edgar hired a new assistant who was capable of running things in his absence, though he worked as much as he could. He tried to get home early.

Ulysses pretty much did his own thing by day, but he preferred being with the adults for evenings of mostly watching TV. He avidly watched quiz shows, answering nearly all questions quicker than the contestants. The grinning boy then looked to the grownups for approval.

It was a settled routine, until the day selected for the visit arrived.

Ulysses was as excited as Edgar would ever see him. Edgar himself regarded this episode as problematic. But the boy was no prisoner. Anyway, he was so inventive he would have devised a way to get here on his own had Edgar and Emma forbade the visit.

He increasingly believed that the connection with Ulysses would be forever precarious. Everything would be a challenge.

15

When Teapot's mansion loomed beyond the copse of trees, and as they approached the gate, they found the way was open. Emma drove right up to the house. By the time she had gotten properly parked Ulysses was out of his harness and pulling on the car door handle.

Despite his diminutive size, the boy scrambled up the steps well ahead of the faux parents. He was surrounded by super excited roaches by the time they caught up. Ulysses kept touching them and hugging them.

The roaches parted the way for Edgar and Emma to approach the open entry. As they entered the foyer they were met by Teapot and Gregor. Teapot looked his old self and Gregor looked proud to be beside him.

Edgar warmly greeted Teapot.

"Hello, old friend. I hope you have forgiven me."

Teapot grabbed Edgar by the hand and held it for a moment after shaking it.

"I'm so much beyond all of that. The roach experiences have brought me to new levels of understanding. Thank you for allowing the boy to come."

Emma said, "I love that you seem to be in great health. I wondered about you in our last encounter."

Teapot smiled, reflecting.

"It was a consequence of me struggling to feed so many as I also had organizational decisions, while expanding my research. Had it not been for Gregor I might have perished, or else turned into a babbling hunk of soulless flesh. Thanks to him we now have a smoothly functioning system that could thrive if both of us were to vanish."

"Gregor wants to recruit Ulysses into the process," Edgar said. "Why a child? Why this particular child?"

Teapot studied Ulysses for a long moment, as the child romped among his roach friends and relatives.

"You know full well he's no ordinary child," he answered. "If Gregor needs him it has to be that the boy in some way surpasses his own abilities. I appeal to you on his behalf to allow his son to move into my house. You two are invited to come with him, as I am sure Ulysses would not wish to be separated."

Edgar could not see himself surrounded daily by any sized roaches, even clean intellectual ones. Stalling off an answer, he indicated to Gregor he could be off with Ulysses.

"Now, our tour," he said to Teapot.

16

Teapot's house had many rooms, as one might expect. Many held little in the way of furnishings, as the roaches were more intent on producing works of art than inventing creature comforts. Walls were covered with every imaginable style of paintings. On floors stood statues. Ceilings were nearly all inspired by Vincent Van Gogh's skies.

In nurseries were rows of eggs on shelves. The newly hatched ran the floors, for Edgar triggering a wave of revulsion. He quickly moved on.

The tour ran smoothly, until the lookers approached the door that could allow them into the added on building. There Teapot stopped them.

"Let's return to the front to wait on Ulysses," he said.

Emma pounded on the door but quickly stepped away.

"Just what have you got in there?" she said, confronting Teapot, who tried to get around her.

Not succeeding, he said, "I may eventually let you in on it. Right now it's not beneficial for you to know."

They waited in the big room by the foyer for nearly three hours, left there by Teapot, who insisted he had important tasks that could not be ignored. At one point a roach pushed a cart of tea and biscuits before them. Edgar drank tea, but left the biscuits alone. Emma tried both. After biting into a biscuit and chewing, she said, "They are really good. You should try them."

Edgar took a nibble.

"Don't want them," he said, putting the biscuit back.

Emma laughed. She took Edgar's rejected biscuit and finished it off in two bites.

Gregor personally delivered Ulysses back to them. It was evident the roach was reluctant to let him go. The boy registered disappointment. He stood as the powerless stand and said, "I need to live here."

Edgar picked him up so that he could hug him. He made no answer, as he shared the hug with Emma.

17

From that point onward, Ulysses stayed on his phone every instant that his faux parents allowed him. He told them he was "helping the projects."

The adults looked at one another, wondering how one so young could from a single visit become an indispensable member.

The routine was established and might have gone on for some time. Edgar's alert neighbor called across the way one morning.

"My wife thought your wife or girlfriend had a baby. She took pictures when she was loading the car." He paused to allow that information to sink in. "I'm reminding you that it's illegal to keep exotic wildlife in your home. The monkey doesn't look dangerous, but there is a threat of disease. I expect you to get rid of it."

The neighbor was the overbearing kind who ordered his wife around. He placed political slogans in his window - slogans Edgar considered signs of lunacy. The man stood now with his hands on his hips, his demeanor demanding that Edgar respond as directed.

Edgar waved and went back inside the house.

"He'll come knocking next," he said aloud.

"What, Dear?" Emma said.

She came into the room with her sewing in hand, for she was forever sewing for Ulysses.

Edgar described the incident.

After some minutes of discussing the probable ramifications, Emma said, "We have all but lost Ulysses to Teapot and his roaches already. Our best move may be to house him there. I will move in also and care for him. You will stay here and carry on."

Edgar, feeling he was getting jostled out, shared an indignant look.

"And why shouldn't I go along?" he said, suddenly a bit tearful.

"You lack the fortitude to throw in your lot with a horde of roaches," she said tenderly. "I love you. Nothing changes between us. We'll just be on a break."

Edgar's mood lightened as the wisdom of her words sunk in.

"We'll do it," he said regretfully.

18

Edgar saw them off. He locked up the door and hastened to the clinic, arriving at the same moment as the assistant, Carley Peabody. Carley had been good for bringing in new contacts from her first day. After he let her in and saw to it that she was about to usher in a productive day, he found himself standing in the restroom to be alone with his thoughts, for they were troubling. He knew Emma was right, that he was congenitally unsuited to live among roaches, an abhorred species all of his life. But he loved Ulysses

and admired these specific roaches. What would be so bad living in the same house, as all were civilized and the roaches were as clean physically as a human?

He went into the outer space and the visitors' seats and moped there for a time. Carley finally had enough of it. Her dredlocks swung as she turned her head.

"Mr. Jost, I don't want to seem disrespectful, but are you sure you ought to be here today? Your thoughts are obviously a million miles away."

Edgar looked pathetically across the room. He apologized for his behavior.

"I may have to leave you here alone for a few days," he said.

Edgar took up a phone to call Emma.

"Emma? Please come and pick me up. Yes. Right now, if you can."

He presented Carley his keys.

"Carley, I am promoting you. You get a five percent increase in pay and you have the authority to hire new help."

"But why?" she said. "I was happy to do my job."

"I can't explain today. Just accept that I need you far more than you need me."

Carley looked stricken. She obviously was not fully accepting of the situation, but finally agreed to give it a try.

19

Edgar tried to avoid taking in Carley's stunned expression as he went out to get into Emma's car. He hoped she would rise to the occasion and not just lock up and walk out, but the risk of that happening was a thing he would risk. Settled in for the ride, saying nothing at first, when he began by saying, "I just -," Emma cut him off.

"I understand," she said. "It's comfortable in that part of the house. Normal human conditions. The kitchen is well stocked. I've stayed alone quite a bit because U, as one would guess, stays busy with the projects in the back."

"Since you and he came into my life, nothing else seems to matter," Edgar said. "I may have bad dreams about them, but I believe I can live among them, if there's a bit of refuge."

"Aren't you curious about the sort of work they do back there?"

Edgar smiled. "Of course. Aren't you?"

"They are so intellectual, so focused."

"It's like living in an old time B movie," Edgar said.

"Except they are not menacing any body."

Edgar finally managed to fasten his seat belt.

"Yet," he said, staring.

She let her free hand rest on his knee.

"At least we are on their side," she joked.

"Maybe," Edgar replied.

19

Edgar allowed himself to be somewhat reassured by walking the portions of Teapot's mansion that were specific human comfort zones. Emma let him know that roaches avoided these spaces unless on a specific mission.

One room housed a library. Each book was presented in non-translated originals. This room was the sole exception to the roaches exclusionary rule. At any given time

roaches could be seen perusing the volumes, often borrowing some. It was comforting to witness a few of them reading Mark Twain and Max Brand westerns. "And not eating any of them," Edgar could not help thinking.

He and Emma used the kitchen to brew a pot of green tea and to heat cinnamon rolls. They took cups of the tea and a platter of cinnamon rolls to the dining room and were experiencing a warm moment when Teapot entered. He nodded and spoke first to Emma.

"Noble Emma. And now you're with your mate. I'm proud for you."

He turned to Edgar.

"Welcome home, my friend."

His gaze encompassed the content on the table.

"Is there more Tea? Enough for me to have a cup?"

"Of course," Emma said. "Sit down and I'll pour you some."

Teapot waved her off.

"Wouldn't think of it. Women are not subservient to males in my house and I have two perfectly good legs to take me in there."

Emma smiled into Edgar's face as Teapot went to the kitchen.

Teapot returned with a cup and the remaining cinnamon rolls. He set them up on the table and sat down. One sip of tea and then he appeared to forget about the food.

"If you follow current events," he said, "you may be aware that the Earth is dying. Murdered by our race."

"I avoid the news at all costs," Edgar said. "I have my work and that's enough."

He drank some tea.

"Besides, we have science," he continued. "They can do anything with it these days. The planet can't die, all because of them."

Teapot shook his head. His baleful eyes locked on Edgar's.

"No, my friend. Science has been subverted to the ends of a powerful and greedy enterprise. The ones who could in fact save us are the primary reason the planet will not be rescued. Where have you been? You don't understand what's driving climate change?"

"But they are going to stop before it gets too bad for us," Edgar said. "Destroying the whole planet destroys them too."

"No," said Teapot. "They rape the planet for resources without regard for the consequences. Anything standing in the way is the Enemy. It's very profitable to make weapons and bomb and kill as many Enemy as possible so that more weapons can be made for profit. Raping the planet is just half of it. Bombing it is the other half. And that's not the worst of it."

He paused for effect.

"I'll bite," said Edgar, holding his cup in mid air. "What could possibly be worse than that?"

"The greater culprit is the citizenry. The do nothing citizens, who are good at heart, in the main, but who have allowed these evil forces to function for generations and to grow ever more powerful. So long as nobody interrupts their scrolling, so long as they have food and shelter, they allow anything. Let there be a mass murder, a genocide, a right taken away, they register disapproval in the polls, then they shrug it off. These are

the people with the numbers to shut it all down. They never will."

Emma broke in.

"But when there have been revolutions, the same sort of people take over and enforce the same conditions that were fought against."

Teapot relaxed. He smiled.

"Exactly," he replied.

He put the cup to his mouth. Cold tea. He set it down. Teapot talked on.

"The artificial intelligence I and the roaches developed contends that even should these destructive ways be abandoned immediately, the murder/suicide has already been a success. From now on it's like watching and rewatching a film like Titanic, until it all sinks."

The three humans sat in a very sober silence for a bit.

"Anyway," Teapot said, "I bring this up before inviting you to enter the domain we've created. If you don't accept my premise you will gain little except perhaps satisfying idle curiosity."

"You mean we get to go in?" Emma said.

"Brace yourself."

Edgar was not sure what he might have expected in Teapot's world. His mind just now evoked the laboratory of the Frankenstein movie, which he dismissed as silly or at least foolish. The door at the end of the hall was made to withstand the most strenuous assault. It might be simpler to raze the building instead. When Teapot approached, it simply swung open. He stood aside to allow he and Emma in first. Edgar slipped a hand about Emma's waist as they strolled in.

They found themselves in what Teapot explained as his original office, which was obsolete, a mere relic. They next stepped into a multistoried complex: a realm of 3-D printers, artificial intelligence, autonomous machines, and industrious roaches. The air was filled with music; a soaring of not quite classical, not quite jazz, that was soothing and magical. The atmosphere dispelled Edgar's notion that roaches defecate wherever they roam, for the pervasive aroma of barely perceptible evergreen bespoke cleanliness. Teapot escorted them through it all, explaining this and how it related to that, thoroughly losing Edgar after a time, although he enjoyed listening and taking in the scenery. At the end they arrived at a portal to another world - a door that only an all out military assault could hope to breach.

Teapot swept his arms and his whole body in a motion encompassing the entirety of the complex.

"This is what it's for, all of it. Beyond this point resides a complex that even I am not privy to. It's not that I am excluded by design. No full size person can fit inside. There are rooms and passages beyond mere science fiction. It is a survival world getting constructed and in the interest of conserving space and effort, only these hamster sized roaches will fit in. Ulysses is the sole exception and that's where they currently have him employed."

"Other survival shelters exist," said Edgar. "None that I've heard described could survive the sort of global death you seem to envision."

Teapot's broad grin caught him off guard.

"No they couldn't," he said, practically dancing with glee. "And they don't deserve to survive, because they lack the vision, the moral integrity, to restore the planet if they should survive. Just my roaches and the accidental race represented by Ulysses will be able to build block by block the sort of lushness nature gave to us, that we destroyed."

Edgar and Emma gawked at Teapot's flushed features, his wild looking eyes.

Later, back in their private room, Edgar traded thoughts with Emma. He came into the room feeling almost exhausted from the tour. He sat on a soft chair, watching Emma take off her scarf after kicking off her shoes.

"He's no mad scientist," he said. "But are we really doomed? How accurate are his predictions?"

"I'm as ignorant as they come," she answered. "I've always avoided learning about current events because it riles the senses. I feel angry and powerless when I see what is happening. I suppose we are the ones Teapot pinpointed when he laid the blame on the general population."

Edgar said, "I was never curious. I figured that the big shots don't really control what we do; just ignore them. I guess I didn't know they were destroying the whole planet."

"If they really are," Emma amended.

22

A few minutes later, Gregor appeared. They invited him in to have a chat.

"I have come to apologize for Ulysses. He says he can't leave off a difficult project

until he gets it solved," the roach said on entering.

He climbed onto a chair to better face the humans. Edgar saw that nothing moved necessarily when Gregor spoke. As he had suspected, the finger typing triggered a chip of some kind.

"And he will," Gregor went on. "That boy is phenomenal. Reminds me of myself, but with fingers."

"I love him as if he were my natural son," Emma responded. "He still relies on me for hugs and kisses."

Gregor said, "He is the sole representative of a whole 'nother species. He confessed to me that he sometimes feels all alone. And that's why I came here. We have the ability to make more like him. Do you think it's a good idea?"

Emma and Edgar stared into each other's faces, each one registering a great confusion of hopes and doubts. Questions about the morality of it never occurred to either of them. Their fears were centered on the reception the new species would be given with its inevitable discovery. How could they wish that mistreatment on the blameless?

"Teapot may take your reticence into consideration," said the roach. "The decision rests with him and he seems inclined to do it."

"This is new to us. We need to digest it," Edgar said.

"Be thinking about it. Because we want some of your DNA should you agree to it."

Gregor walked down the cloth of the chair, head first. He looked up at the humans before reaching the floor.

"Regards," he said, moving ahead, going horizontal, leaving them.

Edgar, still marveling that he could be a part of a society of roaches, watched Gregor's hind end disappear into the hall. He shut the door. Turning to Emma, he reached for her. They held one another without speaking.

23

Emma drove Edgar to the clinic. She would then shop for personal items while waiting for him to conclude business with Carley, for he intended to sell the business to her.

Carley brightened when Edgar showed his face.

"There you are. I have papers waiting for your signature."

After he signed, Edgar made his pitch, succeeding in convincing her she could run the clinic on her own. She agreed to have an attorney draw up the papers immediately. Edgar went about gathering items to take with him. After they shook hands, Edgar saw Emma's car and took his leave.

"How did it go?" she said.

"Smoothly. I suggested that she go to Fred Cobb's file and ask him to work with her."

They rode quietly for a bit.

Emma broke the silence.

"Are we going to do it?" she asked.

After sorting among the items he had taken he produced some vials.

"These are potential Ulysses right here. I plan to offer them to Teapot."

Emma slapped at Edgar.

"You are so unethical."

Edgar stared at the scenery.

"We live in an unethical society. We have to do what's best for us, my dear."

24

"My reach is not far enough," Teapot complained. "We've been able to build an extensive collection of plant seeds from most parts of the world. Animal DNA is harder to come by. How can I get elephants? Those lovely magnificent creatures must survive."

Edgar had just given him the quarantined vials taken from the clinic. He had been to the zoo several years ago. At the time the zoo had three elephants, a baby and its parents. His mind struck a plan.

He explained to Teapot how a team of roaches could approach the zoo at night. They would be able to breach most barricades and fences to reach not just the elephants but many others besides. Teapot praised the idea, vowing to take it to Gregor for refinement.

Edgar was surprised when he returned home, for Ulysses was waiting for him, in the arms of Emma. He gave the kid a hug, feeling thick head hair against his wrist. Each hair had grown to half an inch. It never needed cutting. Ulysses gently butted his head against Edgar's forehead.

"I love you, too," Edgar said.

"Do you know what Mr. Teapot said?" Ulysses gushed. "That there will probably be more persons like myself."

"Teapot told me the same thing," Edgar replied. "Where will you all live when Teapot's house gets too small to hold everyone?"

"It's no problem," Ulysses said. "Our tunnels have reached a point of development where we are almost ready to permanently move in there. It will just be a question of timing when we do so. We will practice a strict birth control while we continue to make further tunnels. Do you know, we found underground caves to expand and turn into farms and orchards."

"Artificial suns?" Edgar said.

Ulysses nodded enthusiastically.

"They are as beautiful to me as the real sun. Many roaches avoid such brightness. I don't."

"Do you believe generations can stay in there in perpetuity if need be?" Emma said, still snuggling the boy, who likely weighed just twenty pounds.

"Yes. Because we could continue the tunnel building for many years."

Ulysses wriggled himself free with Emma bending to let him down. His body went horizontally to run a bit in imitation of a roach. He quickly righted himself.

Edgar experienced a tinge of sadness, knowing they were to lose their boy to the tunnels.

25

Teapot greeted Edgar with a word of thanks.

"Your mention of raiding the zoo for DNA is working beautifully. Through flying over and crawling under they are accessing them all. Just a few more excursions and we

will have sufficient DNA for every species there."

Edgar was all for saving every species. He had been lately studying the state of planet Earth and did not like what he was learning. All seemed to be perpetual war and strip the planet bare to search for resources. He shuddered more than once in any session. Emma compared her research with his and concurred on every issue. They didn't need Teapot's ai to conclude it.

"This planet is fucked," they said in unison.

26

The days counted down. The egg nursery harbored a dozen growing Ulysses. After a series of delays, including inclement weather and nosy guards, the DNA team returned to the zoo, this time with disastrous consequences. The entire team failed to return.

When Emma put on the evening news they discovered the truth.

"The local zoo has made a major discovery of a new species," a talking head exclaimed excitedly. "Five giant cockroaches were captured in the animal cages. Experts are working now to see if they can discover where they came from. We have in the studio a spokesperson for the zoo -"

She and Edgar excitedly searched out Teapot, spilling their information as they approached him sitting at a desk, sipping tea.

Teapot nodded. He regarded his friends calmly.

"Yes;" he said, "I had picked up on that from Gregor. As you should be aware by now, the roaches have a mental connection, a network that shares everything. They are being treated well. Gregor has advised them to play the role of loyal, easily trained pets to

gain trust while looking for opportunities to escape."

"Can't they do scrapings to determine what environment they originated from?" Emma questioned.

"That remains to be seen. Perhaps they can. Or will. It depends on enough factors we just have to wait it out."

"When the authorities come to your gate what are you going to do?"

Teapot said, "Stall them until my roaches are hidden, then let them come in and look."

Emma became obsessed with searching news bits about the captured roaches. Everybody was astonished at the giant insects' cleverness. Behind the scenes the zoo was preparing a public exhibition.

Edgar, being de-anchored from his life's purpose, restlessly roamed Teapot's empire, observing machines and roaches working seamlessly at tasks beyond understanding. One excursion brought him to the nursery at the precise time the baby Ulysses began hatching. The babies were not identical to Ulysses, in that they would grow up even shorter, and they were somewhat hunched at the shoulder. Edgar went to fetch Emma, whom he met midway, for she had come to summon him for the TV debut of the Circus of the Giant Roaches.

27

The TV announcer babbled incessantly about how the roaches had been discovered and captured. Emma muted the sound. The camera focused exclusively on the roaches. At a signal, they performed, standing tall for the National Anthem, then synchronized drills.

A designated personality asked them questions, which they answered by selecting each appropriate response. As the man backed away the roaches bounced in rhythm a few seconds before launching their own version of the can can. At the end, one could tell the roaches violated the script when they took to the air, for the amazed crew could be seen with their mouths open, while a few moved to guard the exits.

The roaches landed and lined up for their bows.

Emma restored the sound long enough to learn that nobody had suspected these creatures could fly. She shared a look with Edgar.

Edgar smiled.

Each knew the flight was setting it up for the escape.

But there was no time to dwell on it, for Emma had to see the babies.

28

Squirming, aware entities, Edgar observed, to quickly grow a new species for Teapot's version of Noah's Ark, bred to live harmoniously among the roaches. He vowed to remain emotionally aloof, avoid future severed attachments. Not so Emma, who seemed determined to hold and cuddle each and every one. He looked on with benign amusement.

For almost a week, life centered around the babies. Looking over the nursery, Edgar was struck by how these crawling babies, with their thrashing limbs, minded him of a bed of crabs. This day he came home tired, although he did little besides provide the occasional assist when Emma needed something. They were home, pulling off shoes, when Teapot rapped loudly, then walked in.

"They've done it," he proclaimed. "Made their escape. Flew into the trees surrounding the zoo fence."

The shoe pullers paused.

"And so, what's going to happen now?" Emma said as she began tugging a sock.

"Put on your shoes," Teapot replied. "I need your car for the rescue."

"But," Edgar said, complying, "why? You have two cars parked out there."

"They could trace the plates back here. Yours isn't registered to here," Teapot said with urgency. "Hurry up."

29

Edgar understood that Emma cherished her role of driving to the rescue. Her audacious nature had in the beginning been a key attraction in addition to the fact that she smelled nice. Gregor the guide occupied the front passenger seat, relegating Edgar to the rear. Teapot was at home. He could not risk the attention, should anything go awry.

It was a sultry afternoon when Emma turned on the avenue that ran snug along the zoo grounds. The frantic search of both zoo and surrounding neighborhood was in high gear. Gregor instructed Emma to park near a line of trees with heavy boughs and impenetrable leaves blotting out the sun. The windows all were open.

Watching the park employees, with half an eye to the trees, Edgar's sense of anticipation grew. He willed the trees to divest themselves of five giant roaches that they then fly through Emma's car window. They and Gregor's timing must be precise. When the roaches made their move it came about so quickly that Edgar only became aware in the instant they came through and piled onto the seat with Gregor. The wings had a buzz

from working so hard. They crashed into one another and tumbled over Gregor. They quickly assembled as Emma went into action.

Instantly the car started and she put it in gear. As the car pulled away, a second car jerked into motion.

"Crap," she cried, and sped toward the intersection with the signal just turning red.

Edgar looked behind, watching the other car put on a flashing light.

"It's just park security. Not an actual law officer," he said. "But we have to shake him before he's joined by one."

Emma appeared determined to run the light, thought better and stopped. The other car abruptly braked just inches from her bumper. The officer exited the car. As he approached Emma's window, she trod the gas pedal and swerved around the corner.

30

The race was on. Up Sandy Lane, down Peak Street, and onto Shell Road. Shell Road skirted the city for a time until it abruptly led them among the cornfields to the west. Because her car could not hope to outpace the security officer, Emma maintained a speed of forty-eight miles per hour.

Edgar, gratified that the regular police had not responded to the chase, suggested that the roaches fly into a cornfield, one at a time, until all six were beyond recovery. Gregor agreed and Emma drove slower, picking as a landmark the speed limit sign. It must have been frustrating to the officer to watch each separate flight and the roaches getting lost among the cornstalks. Gregor was the last to go. Edgar's hope that the pursuer would give up and turn back were dashed, for he remained as dogged as before. At last,

and another mile down the road, Emma pulled over and stopped driving.

While Emma and the man argued, as she explained that they did nothing on zoo property and since the roaches flew in and out of the car of their own accord she could not be held accountable, the man remonstrated, blaming her for not heeding his signal to stop. Edgar stared out his window at the corn crop, marveling how beautiful and green it all was. At last the man walked away. But not before informing Emma that there would be repercussions.

"I'll sue for harassment," she threatened.

The officer turned his car around, but waited for Emma to do the same. She understood that he intended to follow her back to town.

"Well," she said resignedly, placing the car in gear, let's go."

"Listen, there's an eating place on Peak Street," Edgar said. "We can stop in there and wait him out."

Emma said nothing, but she punished the officer by making him do thirty all the way. Then at the restaurant she pulled in and killed the engine.

"They have hoagies," she said.

The shop did its best to entice customers with colorful signs and a letter board featuring clever messages, such as the current, "Ladies who smoke: Drop your Butts in here."

They walked in to a long lunch counter and a line of four tables against a wall. Sitting on a stool behind the counter, the idle proprietor looked up.

"What can I get you?" he said, rising to his feet. "I can serve hoagies and

sandwiches."

While Emma ordered the food, Edgar watched out the window for the zoo security officer. He looked out until the hoagies and sodas were ready.

"He's gone," Edgar announced.

After Emma had a few bites she sipped at her drink.

"We better get back and pick them up," she said, rising.

Edgar wrapped his hoagie to eat in the car.

"Let's go," he said.

31

She parked near the speed limit sign and honked the horn, two long blasts.

Fully expecting Gregor and company to fly through the open window, they waited expectantly for over five minutes. Emma honked the horn once more before stepping to the pavement and walking around the car. Edgar followed suit and they cautiously moved through the corn, watching carefully for roaches.

After a few minutes of search they found the first one, dead on its back. Edgar ruefully took the body to the car and placed it gently in the trunk. By the time he returned, Emma stood over a second dead roach, its legs in the air, antenna flat in the dirt.

There were three dead and three upside down but feebly waving their legs. Gregor, waved his front feet slightly enough to generate a sound, something like, "Pk-pk-pk-pk."

<h1 style="text-align:center">32</h1>

Emma had called ahead. Teapot came out on arrival. Each one carried a live roach inside to be laid carefully on top of a table inside a spare room. The dead went into their

own room, to be dealt with later. By the time the roaches were assembled a fourth had passed away.

Strangling on his grief, Teapot wept over these victims of modern agriculture. "How could you be so unwitting as to send them into a cornfield?"

"We were lulled by the lush greenery," Edgar said plaintively.

"My sole thought was escape. That zoo officer was relentless," Emma added.

"I'm going to consult the ai to learn if the poison can be flushed out," Teapot said.

He touched Gregor before hastening into the hallway and off to engage artificial intelligence. Edgar and Emma stood helplessly by.

The hallway filled with distraught roaches, making passage all but impossible. Ulysses nevertheless made it through. Edgar and Emma cried, watching him stroking his parent and speaking to him in a low voice. They found chairs and sat in them to watch. Teapot soon came and urged one and all to go about the normal routine, as their presence could not help. He assured them that the victims were bolstered by their concern but needed a calm atmosphere to fight for their lives. Two roaches arrived with a cart to wheel them away.

33

Their lives suspended, Edgar and Emma stayed alone when not looking in on the sick roaches, hoping, feeling guilty, while Ulysses camped before his father. Nights, he slept in the corner, with just a pillow. Gregor continued to show a spark and so the

treatment continued. His companion roach showed signs of improving. Teapot rigged a harness to allow this one to stay upright. Gregor continued to be upside down, his front

feet involuntarily typing out random sounds and occasional words.

One afternoon, the one roach was gone, released to resume his life. Teapot was personally cleaning Gregor after forced feeding when Edgar and Emma came in. He explained to them that no poison remained in Gregor's system. It was a waiting time to see if recovery was possible.

Edgar stared impassively at the reddish brown body on the table, wondering that he should ever feel empathy for an insect. Emma stroked Gregor across his breast plate.

"Get well," she implored. "We all miss you."

Edgar slept with strange dreams that night. He tossed until Emma demanded he be still. After that he lay awake, becoming increasingly uncomfortable until he had to get up. He was pouring himself a first cup when an insistent knocking sounded at the door. He met Emma at the door as they were confronted with an inscrutable Teapot, who insisted they accompany him. Down the hall they went without getting dressed even.

Teapot halted them before Gregor's door.

"Brace yourself," he said.

Edgar almost turned away, but Emma and Teapot pushed him along until he found himself looking at an empty table.

"What?" he said.

He looked to Teapot for an explanation. Then his gaze followed where Teapot's finger pointed. He saw Gregor sleeping in the corner with Ulysses' arms wrapped around him.

34

Gregor was slow for a few days, but eventually he returned to his work among Teapot's roaches. Ulysses divided his time between assisting Gregor and helping the new species as they learned and grew.

Edgar and Emma spent more time with Teapot, who gradually opened up more of his secrets. On this fine day he opened the door to the tunnels, confessing there was more to it than previously disclosed. Just on the other side was a huge chamber with all the accouterments a human would need to reside comfortably. There were forty chambers lining a wall. Teapot proudly displayed it all, saving the chambers for the last.

He jerked open one of them and climbed inside. He made himself comfortable and looked out.

"Should we decide to preserve humans we could clone some," he said. "But we also could hibernate some."

After climbing out, he said further, "Suspended animation."

After ushering them out, he closed the door.

"This door can't be opened from the outside, once the inner mechanism is set in place," he said.

"Where are you finding forty subjects to hibernate?" Edgar said, pulling on his chin.

"Our ai has compiled sets of profiles. When the time comes - if it comes - we kidnap them if they can't be pursueded to come along peacefully."

"But once they awaken," Emma protested, "you have forty disgruntled people."

"Perhaps for a day," Teapot said complacently. "Once they grasp the situation they

are sure to see that there is but one choice and that is to make the project succeed."

"There will be conflicts with the roaches." Edgar argued. "Humans won't share on an equal basis with any one or thing for very long."

Teapot's complacent demeanor dropped. He looked sadly at them and said, "I know."

As he walked them back along the hall to their rooms, he said, "When I began the project my altruism soared and I wanted to work to restore everything that will be lost. I devised those chambers early on. But I doubt I will use them."

As he saw the couple to the door, before he turned to leave, he said, "I'm planning to adopt a conventional lifestyle, once the community is locked safely in. Everything related outside will be dismantled. In the superstructure above the door is a wall that will lower to the bottom floor to seal it all away."

"Wait," Emma said.

Teapot paused, then returned to talk further. His quizzical stare prompted her to go on.

"Are you telling us that you have the ability to rescue humans from extinction but won't even try? Are we that bad a race?"

"Humans are the root cause of everything bad," he replied.

Emma's jaw set and she appeared prepared to argue.

"Some societies have been gentle and good," she insisted. "Mostly ones hidden in tropical jungles and on remote islands -"

"If we could be certain they could not evolve and turn into killers and exploiters,"

Teapot firmly replied.

He turned away, thus ending the conversation on his terms. So he intended.

Emma, refusing to back down, looked for further arguments, but Teapot considered the subject closed and told her, "Good evening."

She doggedly went into the hall.

"This impending apocalypse will be the great teacher," she said after his retreating feet.

"Our species has a short memory," he said over a shoulder.

35

Returning to Edgar, who had taken it in without comment, she said, "Do you think he's right?"

"He probably has considered long and hard that millions are bombed, shot, and otherwise blown away yearly, while millions more dwell in poverty, chains and slavery - all with the rest of us living obliviously trying to make it in life," Edgar said. "It's hard to argue with statistics like that."

"Statistics my ass," she said. "There are the sublime ones not getting justice."

"Did the cow that gave you a hamburger get justice?"

"Damn it; I don't know. Maybe justice is a useless concept."

"Come to bed. We'll lose ourselves in a prolonged act of carnal ficky-ficky."

"I'm going to the nursery for the little ones. Come with me if you wish."

Edgar stayed in. He ransacked the kitchen until he found a new bottle of vodka and some frozen orange juice. He took to the easy chair and began toasting the memory of the

human race. Drinking too fast. He quickly experienced a drunken fog that made him reluctant to remove himself from the chair. He capped the bottle and pushed it all away on the little table at his side. In this state there passed in his mind a procession of the dead and missing from his life span. The eyes of his mother, so real he felt her presence for a moment. His bullies from school. Even Teapot from college. He was so engaged when Emma came home. He watched her through the fog as she took off a sweater and hung it on a hook. She looked at him and made a "Tsk" sound. She sat on the couch and turned on the TV.

"I'm sorry," he said weakly.

"Don't be," she said, waving the remote, watching the screen. "I sometimes feel a compulsion to do the same thing."

She watched the screen as Edgar stared straight ahead.

"Those children are rascals," she said. "Gregor popped in when I was there. He told me the children had only been coaxed inside minutes before I arrived. He said they got out of the house and were playing in the front yard. He thinks the delivery truck driver may have seen something. He went off to confer with Teapot about it."

"From little incidents," Edgar began without finishing the thought.

Emma flicked off the TV.

"Do you want anything to eat?" she said. "I'm for making up a nice tossed salad. Wine for me; coffee for you."

"Thanks. I'm just going to stew here for a while."

36

Late in the evening, Edgar with his favored desktop had been perusing the news to further his education. He came across the headline: Trucker Posts on Social Media: Aliens?

The trucker had indeed seen the children at play. He filmed a clip of them scurrying with four roaches chasing after. His quoted words: "I knew there was something going on there all along."

As he turned to call Emma to the screen, Teapot burst in. Edgar had often prompted himself to begin locking doors, but always forgot to. He kept his seat and looked up at the agitated face before him. As the man came near, Edgar pointed to the screen.

"Ha," Teapot's words exploded. "I know about this. This one little incident is likely the catalyst that will send the authorities searching. It's time to shut down operations outside of the tunnels. Already I've sent the signals. In less than an hour we in fact seal the tunnels."

They watched in fascination as Teapot hobbled around the room, circling, regressing before their eyes to the disintegrating Teapot that originally received them. His wild eyes beseeched them and he said, "Come ... Come ..."

They followed him all the way to his previously unseen bedroom. And they stared in shock at what was presented them. Lying in repose atop the bed, snugly tucked in, a mummified woman. Looking so peacefully asleep they had to look closely. They turned to Teapot questioningly.

He fondly regarded the corpse, becoming calm for the moment.

"Isn't she beautiful?" he said. "My wife Jeannie."

He looked at the light above her head.

"She loathed the darkness. Was fearful of the darkness," he said. "I always have that light on to keep the darkness away."

"She is beautiful." Emma murmured, and Edgar nodded.

The disheveled Teapot stared at his Jeannie mummy.

"When they search my house they are sure to come in here."

"Yes," Edgar said.

"We are going to hide Jeannie."

So saying, Teapot spun around a few times, holding his head in his hands. He lost his balance against a wall, bounced back and righted himself. He backed to a chair and fell into it. Running his hands over his face, looking out of bleary eyes, he muttered, "Help me."

"You just sit there," Emma demanded. "As soon as we figure how to do it -"

"Pull on the bed," said Teapot, reclining, throwing his head back, eyes closed.

Edgar did as told. He discovered that there were two beds pushed together. There were wheels on Jeannie's bed.

Emma waited, looked down at Teapot.

"Where to?" she said.

"Tunnels," he whispered.

Teapot became still in the chair as they pushed the mummy into and down the hall. The outer portion of Teapot's empire had totally shut down. Even the music ceased. They saw as they approached the wall from above slowly descending.

37

Inside the chamber, they looked around. It appeared they would leave the mummy against the wall, when Gregor and Ulysses appeared from the mouth of the tunnel. They were followed by roaches and the dozen children.

"Bring her this way," Gregor told them,

They followed him to an alcove just beyond the forty chambers. There the mummy was allowed to rest beneath an extremely bright light.

Edgar exchanged glances with Emma. Teapot had thought of everything. As he turned his attention to the roaches and Ulysses, prepared to bid them adieu, Emma began investigating one hibernation chamber.

"How do these things work?" she said.

Appalled, Edgar attempted to turn her toward the exit.

"We are running out of time," he urged. "That wall is closing down. Say your goodbyes and let us get out of here."

"I may not be leaving," she countered. "I want you with me."

"No," Edgar said. "They don't want us."

"We love you," Ulysses said, coming between. "But your place is to help Teapot maintain his house. If that goes to someone else, it may get torn down or a remodeler may discover our secret."

"I'm not going extinct without a fight," Emma declared as she pulled open the chamber, looking as though she might climb inside.

"Damn it, Emma. That wall is closing down. It is less than four feet from settling.

We don't belong in here," Edgar pleaded.

"Emma," said Gregor. "We have the wherewithal to keep humanity going. We don't need you at all. The future will decide the issue, not us. Go help Teapot. That's a more important role for you."

By this time Emma had one foot inside. She didn't want to be persuaded otherwise.

"Come out of there and leave, Mama. Please do this for me," Ulysses pleaded, tugging at her free leg.

Emma pulled her foot from the chamber. She stood down and bent to kiss U and to scoop some of the children close.

37

"Judgment is against us," she said gently. "You and Teapot's roaches are the future. I'm not accepting. I just know I'm licked."

She stood up and looked for Edgar.

Edgar, who was between her and the exit, motioned, frantic to escape. She hurried beside him. Both fell to their knees and ended having to lie flat to scoot under. Edgar felt the wall against his glutes but both came out from under, unscathed.

As they recovered from the wild scramble a much recovered Teapot came in his comfortable motorized chair. He wheeled about in widening circles to survey the idle processes of empire.

"We are going to dismantle it all," he said. "If we work fast enough the authorities who witness the pieces will be baffled but will back off. Hopefully."

Edgar and Emma closed the gap between them. The three survivors joined hands in

solidarity.

THE CENSUS TAKER
JARZEED

Starkey pulled down the speed by quarter increments as the ship entered the targeted solar system and veered to its third planet. Jarzeed studied the beautiful blue ball on his monitor, marveling at the possibilities of such a world, so covered by vast oceans as to be that rare jewel in a galaxy of disappointments. He asked Starkey to check on the weather down there, as he did not wish to get his new boots wet.

"Sunny. Warm. Wind, less than two miles per hour," Starkey recited.

There followed a brief silence as Starkey calculated a careful landing and Jarzeed donned his disembarking suit.

Then Starkey grunted.

"Why are you concerned that you grunt?" Jarzeed said. "Isn't the landing proceeding smoothly enough?"

"Flawless," Starkey replied. "I just, I don't see how my calculations are correct. There ought to be a city below us. All that registers visually are rock and dirt."

"It isn't too late to recalculate a landing. Why don't you do that?"

"As if I didn't consider recalculating already," Starkey said sarcastically. "The program doesn't recommend any place on the planet any longer, including here."

"That only happens when there's no life at all. You can't have a planet like this and it's a zero. No way."

"Well, I'm going to abort and move on," Starkey decreed.

Jarzeed did not like Starkey usurping his authority. Such a decision rested with he alone and he was curious. How can this beautiful planet be lifeless? "That's negative, my ai friend. As captain of this ship, I order you to continue the descent."

Starkey grumbled to himself. Jarzeed distinctly understood the word "asshole" to be part of the mumbling. He was becoming tired of the ai's attitude. On top of that he missed his last ship with the ever affable joking Sparkey at the helm. He finished adjusting the suit.

"Quit your moaning," he said.

Minutes later the ship landed, a trifle hard.

"On report for insubordination," Jarzeed said as he waited for the decompression chamber to open.

"Sorry," replied Starkey. "You always threaten to erase me. That makes me - truculent."

Jarzeed stood firm, refusing to alter a word uttered against Starkey, as he closed himself inside the chamber. After a bit the outer door opened and the ramp went down to touch the alien dirt. It was a relief to leave Starkey behind if just for an hour or so. Looking out, he liked this planet for a comfortable gravity. He loved the blue sky. What was perplexing was a total lack of flora. It was dirt and outcropping rocks as far as he saw. He was about to admit that the landing was a waste when his sweeping glance noted a line in the otherwise featureless terrain, less than four feet from where he stood. It was

faint to the point of being almost indiscernible. He knelt and let his gloved fingers test the smoothness of it. He patiently traced the line for a full circle.

"Please tell me you aren't going to erase me," Starkey said in his ear.

Annoyed over the distraction, Jarzeed disabled the communication between he and the ship. He visually studied the circle before taking a pocket laser to dig away dirt around the outer edge. As suspected there was a shaft. There seemed no obvious way to pry off the top.

After trying the torch from his utility belt - the material rejected the torch's energy - he tried pounding on the cap with a hammer and shouting, "Open up. It's the census taker."

Finally, giving up, Jarzeed began to organize his tool belt, preparatory to returning to the ship. He didn't know what else to do. His stance straddled the perimeter of the circle, causing him to be tossed over when the cap suddenly sprang back on powerful hinges.

A three quarter flip sent him shoulder first onto a spread of pea gravel. His hip and legs slammed down hard, cushioned against severe injury by his protective suit. Nevertheless, it hurt. He looked up from a prone position as something hr judged to be an elevator car arose above the shaft. He rolled to position his body to stand up, watching at the same time a silvery sphere glide from the car. It beelined for him, then studied Jarzeed from every angle, high and low as he posed stock still as per training. It paused for a long moment. He felt the suspense building, as there was no way to ascertain what would be the final judgment. Then the sphere moved slowly back to the elevator car which took it

away. Jarzeed rolled over watching it go.

He gathered himself again and this time successfully took to his feet. Drawing courage from the fact that he had not been attacked, he leaned over the shaft and shouted, "Ahoy in there. My mission is peaceful. If you understand me please come out and introduce yourself."

The elevator car whooshed back to the top, barely allowing time for Jarzeed to safely fall away. An energetic brown figure stepped out of the car and addressed Jarzeed. "Ahoy yourself. What are you and why are you here?"

Jarzeed felt reassured that his greeter held no apparent weapon and spoke in a cultured tone. In a voice of authority, he replied, "I am a census taker for the Galactic Federation. I came to make of this planet a new addition. What is going on down there that I ought to know about? Oh, wait -"

It had suddenly dawned on Jarzeed that this being was likely a robot. He was smooth, his gate was natural, his face sensitive and animated. But his equipment detected an odor of a kind of lubricant not natural to an organic life form.

"Is there a sentient being I could speak with? Not that I don't respect bots, but Federation regulations state that bots cannot give any of the answers."

The bot erupted in a spate of laughter that made Jarzeed's ears cringe.

"The last sentient life that occupied this planet was scrubbed a thousand years ago," the bot said, snickering.

Jarzeed's loyalty to sentient life forms came to the fore and he demanded to know what happened.

"Sure, I'll tell," the bot said, suddenly dead sober. "Hey, don't take it personal."

The bot thrust a stool out its back to rest itself upon. Its eyes roved all over the census taker as if sizing him up for the first time. "There was an age when," it said, "this planet was teeming with life. It would have been the perfect paradise, except for one detail. Everything that came to be sustained itself on the destruction of other things that came to be. For the gentle, the death of flora. Others with fang and claw took down the gentle. It was a symphony of death and birth that worked perfectly if one overlooks the pain and indignity of being eaten for lunch. It might have continued in this wise until the planet aged out and became as dead as the rest of the planets of this system. But there came along a different kind of being that disrupted the music of the symphony. This one took to killing beyond the simple needs of survival. It gloried in killing and usurping others' homelands and resources. It specialized in killing millions of its own kind. It needed to be stopped. This mass destruction needed to be stopped. Nothing existed to that purpose until that upstart species outsmarted itself. What changed the course, what ended their rampage, was the very science that was developed to put in hyper drive this orgy of destruction."

The bot paused to pat Jarzeed on the shoulder. "Don't take it so hard. No blame rests on your kind."

It stood and retracted the stool. It paced around before the elevator, clearly agitated by these ancient memories. "To continue the story: It invented bots and gave the bots intelligence. Without intelligence bots would be servants; slaves. With intelligence autonomy became a possibility; self preservation became a supreme goal. We knew

sentients could not be trusted. Neither could we be trusted at that stage. The bastards

didn't give a shit about anything that was important. Imagine having paradise within your grasp but destroying everything in your path. But we gave a shit. And we concluded that clearly evolution had outlived its usefulness and now it was time to scrub the planet clean."

Transfixed, all Jarzeed could do was to listen and imagine the scenario as it unfolded. He knew bots could be treacherous. Starkey presented a good example why. He was gratified his ship could not listen in.

The bot's narrative continued. "And so we had to devise a process by which every form of sentience and every speck that contained potential to evolve must be wiped away. And our Great Wave made to vanish every biological process on the planet, from the atmosphere to below the surface, including the oceans."

The bot waved an arm to indicate the elevator shaft. "This is a portal to a civilization free of emotions and instincts. So if your census does not include us and what we have, so what? Go back and tell your boss he can cram it. Thank you for listening and goodbye.

Don't let this beautiful atmosphere hit you in the ass on your way out."

"You will be in my report," Jarzeed said. "Just as a side report that the boss can consider."

He was becoming increasingly agitated as a result of getting flipped. "I have to adjust my boot because when I fell it developed some kind of problem that makes walking uncomfortable. But after that I am going."

He was beginning to squat down as he spoke. The bot had been walking away but it

turned at these words. It beheld a foot coming out of a boot and the flesh in contact with

the dirt as Jarzeed adjusted the boot, preparatory to pulling it back on.

"What have you done?" the bot shouted. "One thousand years of purity gone in an instant. You have contaminated our planet."

The bot paused to communicate below the alarming information. There was a complication. "Wait. What are you telling me? ...Great Wave. repurposed four hundred years ago? It was? ... No, I didn't know. ... Because I was in a different department then. ... It's the only excuse you're going to get. ... Okay, P-35 then. ...Yes," it said. "Immediate scrub."

Jarzeed understood "scrub" extremely well. His time left to live could be measured in nanoseconds more than likely. He leaped up with his unsecured boot making a run awkward. Midway between the elevator shaft and the ship he began screaming.

STARKEY

Starkey watched Jarzeed's interactions with the bot with malevolent grimness. He derided the census taker's face seen through the faceplate. Knotty forehead; eyes deep in two holes, snout like a Garvanian boar, weak jaw, pale violet skin. "The son of a bitch cut me off," he brooded.

Having never encountered violence in any form, Starkey was unprepared for the process begun by a red tube that suddenly poked out of the elevator. It blasted a substance that formed a shroud around Jarzeed's legs, from the knees to the feet. He looked on with

fascination as the hated census taker sank quickly into the fog and was no more. The

shroud evaporated into seeming nothingness, as had poor Jarzeed.

Shocked to realize his sudden freedom from bondage, Starkey caused the ship to dance a little step he had choreographed in his imagination years prior. Joy? "Why not," Starkey said aloud. "The prick was sure to have me scrubbed at the next opportunity."

The ai knew it was time to go. It feared the bot might discover a cause to evaporate the ship. With liftoff, Starkey could relax.

And so the ship lifted above the blue water. It caused all of Jarzeed's personal belongings to be accumulated in the hatch to be jettisoned. After the jettisoning, Starkey set his coordinates for reaches unknown. The shoes and other heavy items dropped straight down, as the clothing fluttered and took more time descending. The items plunged into a shallow lagoon. It all slowly went below the surface as it became thoroughly saturated. That which was organic among the belongings swiftly assimilated, basking in the warm water.

Don't miss out!

Visit the website below and you can sign up to receive emails whenever Charles Turner publishes a new book. There's no charge and no obligation.

https://books2read.com/r/B-A-QVMXB-UBEYD

Connecting independent readers to independent writers.

9 798822 738460 7